Hope Street

Mike Mitchell

Published by TDM Books

ISBN: 978-0-9928617-0-4

DEDICATION

To Angela my wife and Laura my daughter.

ACKNOWLEDGMENTS

Thanks to Chris for the gifts of Harry and Hope.

PREFACE

No scene of Grimsby docks has ever graced the lid of any jigsaw puzzle box that I have ever seen. To put it plainly, Grimsby is not a pretty town. No swathes of white sand here, no smuggler's coves, and no rows of jellybean coloured fishermen's cottages. Nor does Grimsby boast any quaint old coves harbouring brightly painted wooden vessels like so many life sized children's toys. This town is built instead, in the monotone greys and browns of the brick and slate tenements that sprawl in flat ranks across the drained marshlands of the Humber estuary.

By the middle of the twentieth century Grimsby had become the greatest fishing port in the world. It was an Industrial Age marvel and a grimy, smoke blackened bastion of iron, brick, steel and coal. The docks themselves, a network of manmade basins shielded behind a formidable concrete sea wall were the home base of the great Northern Trawl fleet, a triumph of man's dominion over nature, and the nemesis of the cod and the haddock.

If it were not for the fishing industry, this town would not exist. At most, it would be a blasted and remote coastal hamlet perched on a sand-spit, trapped between the sea on one side and treacherous marshlands on the other. By the middle of the nineteen-sixties though, after almost a century of growth, Grimsby had become populous, comprising some hundred thousand souls, mostly scraping their livings from the fishing industry, toiling on the boats and in the fish processing factories that had grown up around the docks.

The inhabitants of Grimsby are insular. There is a uniquely rugged independence about them, borne from generations of isolation, and of the stoicism and single-mindedness required of those who earn their livings and offer their lives in the service of the seafaring industry.

Hope Street tells their story. It is 1964 and Britain stands on the threshold of a new technological era, but in the dockyards and on the distant water trawlers of Grimsby, life is still hard and the men and women who live and work there, harder still.

"...over there, beyond the squalid alleys, the warehouses, the railway sidings and the cranes, is something infinite and old, that moulds the lives and thoughts, the hopes and fears, of all the sturdy, soft-voiced people that pass to and fro amongst them. There is the sea – their life and death, their salvation and their doom. There is no escape from it. It possesses them so completely that most of them would not forsake it if they could."

From: North Cape by F.D. Ommanney (1939)

PART ONE

CHAPTER ONE

March 1964.

It was before dawn and still midnight dark, but the vessel was brilliantly lit with a multitude of electric arc lights. A sharp easterly blew in from across the North Sea, bringing with it a numbing coldness, straight from the steppes of Central Russia, and although it was only half past five in the morning and most reasonable people were still asleep in their beds, the men who unloaded Grimsby's trawlers were already busily about their work and the docks were clamorous, alive with the tumult of activity.

Above the din of the workers, gulping waves sloshed and slapped between the concrete quayside and the steel hull of the massive trawler berthed there. Men swarmed over her deck, unbattoning the fish-room hatches and readying the vessel to discharge her cargo. Shirley Lofts stood and watched them from the quayside, shivering in her thin coat, her still slightly tired eyes busily flitting from figure to figure. She was looking for one person in particular and was beginning to think that she must have missed him when at last he appeared, swinging down the narrow gantry towards the dockside with the unsteady gait of a man who had been at sea for a very long time.

He smiled at the sight of her early morning face, white and pinched with the chill, salty wind blowing in from the estuary. Shirley was just eighteen years old and was very pretty, even with her fair hair twisted into the white linen turban that covered her head and terminated in a neatly folded knot above her brow. She was on her way to work and had arrived early at the dockside to meet her friend Harry Coulbeck, it had been over three weeks ago when she had waved him away on this trip.

Harry was older than Shirley by just three years and his young frame was beginning to fill out with the strenuous work of the fishing. He trotted towards her with his canvas kit bag slung easily over a strong shoulder. Despite the cold he was wearing just a pair of jeans and an open necked shirt.

'Now then Shirl!' he hailed, and with his kit bag still on one shoulder he snaked his free arm around her waist and hoiked her clean off the ground in a swirling embrace. He spun in a full circle and placed her gently back down, exactly on the spot where she had started from.

'You daft bugger.' She smiled and punched his free shoulder with a girly fist, her eyes now sparkling in the electric arc lamps, suddenly looking less tired than before. 'Good trip?' she enquired.

Harry did not have the time to answer. With a squeal of brakes, a bicycle suddenly shuddered to a halt beside him and was cast, clattering to the floor by the young rider, who, with flailing arms, leaped energetically towards him. The two men locked on impact and Harry was forced to stagger backwards; he dropped his kit bag but managed to retain his balance. Laughing loudly, he gripped his young assailant by the jacket and pushed the slight figure out to arm's length.

'Jens, you soft bugger,' he said, beaming into the face of his young friend. 'Calm down mate, I haven't got me land legs back yet. You'll have me arse over tit and in the dock!' Delighted by this, Shirley clasped her hands to her mouth and laughed out loud.

'You should get yourself off home Harry,' she said. 'We're all going dancing at Pearson's tonight if you fancy meeting up. But you look like you haven't slept for a week.' She rubbed her face to feel the rawness where his sandpaper cheek had scraped along it. 'And God you need a blooming shave!'

Harry rubbed his chin, smiled and cuffed Jens around the head, catching him with a playful blow just as he was scuffling away to pick up the tangled bicycle.

'It's great to see you back safe Harry,' said Jens, straightening up the handlebars of the cycle. 'What was the catch like? Have you got lots of beautiful big fish for us?'

'You'll see, and you'd better get off to work you two, you know what this lot are like.' He nodded towards the new ten-storey Hansen Group office building that loomed above them. 'They'll dock you a quarter of an hour if you're a minute late, they don't get money to build swanky new offices like that by chucking it at you bloody factory monkeys.' He laughed and picked up his dropped kit bag, swung it over his shoulder and walked towards a waiting taxi.

*

A box of fish trundled down the roller conveyor and jarred to a halt in front of Jens' station. He reached forward and hauled the box onto his rostrum, taking out one of the fish, a mottled green codling. North Sea, off one of the near water boats, he thought. Positioning the fish in front of him on the wooden block, he made a neat incision behind the head, twisted the knife and sliced in a single cut down the length of the back, exiting at the tail with a flourish. His thumb went into the incision behind the head and lifting the thick loin, he flashed away at it with the tip of his knife, paring the fillet free from the rib cage with short, deft strokes. He flipped the fillet onto the block and with a few final trimming cuts to remove the pelvic fin and the belly wall the job was finished. He flicked it through the air with the back of the knife blade into a waiting box and turned the fish over so that he could begin cutting the other side.

The actions were becoming more mechanical with practice. The knife was sharp and dangerous when working at speed but he hadn't cut himself all week and felt that his speed was building as he became more confident and developed his rhythm. A quick look up at the other men down the line showed that each had their own distinctive style, some rocking from side to side like rolling, drunken sailors, some jitterbugging, some dancing like boxers bobbing and weaving in the ring. Jens wandered what he looked like in full flow. The experienced men could have both fillets off in a matter of seconds and their work rate was relentless. Jens wandered how they could do this; fish after fish, hour after hour, year after year. But they did, and the top cutters made a good living – the more you cut, the more you got paid. Jens wanted to be a good cutter but worried that he might not have the staying power.

'Oi, Snowy! Less of the bloody day dreaming and more bloody filleting!' The voice was Ken Flett's, one of the filleting line supervisors. A dour Scot, he had noticed Jens looking around in between fish. 'Yer not bloody paid to gaze at yer boyfriends, yer paid to cut fish, and the way you're going on today, you'll end up owing the company money!'

There was no humour in his voice; the insults were barked out, challenging and aggressive in his thick Scottish accent. The other filleters didn't break their pace on the filleting boards but Jens' cheeks reddened and he moved on to his next fish with a little less fluidly than the last one, hacking slightly over the ribs and leaving too much white flesh on the skeleton.

Ken was on him again. 'What the bloody hell are you doing to that fish Thorsen? I could make a better job at filleting that with me fucking bike pump. Here, give me that knife!' He snatched the knife from Jens' hand and flicked the pad of his thumb across the blade. 'Thought so,' he spat. 'Yer knife's blunt, I could ride bare arsed to London on that bastard. Get it sharpened!'

Jens reached for his steel and began the sharpening strokes, flicking the blade left and right, up and down its length. He knew he was not as skilled at sharpening as he should be and so he waited head down in anticipation of another attack from Flett, not daring to take his eyes off the shimmering blade. Once he was satisfied that he had achieved a keen edge, he looked up to see that Flett had moved on and was apparently haranguing one of the new starters for spilling ice onto the factory floor. Jens was relieved that the overseer had tired of humiliating him in front of the other men and he tried to get back his focus on improving his filleting skills.

'Don't pay any attention to that Jock bastard,' he

heard the man on the next board say, loudly enough for a few other filleters to hear. 'I've been watching you Thorsen and I reckon you've got the makings of a good filleter. He's just a bully; he'll get his comeuppance one day if he can't speak nicer to people than that. Grimsby men don't take kindly to being treated like shit by scum like him.' There was a general round of agreement from the filleters in earshot and Jens was heartened by the support of the older men around him, he liked the feeling of being one of them. If only he could settle to the repetitive work, fish after fish, hour after hour.

*

Break times were staggered so as to avoid overcrowding in the canteen, but even so, Shirley and her workmate Doreen struggled to find two seats together. Shirley had a quick check around the room and realised that Jens wasn't there; he must be on second serving she thought and couldn't help feeling a little disappointed. The food was served from a counter where the canteen ladies doled out meals not dissimilar to school dinners, simple but good fare and the cold work in the factory made a warm meal very welcome. The girls had both chosen egg on toast and still wearing their white cotton overalls and turbans, they settled down together to eat.

It was Friday and although they still had half a shift left to get through, it was nearly the weekend and their minds were already preoccupied with thoughts of their two days of freedom from work.

'You off to the Palais tonight Shirl, or the pictures?' asked Doreen between mouthfuls. Shirley's mood immediately lifted at her thoughts of the weekend ahead.

'Probably go dancing Dorrie, there's nowt on at the

flicks and Jens will just want to go and see the one that's on at the Tower again if we did.'

'You mean the one about the Vikings with Richard Skidmark in it?' Doreen sniggered.

'Yeh, that's the one. I wouldn't mind, but he's seen it about a hundred times already,' she exaggerated. 'He says he's a Viking and he's interested in it 'cos it's his history.' Doreen was confused.

'What do you mean he's a Viking? How does he make that out?'

'Well think about it Dorrie,' replied Shirley, 'he's called Jens and his dad was from Denmark.'

'Oh yeh, I suppose so,' Doreen acknowledged. 'I never really think of Jens as a scrob, he seems just like one of us.' Another thought occurred to her. 'And anyway, if he's a Viking where's his helmet with the horns on it?' The two girls giggled.

'What's tickled you two?'

It was a man's voice, one they were familiar with but one they wouldn't have expected to have been addressed by. The girls looked up to see Ken Flett seated opposite them. He was drinking very strong, dark tea from a blue and white, hooped mug. A smile flickered across his lips. 'It's either something very funny or you've both got feathers stuck down your knickers.'

Ken's accent was thick Scottish, from the North East and the girls struggled to understand his meaning. It was only his laughter that gave them the clue that this was intended as a joke, prompting them to respond with polite smiles. They only knew Ken by reputation, he was thought to be a hard man, surly and unsociable with the men he commanded. Not at all like the other supervisor Percy Bennett who was amiable and well liked by the filleters. Other girls in the factory said that Ken was married and lived with his Scottish wife in a big house near the park, but this was only gossip and they had never met anybody who had actually been to his home or met his wife. Others said that the couple had a baby. Sheila Johnson claimed to have seen them buying 'baby stuff' in Pramland.

'Well girls, much as I'd like to sit here chewing the cud with you two beauties all day long, some of us have got jobs to get on with.' He stood up, keeping his very pale grey blue eyes fixed on Shirley as he did so. 'See you later doll!'

'Did he just bloody wink at you Shirl?' Doreen asked as soon as she felt he was out of earshot, almost not believing her own eyes. 'I'm sure he bloody winked at you.'

'No he didn't Dorrie, don't be daft.' Shirley was a little flustered but was trying not to show it, although she felt the warmth in her cheeks and was worried they were glowing red. As indeed they were.

'How old do you think he is?' Doreen asked.

'Don't really know but he's ancient. I reckon he's at least thirty.'

'Do you think he's good looking Shirl?'

Shirley didn't know how to answer. If she admitted that she thought Ken was good looking, then Doreen would suspect her of fancying him. If she denied it, Doreen would think that she was lying to cover up the fact that she fancied him. She decided to say nothing on the subject and instead gave Doreen what she hoped to be a haughty look, and then she returned to their earlier conversation.

'So, dancing tonight at Pearson's then, are you and Colin going to be there or what?'

CHAPTER TWO

'Get the kettle on Mum, I'm back.'

Harry pushed through the back door and bustled into his mother's small kitchen, he dumped his kitbag onto the lino as he went and swept her up in a big embrace. She was wearing a dressing gown over her nightdress and had risen early especially to welcome her son back from the sea and to make sure that he had a decent breakfast inside him.

Before long, the kettle was whistling on the gas ring and Harry and his mother Dolly were nattering away whilst she fried the bacon. Once it was sizzling away nicely, she cracked three eggs into the pan and flipped the spitting hot fat over their yolks with a wooden spatula until they were basted to a delicate opaque shade of pink. 'It's so nice to see you back safe and sound son', she said over her shoulder. It was the closest that she could ever allow herself to the articulation of her constant dread.

Whilst he ate, they chatted about his trip and how he planned to spend his time on shore. Harry's father Sid was away at sea on the seine netter Morning Glory, so

Dolly was happy to have the company of her only son. By the time Sid got back, Harry would be leaving again, sometimes it was like this and weeks could pass without father and son seeing each other at all. It was just the way it was.

After breakfast, Harry headed up to bed, where he soon fell asleep in the small bedroom. He was born in this house and had known no other. The room was sparsely furnished with just a single bed, a wardrobe, a chest of drawers and a small wooden table supporting his Dansette record player. The wallpaper had a bunny rabbit motif in a shade of baby blue. A photograph of the beautiful Italian film actress Sophia Loren cut from a magazine was pinned with brass thumbtacks to the wardrobe door. Harry slept lightly and woke up after just a few hours; he got straight up and headed downstairs to the kitchen for a wash in the big sink.

'You up already son?' Dolly was still in the kitchen, peeling potatoes at the kitchen table, getting ready for tonight's tea and listening to the news on the radio.

'Aye,' he answered, rubbing sleep from his eyes with the back of a hand. 'You know me Mum, can't sleep when I know there's beer to be drunk and hearts to be broken.'

'Well, it's about time you stopped horsing around Harry and thought about finding yourself a nice girl to settle with.' She was only half joking. He was twenty-one years old, a fine looking well-built lad, growing stronger by the month with the rigours of the fishing, and doing so well at Hansen's, quite the skipper's favourite. He was already earning good money on the big boat Apollo and could afford a place of his own if he'd wanted.

Harry turned to look at his mother, ready to answer her with a typically dismissive quip, but before the words could be spoken he was suddenly overtaken by a strange feeling of presentiment. A half remembered dream had suddenly returned unbidden to him, surfacing as if belatedly from his recent spell of restless sleep. It was something about Shirley. Just a fragment, but he recalled it with such clarity that he was unsure whether it was the memory of a dream or of a real event. More clearly than events of the dream though, he felt the sensations and the feelings it had aroused in him come flooding back, he experienced anew, the sheer emotional charge of it. They had been sitting in this very scullery, just the two of them; Shirley had been sipping tea from a china cup. She had smiled. The twinkle in her pretty blue eyes had taken his breath away. He had never seen her like this before, never realised that she had become such a woman. What had he been waiting for? It all seemed so clear, so obvious.

'Ah Mum,' he said at last, bringing himself with an effort back to reality, 'you're the only girl for me. You know I'd never leave you. And anyway, you'd miss my rent money.'

'Get away with you, you bloody noggin.' She laughed back at him not seeming to notice his moment of abstraction. He poured some hot water from the kettle into the basin for his wash, turned again to look at his still smiling mother and with a serious tone in his voice that she did not expect and could not fail to detect, he said.

'You know what though Mum, you just might have a point.'

The smile broadened a little on her face and her eyes took a more intense interest in her son. But he had already turned his back on her again and was stooping over the big sink, splashing water all over his face but mostly onto the kitchen floor. Although she had a mother's intuition and could sense a change of mood in him, she knew better than to press for more information right then. If he had something to say, he would tell it to her when he was good and ready. Typical bloke she thought, just like his father.

Washed and shaved, he headed back upstairs to dress. With just three days on shore and a pocketful of pound notes to spend, Harry was in a good mood and was looking forward to the next few days. He had plans. First, he would meet up with his Hansen Apollo crewmate and childhood friend Bill Osborne. They would head off down Freeman Street for a few pints and hopefully bump into a few of their drinking buddies. Then later on, with thoughts of Shirley still fresh in his mind, he planned to meet up with her, Jens and a few other mates at Pearson's Palais de Dance. Harry was no dancer himself but he enjoyed the atmosphere, the music, the girls and of course the beer.

He put on a record. Johnny Cash singing 'Ring of Fire'. Then he selected a plain white shirt of very good quality cotton from a wire hanger in his wardrobe; it had been ironed to crisp perfection by his mother. He opted for a midnight blue serge suit, cut like all of his suits in the style favoured by the fishermen of the port. Many young men in the town were now sporting sharper cuts influenced by Italian tailoring, with clean lines, slim trousers and narrow lapels, but Harry liked his trousers cut generously wide and paired with a broad shouldered jacket with two twelve inch side vents. He didn't put on a tie but instead pulled his shirt collar up and laid it flat on top of his suit jacket collar. Harry's clothes were expensive. It was important that fishermen had swagger when they were on shore. They had money to spend and they lived like millionaires for the three days between fishing trips.

Taking one last look in the mirror, he slid a comb through his Brylcreamed hair, slicking it back at the sides and flicking it forward at the fringe into a cowlick quiff. He gave himself a cheerful wink of approval, ejected the Johnny Cash record, slipped his feet into a pair of crepe soled creepers and bounced down the stairs three at a time. 'See you later Mum, I'm off to pick up me wages and to grab a few beers with Bill,' he said, giving her a smacking kiss on the cheek.

'Are you coming back for tea love?' she asked.

'Don't think so, we'll probably get a bag of chips or something. I'm just going to pop round to see Gwen. Then, I'm off out.' He picked up a parcel of fish fillets wrapped up in newspaper, a gift for Jens' mother from his trip, kissed his mother again on his way out of the back door and then he strode happily off down the passage whistling an approximation of the tune to Ring of Fire.

*

Inside half an hour, Harry and Bill were walking briskly together down the main shopping street of the port of Grimsby town. This was Freeman Street, beginning at the entrance to the docks and stretching for almost a mile towards the North Lincolnshire countryside; the fishermen loved this street, there was a pub on nearly every corner. It had been a short walk for the young men by way of the Hansen Group wages office on the docks, where they had happily pocketed the fat packets of their settlings. Normally, they would have taken a taxi but the morning was fine, a crisp late winter morning that seemed remarkably mild to the two fishermen so recently returned from the Arctic Circle.

They were both wearing suits with no overcoats and were enjoying the feel of solid ground beneath their feet. Their breath trailed in steamy wisps behind them as they walked and chatted.

'Where to then?' asked Bill.

'Reckon we'll start in the Corp and take it from there.'

'Are you sure? Remember what happened last time we were in there! I'm not sure Jim will be too pleased to see us.'

'Yeh, but that wasn't our fault was it,' he was laughing as he added, 'it was them Scrob bastards who started it.'

Bill joined in with the laughter at the memory of the fight which had started with Harry throwing a punch at a Norwegian fisherman for nudging his elbow at the bar and causing him to spill his freshly pulled pint. It had ended with Harry and Bill being dumped onto the pavement outside the pub by the big landlord and a couple of the regulars.

'Hard as nails that Jim Smith,' reflected Harry, 'he's been tipping out the likes of us for so long, it's just part of the job for him now. We'll be alright, he's a mate of Dad's anyway.'

Harry and Bill entered the Corporation saloon bar with broad smiles on their faces, pleased to be back in port, ecstatic to be back in the boozer. The pub stood on a corner adjacent to Freeman Street's big covered market, it was a classic and stylish working class Victorian boozer, with barley twist mahogany woodwork, beveled mirrors behind the polished wooden bar and large frosted plate glass windows on the two street sides, emblazoned with emblems urging the locals to 'Drink draft Bass.' Harry didn't need much encouragement to do that, Bass was one of his favourite beers and the Corporation his favourite boozer.

It was still early, just after eleven o'clock and the towels had not been off the pumps very long. The pub was still relatively quiet for a Friday dinnertime. Jim was pulling a pint as the lads walked through the door; his expression barely changing except for a raised eyebrow in Harry's direction. Harry held both of his hands up and smiled at the landlord who continued to squeeze the frothing ale into the straight pint glass, topping it up with smaller pulls on the pump, teasing the foaming head over the rim and down the side of the glass where it oozed frothily over his knuckles. He returned Harry's silent gesture of conciliation with a nod and a cheery 'What will it be then boys?'

'Two pints of Bass please Jim,' Harry dug out his wad of ten shilling and pound notes and offered one to the big barman. 'And have one yerself mate, sorry about last time, won't happen again …promise.'

'Aye, and grunters will fly.' Jim took the money and counted out the change, tinkling a few coppers into a half-pint glass next to the till as he did so.

A galaxy of sparkling dust particles swirled and eddied around the two friends as they took their seats in the corner of the bar. For a while, neither of them took a sip, they were waiting for the creamy foam to percolate towards the rim and to condense into a head. This was the delicious, deferred gratification for fishermen after weeks at sea, to watch and wait for the perfect moment to suck into that first pint, the best pint they would drink until they returned again from their next trip. The immaculate first pint back!

They raised their glasses together, pausing for a second or two to ensure that the ale was perfectly settled, holding the glasses at eye level so that they could inspect the clarity of the deep amber fluid against the brilliant March winter light. The glasses were ceremoniously chinked together and both men simultaneously toasted, 'Cheers mate, down the hole,' each quaffing half a glass in one long suck before pulling back with satisfied 'aahs'. To finish the ritual they both wiped the backs of their hands across their frothy top lips.

The pub was beginning to fill up now. Men were lining the bar waiting for their beers to be pulled, Jim shouted for his bartender Mal to join him and the sound of animated conversation began to swell and amplify in the wood and glass saloon. The door swung open and three large men in knitted sweaters entered. Their jumpers were of a distinctive heavy knit with crisscross patterns at the hems and cuffs. They were wearing denim jean trousers and leather clogs with wooden soles on their feet.

'Fucking skinfoot Icelandic bastards,' Harry commented to Bill who nodded back.

Icelanders were not popular in Grimsby. The port had a closer historical and cultural affinity with Denmark and Icelanders were seen as somehow more foreign and strange than their Danish or even Norwegian cousins.

'I don't know who they think they are, robbing us of our fishing grounds.' He struggled to contain his resentment. 'I mean, they act as if they own the sea. Nobody owns the sea!'

Bill shared his friend's anger on this point. 'They're good grounds up there Harry, Dad says they used to get spanking cod and haddock up on the North Cape, and some good flatties too off the Westfjords, big plaice with black backs and spots like coal dust, big as dustbin lids. Can't go there now, thanks to their bloody fishing limit.'

'They've got no right' Harry concluded. Bill agreed.

Jim paused before he served the three Icelanders who all appeared to be in good spirits, enjoying their shore leave and clearly planning to get some quality English ale inside them. He looked over towards Harry with a cautionary expression. 'Don't worry Jim, we're on our best behaviour today, we're going dancing later and we don't want to mess up our best suits.' Jim seemed to be appeased by this and began pulling the beers for the unconcerned visitors.

'Don't know why they don't fuck off to Hull though,' Harry shared this thought with Bill, but not loud enough for Jim to overhear.

'So, what's with this dancing lark then Harry?' asked Bill, changing the subject before the Icelanders realised they were being talked about. They looked like hard men and Bill knew that despite being outnumbered, Harry was liable to start something if he wasn't distracted. 'I don't know why you bother going up the Palais,' he added, 'you can't even dance.'

'I just thought it would be a laugh, we'll meet up with Jens and Shirley, it'll make a change.'

'Definitely make a change. A change from us getting pissed and scrapping with scrobs.' He laughed at his own joke and taking another swig from his pint he suddenly became thoughtful. 'Reckon those two are getting very close lately, don't you? I bet Jens is filling his boots.'

It was as if Bill had stabbed Harry in the heart with a shard of ice. He visibly stiffened but answered coolly enough. 'No way Bill, they're like sister and brother, known each other forever. And anyway, they're still just kids.'

'Not that much like kids nowadays, haven't you noticed? Jens is filling out nicely since he started at the factory, he'll never be a big lad but he's wiry like his old man was. And as for Shirley …well she's turned out to be quite a stunner and you could say that she's filling out quite nicely too. She certainly fills out those sweaters she wears.'

Harry felt a powerful and sudden compulsion to grab Bill by the throat and pin him against the back of the snug seat. He frantically fought the urge. He imagined his grip closing around Bill's neck, the half raised glass falling from his hand before it reached his lips, the beer swilling and slopping onto the floor, the exploding shatter of broken glass.

'Watch your mouth Osborne!' His voice was not loud, but it was harsh and it attracted the attention of Jim Smith behind the bar.

'Harry! Anything up?' Jim's shout was like a slap, it recalled Harry from his red mists and back to the clarity of the here and now, breaking his inner tension. Bill looked confused and hurt by the reproof; he didn't know what he had done wrong.

'Sorry mate,' Harry apologised to his best friend, 'I didn't mean to sound arsey, it's just that …well you know, I've known her for a long time too and I guess I must think of her like a little sister myself.'

Bill was a good-natured lad and had come to tolerate if not to understand Harry's moods. Harry was fiery, like his father Sid Coulbeck who as a younger man had a reputation in the bars of Freeman Street as something of a hard case. Bill got up and sauntered over to the bar to order two more beers and when he returned Harry's temper had completely subsided and the conversation soon shifted to the events of the fishing trip they had just returned from.

At the back of his mind though, Harry was

disquieted by his own reaction to Bill's relatively harmless comment about Shirley. What was happening to him? Was this something to do with the dream? It had all seemed so clear, so obvious when it had first come back to him in his mother's scullery, but suddenly, after the surprise of his emotional outburst, things didn't seem quite so straightforward. Was there anything more than friendship between Jens and Shirley? How would he feel if there was? There were too many questions; and all he knew for certain was that right now, all he needed was seven or eight more of these pints of beautiful beer. Maybe then he would be able to think more clearly.

*

At half past three Harry and Bill found themselves draining their last pints of the afternoon in the Albion. It was kicking out time, the towels were on the pumps and the lights were already off. The afternoon had clouded over, threatening rain as Harry and Bill, oblivious to the cold, were ushered onto the street. They squinted in the fading March sunlight, trying to decide their next move. They had made their way to the Albion by way of four other public houses after leaving the Corporation; they had consumed a total of eight pints of bitter each.

'Where next?' Harry posed the question to a grinning Bill.

'Wouldn't mind a bite to eat Harry,' he answered, 'I could eat a scabby dog, I haven't eaten since I got home this morning.'

'Me too.' Harry agreed and they set off at a brisk pace without further discussion towards the café just a short walk away, close by the main road junction at the entrance to the docks. It looked inviting from the outside, the windows illuminated against the fading afternoon light and the condensation on the glass telling them that it was much warmer inside than it was outside on the street.

They found two seats together at a red Formica table and squeezed themselves between the other customers, a mixture of fishermen who like Harry and Bill had just been evacuated from the nearby pubs, and shoppers, mainly women in big coats and full shopping bags. Bill's eyes became alert; he was checking the room, apparently looking for somebody in particular.

'Don't worry mate, she's here, I've just seen her.' Harry was smiling as he said this, teasing his friend.

'What you on about Coulbeck?' he replied, his already beer-flushed cheeks reddening to an even deeper hue.

'You can't fool me Bill. I've known you way too long for you to be able to pull the wool over my eyes. I know it was no coincidence that you just happened to fancy a bite and let's face it, you nearly did the hundred yard dash to get here!'

Bill knew that he had been found out. 'I don't know why I bother,' he said, a little forlornly, 'she never even notices me anyway.'

'Why don't you just say something man? She's not a bloody mind reader.' Harry was still smiling but a little more serious now.

'There's no point, I don't even know her name.'

Harry exploded with laughter. 'I don't bloody believe it,' he said, 'you mean we've been coming in here for weeks on end 'cos you're mooning over some bloody tart and you haven't even had the gumption to ask her bloody name!' He was incredulous. 'Oi, darling!' He shouted, leaning back in his chair and gesturing at the pretty young red haired waitress who had just stepped out from behind the counter.

She came over to the table, an order pad in her hand, and with a flourish of her pencil stub and a slightly haughty look at Harry she asked, 'What'll it be gents?' The word 'gents' was stressed with barely disguised irony.

Bill's face glowed two shades deeper red and he sat dumbstruck in an agony of embarrassment. Harry was unabashed.

'My friend Bill and I,' he looked conspiratorially across at Bill as he said this, 'are famished and would like you to bring us the works. Pie, spuds, veg, the lot. And make 'em man sized portions darling, we're working men!'

'Drinking men more like,' she answered only half under her breath. Harry heard her and chuckled.

'If you don't mind, we've just got back from risking our lives in the Arctic Circle to put food on your plate milady.' He put on his posh voice for the word 'milady'.

'Oh, fishermen are you?' she replied, 'I'd *never* have guessed.' The banter was good-natured and she wasn't surprised when Harry asked.

'What's your name darling? Me and my mate Bill was wondering. Aren't you gonna tell us?'

She was still smiling as she answered, accustomed to bantering with the clientele, especially at this time in the afternoon, after the pubs had kicked out.

'Maybe I will, maybe I won't. My mother told me to steer clear of fishermen and I know what she means now, I can see you're just the kind of blokes she warned me about. You're all the same you fishermen, you think your God's gift; too much money, too much lip, too much bloody cheek.'

'Maybe you're right, maybe you're wrong,' echoed Harry, 'but the truth is, *I* probably am like that, and I can't blame your mother for warning you about blokes like me, but she's wrong about one thing, I can tell you.'

'Oh aye and what's that then?'

'Us fishermen,' he paused for effect. 'We're not all the same. I might be the kind of bloke your mother told you to avoid, but he isn't.' He nodded towards Bill. 'He's a smashing bloke, make some lucky girl a very happy woman one day!'

Bill exploded out of his seat, his red face radiating heat. 'I'm off to the snooker,' he spluttered, nearly falling over himself in his headlong rush to the café door.

The young waitress was temporarily taken aback by the sudden exit of the nice looking boy.

'It's Maureen,' she said after a moment of thoughtfulness. 'Tell him I'm called Maureen.'

CHAPTER THREE

At precisely two o'clock every afternoon the factory whistle sounds and the shift is changed. People on the way in to work arrive with their faces betraying the fact that they faced an eight hour shift whilst the faces travelling in the opposite direction tell a very different story.

Jens was standing in the men's cloakroom, wrapping his knife and sharpening steel into his thick plastic apron and tying the bundle neatly with the apron's tapes when he felt a hand on his shoulder. Turning he saw the large, genial face of Percy Bennett.

'Now then young Thorsen' he began. Apart from Shirley, Percy Bennett was the only other person in the factory who pronounced Jens' surname correctly, with a hard 't' as in 'torn' as opposed to the way that most Grimbarians pronounced it, with a soft 'th' as in 'thorn'. Percy was concerned about something he'd witnessed earlier and he continued, 'I saw Ken giving you a bit of a hard time lad and I just wanted to check you were alright.'

'I'm fine mister Bennett,' Jens replied, 'he put me off

for a bit but I'm getting the hang of it now.'

'Aye lad, I can see that, I've been keeping an eye on you. I don't know if you know this, but I knew your father. We never fished together but I know he was a good man and a bloody good fisherman, he had a good reputation in this town.'

Jens swelled with pride at this. He loved to hear stories about the father he remembered so clearly, although his memories were those of a child and now he had grown he longed to know more about what kind of a man his father was.

'Thanks mister Bennett that's really nice to hear, it means a lot.'

Percy slapped Jens on the shoulder and said, 'You get yerself off home now Thorsen, that girl of yours will be waiting for you.'

*

Every day, Shirley and Jens met in the corridor outside the cloakrooms, and today being Friday they were even more excited than usual. The factory workers were paid in cash on Thursday mornings, the money was put into brown paper envelopes which were folded and sealed so that the corners of the notes could be counted without opening them. Jens and Shirley had both already paid their board and had a small sum of money left over for their enjoyment. The working week had finished and a weekend of possibilities now stretched before them.

'What do you fancy tonight Shirl?' asked Jens. 'What about the flicks? That Viking film is really good.'

'Jens,' she replied, 'we're not going to see that flipping Viking film again.' She was firm but good-natured with him. 'And anyway, you flipping well know that Friday is the best night at the Palais and we haven't been dancing for ages.'

'We went on Wednesday.'

'That's what I said, it's been flipping ages.'

Shirley loved dancing and she was very good at it, much better in fact than her partner. Even though he had overcome his childhood reticence and had proven over the years to be a competent ballroom dancer, Jens was not as committed as Shirley. In fact, one of the main reasons he continued with the hobby was because he knew it made Shirley happy and this gave him a great deal of satisfaction in itself. The two had been friends since they'd met at Infant School and were put into the same class. It was not very long after this that Jens had lost his father in a fishing accident and despite the fact that she was only just six years old then, Shirley had experienced a deep sadness and empathy for the grieving boy and her particular friendship for him during that time had cemented a lifelong bond.

To outside observers, Jens Peter Thorsen and Shirley Lofts had the appearance of a courting couple. They always seemed to be together and they clearly shared a natural and unselfconscious familiarity, so there was an understandable and widespread assumption amongst their factory colleagues that they were 'going out' with each other.

'So, Pearson's then!' Jens confirmed with a smile. He had of course known all along that Friday was for dancing and they would be going to Pearson's. He had even heard Shirley make the arrangement with Harry earlier that morning, but he couldn't help himself from having this little joke with her about going to the pictures instead. He had seen the Long Ships film twice and had really enjoyed it both times, but he had no desire to see it again. He did however, enjoy his cheeky wind-ups of Shirley, he liked to see her get a little bit feisty with him and hear her put on her bossy voice. It made him smile inside.

'Harry will be there later,' he added, 'it will be good to talk to him about his trip. Just hope he isn't too pissed.'

'Jens! Language!' Shirley reprimanded him. 'Just because you work in a fish factory, doesn't mean you have to talk common.'

'What about you,' he countered, 'with your flippin' this and flippin' that.'

'Flippin' isn't swearing Jens Thorsen, as you very well know,' she replied, rising once again to his bait. He was smiling widely now and Shirley noticed. 'And stop taking the Mickey out of me Jens, you enjoy winding me up too much.' He threw his arm around her shoulders, pulling her into his side as they walked together towards the bicycle sheds.

They set off cycling home together, side by side with the other shift workers, all leaving the dock estate. More than a hundred bicycles accumulated from the factories, large and small around the docks, they snaked through the streets in a bicycle Armada, over the railway crossing and then dispersed in different directions to homes on the East and West Marsh estates of the town. Shirley and Jens headed east. They lived in neighbouring streets on the East Marsh and they chatted breathlessly about their forthcoming evening as they pedaled away towards their respective homes. Shirley was keen to practice the foxtrot in advance of a forthcoming competition she had entered them into. Jens was looking forward to meeting up with Harry Coulbeck. At the end of Shirley's street, she peeled away, calling over her shoulder as she did.

'See you later Jens, give my love to your Mum!'

*

Less than a minute later, Jens turned his bicycle into Hope Street. He wheeled it down the passageway between the terraced fishermen's houses and propped it against the back wall of his mother's house.

'I'm home Mum,' he shouted as he entered the kitchen. 'What's for tea, I'm starving?'

'You're always starving. I don't know where you put it.' Gwen Thorsen was standing at the gas stove, preparing the evening meal. 'But you'll have to wait for our Frank to get home from school, so make yourself useful and bring some coal in will you.'

Gwen Thorsen was in her mid-thirties; she had been just eighteen years old when Jens had been born, the same age that he was now. In her youth, she'd been considered something of a beauty in the neighbourhood and there were still traces of those good looks in her kindly face today, although there was a sadness and a tiredness in her eyes that betrayed her tragedy. Her once raven black hair was now prematurely threaded with steely grey.

Since losing her husband, Gwen Thorsen had remained single and relied on her boys for the heavier jobs around the house. They were both fine lads but were very different. Jens was such a good-natured boy, she still thought of him as a boy even though he was eighteen years old now and was quite a man in his appearance. Her younger boy Frank was seventeen and still at school, he was more studious and serious than Jens, and at eleven years old had passed his Eleven Plus exams to go to the boy's grammar school where he was now doing very well. He had recently confided in her that he had hopes to go to university; this had made her feel very proud, but at the same time worried that she would not be able to afford the expenses of it.

A few moments later, Jens returned with a fully loaded coalscuttle. 'I'll get me wash now if that's alright Mum,' he said. 'It's Pearson's tonight and I want to be ready early. I'm picking Shirley up at seven. Oh, she sends her love by the way.'

'Ask her if she wants to pop by for tea on Sunday Jens,' she replied. 'I've been down the butchers and got a lovely piece of stuffed chine.'

Whilst she would not consider that they were well off, there was no doubt that things had been better in the Thorsen household since Jens had started bringing money in after he'd left school and got his job at Hansen's. It had been difficult for Gwen up till then, bringing up her two boys on her own.

'I'm looking forward to tonight,' he added, 'Harry just got back from sea this morning and he'll be coming up to Pearson's later, probably with Bill Osborne.'

There was a very brief pause as Gwen Thorsen took this information on board and she made perhaps a momentary and almost imperceptible reaction to the mention of Harry Coulbeck. Gwen had known Harry all of his life; she was very close to his mother Dolly who had been a great comfort to her when she'd lost her Kurt. She liked Harry very much and recognised his qualities, seeing him as a hard working young man, loyal to his friends and devoted to his family, but she didn't entirely like the fact that he exerted a great deal of influence over her son Jens, and there were some aspects of Harry that she did not entirely approve of; his quick temper, his drinking and most of all, the fact that he loved going to sea.

'Aye, I know,' she answered, there was no trace of any trepidation in her voice. 'I saw him earlier. He popped in on his way out and dropped off a nice parcel of fish for us, that's what you're having for your tea tonight. Dressed to kill he was. I tell you, he must spend more on fancy clothes in a week than the three of us spend on food in a year.'

'Well he's got it Mum, you can't blame him.' There was no jealousy in Jens' voice, only admiration for his friend.

By the time Frank got home from school, Jens had washed and changed and was sitting in his shirtsleeves at the kitchen table with his mother. They were talking about Frank, and how well he was doing, when he walked into the kitchen and hung a satchel full of books onto the back of the spare chair.

'I've got loads of homework,' he said, but rather than looking depressed at this, he rather seemed the opposite and even appeared to relish the idea of an evening with his head buried in his books. This was his first year in the sixth form and the beginning of his A' Levels.

'How was school today?' she asked him as she served up portions of poached haddock in a milk sauce thickened with cornflour and flavoured with a little mustard powder. Paired with mounds of steaming boiled potatoes, it was a family favourite for Friday tea and was just how their Danish father Kurt used to like it.

'It was good,' chirped Frank, diving into the meal with relish, mashing the potatoes into the sauce with his fork, 'I got an A star for my history essay, it was the top mark in the class.'

'What's the point in learning about history Frank?' asked Jens, 'I don't see what's so important about old kings and queens and all that, surely it's more important to learn something useful, like a trade that'll earn you good money.'

'It depends what you want out of life,' replied Frank, 'there's nothing wrong with learning a trade, but there's more ways to earn a good wage than by doing it with your hands Jens.' He paused, to reflect and continued. 'I've got an idea that I'd like to earn my living from working with my brain. We had a careers talk at school the other day and I'm interested in learning about the law. If I get good A' levels, I could go on to study law at university and become a solicitor or a lawyer one day. And that would be very good money Jens. I know I'd have to study for a long time, but when I did eventually get a job, I'd be earning a lot of money. Just think where the solicitors live in this town, they've either got big houses up top town around People's Park or else they live in mansions out in the Wolds. That could be us one day if I pass the exams.'

Frank's enthusiasm and ambition was touching for both Gwen and Jens. He was a clever boy without a doubt and mixing with the posh boys in the grammar school's sixth form had certainly given him a glimpse of what the world had to offer beyond a life of working on the docks.

'Darling,' Gwen said, her voice very gentle now. 'You do realise don't you, that it costs a lot of money to go away to university, and you know that even with Jens' money coming in now, we aren't exactly rolling in it.' It hurt her to say these words and she was fighting to hold back a tear at the thought that she could be crushing her youngest boy's dream. But she needed to let him know that a university education was beyond her financial means. She continued.

'I know you're very clever Frank and I'm sure that

you could get a degree if you set your heart on it, but there are lots of really good jobs you could get with your A' Levels, you could get into the Civil Service or get a really good job in a bank. They're brain jobs, and if you work hard at them, you could get promoted and be on really good money before long. I'm sorry darling, but you need to know that I just don't think that I'll ever be able to afford to send you to university.'

Gwen was deeply upset at bursting her son's bubble but was somehow relieved to have had the opportunity to make Frank face the reality of his situation. She had been tempted to let him go on thinking he would go away to university after his A' Levels, but she was worried that the longer he was allowed to carry on with his day dreaming, the harder and crueler would be the realisation that it could never be. She was reassured that as hard as it was for her to say these words, it was the kindest thing for her to do.

Frank looked crushed by this but did not challenge back. He could see the pain in his mother's face and knew enough to realise that these words were hard for her.

'Yes Mum, I know you're right,' he sighed. 'It was just a dream; it's what the other boys talk about and I guess I just got swept along with it all. There isn't anyone else in the sixth form like me; they've all got dads and their dads have all got good jobs, going to uni' is what's expected of them. I'm just as clever as any of them though, cleverer than most even, and it doesn't seem fair that they're going to get the best opportunities and the best jobs and the best lives just because they're from rich families. It just doesn't seem fair that's all.' He was nearly crying.

'It isn't fair Frank.' Jens had been silent through this until now, but couldn't hold his tongue any longer. 'It isn't fair that you've got all of those brains in your head and you won't get the best chance to use them. If Dad was alive, we'd have been able to afford to send you to university and he would have wanted you to go.' Gwen shot him a glance at this, she knew that losing his father at six years old had been a massive blow to him and that Jens had been desperately trying to be the man of the house ever since.

'It's not fair that you should miss out just because you haven't got a father,' he continued. 'But I'm going to make sure that you can go to university Frank, so don't you worry about it anymore. Just get on with your school work, study hard and make sure you pass those exams and leave the rest to me.'

'Jens, what are you saying?' Gwen interjected with an alarmed note in her voice. 'You know that we can't afford to send him, you're just giving him false hope.'

'Not if I get a better job,' he replied, 'I've had enough of working in the factory anyway Mum, I'm going to put my name down for a job on the trawlers.'

'Oh no you're not young man!' She was flaming with anger.

'Yes Mum, it's the only way.' Jens had been dreading this conversation ever since he'd had the idea, but he was relieved to get it out into the open.

'You know that I've always wanted to go to sea, and Hansen's are launching new boats all the time, they're making record catches and the crews are making really good money. If I was on the boats, we'd be able to afford for Frank to go to university, so we'd both be happy.'

'But I wouldn't Jens,' she replied, 'I'd be worried sick every time you walked out of that door. Scared that you wouldn't come back. You must be mad to want to go to sea, look what happened to your father, and he isn't the only one, there's hardly a family on this street that hasn't lost a loved one at sea.' There was truth in this and Jens understood how difficult this decision was for his mother to accept.

'It's different now Mum,' he pleaded, 'the boats are bigger and better equipped, they've got safety gear and you get proper training nowadays. It's not as dangerous as it used to be.'

'It is still really dangerous Jens,' Gwen countered. 'Those trawlers aren't floating hotels you know; the work is hard, the hours are long and it's freezing cold up in the Arctic Circle. Danger is everywhere, even on the new boats.' She was transported back in her mind's eye to the terrible days of her loss; the knock on the door from Ophelia's skipper and the subsequent breaking of the terrible news, sitting in the small front parlour of this very house. The young Dane had stolen her heart and she had never even thought of another man since his death. Her life had been her two lovely boys and caring for them and worrying about them had been all she'd known since that day. It was twelve years ago, but felt as raw in her heart today as the day it had happened.

Jens realised that he would never win this argument with his impassioned mother, he saw her retreating somewhere into her memories and knew that she had become withdrawn from them. As painful as it had been, he was relieved though, relieved that he had aired his lifelong yearning and broken the news to his mother that his ambition was to go to sea. He turned to Frank who was looking confused and upset by the chain of events that he appeared to have triggered. 'Don't you worry Frank,' he said quietly, gripping his younger brother firmly and reassuringly on the shoulder. 'Things will work out okay in the long run one way or another. I'll make it happen. I promise.'

They finished their meal in silence.

*

Just before seven o'clock Jens knocked on Shirley's kitchen door and went straight in, calling out as he entered. 'Hellooo, it's only me, are you ready Shirl?' He was summoned through into the living room, which directly adjoined the kitchen. The room was small but cozy; a coal fire burned in the hearth and the television was turned on. Shirley's father Derek had been watching the news but was sleeping now, her mother Gladys was waiting for Doctor Kildare to come on; it was her favourite programme. Shirley's younger sister, fifteen-year-old Sally, was sitting on the settee cuddled up next to her mother, whilst Derek was enjoying the armchair close to the fire, the Grimsby Evening Telegraph unfolded over his face as he snoozed with his feet warming in front of the fireplace. Gladys looked up at Jens and raised a finger to her lips, alerting him to the sleeping Derek.

'She'll be down in a minute love,' she told him, 'she's nearly ready, take a seat.'

Jens slid onto the settee next to Sally and watched the television with them for a while; this was a novelty for him, they did not have a set in his own house. His mind wasn't really on the programme though, he was still feeling unsettled after the upsetting argument with his mother about his ambition to go to sea. His mind was still elsewhere when he was shaken from his forlorn reverie by the creaking sound of Shirley hopping down the stairs and entering the room in a swirl of pastel chiffon.

'I'm ready Jens, let's get off,' she enthused, 'I can't wait.'

Shirley loved to dance and Friday night at Pearson's Palais was her favourite dance night of the week. Jens got up and gestured a quiet good evening to Gladys and Sally, smiling at the still sleeping Derek, the newspaper rising and falling slightly with his breathing.

It was dark outside, and cold after the warmth of the coal fire in the little living room. Shirley and Jens walked arm in arm, as much for warmth as for friendship, to the bus stop at the corner of the main road. They did not have to wait long before one came along and they got on board paying the conductor with pennies for the short trip to Cleethorpes. The bus was crowded with people heading into the resort for their Friday night's entertainment and Shirley and Jens had to stand in the downstairs aisle, hanging onto the upright poles for stability as the vehicle accelerated and braked for the frequent stops along the road.

'Are you alright Jens?' Shirley asked. Although he hadn't said anything, she had a sense that her friend was troubled; he seemed a little distracted by something. She was puzzled. 'Have I said something wrong Jens?' she asked.

'No Shirl, course not,' he replied. 'You could never, ever upset me. I'm sorry, just ignore me, I'll be okay.' The bus lurched and they were thrown together, their faces only inches apart. She put her free arm around him and looked into his eyes.

'Look Jens, I know there's something wrong and you're going to have to tell me what's worrying you.' She paused for effect. 'Because if you don't, we won't be doing any dancing, 'cos I won't be able to enjoy myself knowing that there's something up with you.'

He had been trying not to let his somber mood show, but she knew him so well it was impossible for him to deceive her; he felt that she must have some sort of sixth sense, that she was able to read his mind and to understand his innermost thoughts. Any chance of keeping his secret to himself had disappeared, he simply could not bear for his own problem to impact on Shirley's happiness and to spoil her enjoyment of something she loved so much.

'Well, it's nothing really,' he started, 'it's just that Mum and me had a bit of a fall out over tea.'

'Why's that? It's not like you to argue with your mother.'

'I told her that I want to put my name down to go on the boats.'

Shirley looked shocked. Still pressed close to him on the crowded bus, her eyes were locked onto his but she was speechless. Jens couldn't hold her gaze and cast his eyes downwards. Eventually, Shirley recovered enough to say, 'I never knew that you wanted to go on the boats; you've never said anything. Why? Why do you want to go to sea, and why has this just come out now?'

'I've always wanted to Shirl, I've just never been able to say so. I want to be a fisherman like Dad and like Harry. It's a good life, the money is really good and I had to say something tonight 'cos our Frank has got his heart set on going away to university and he'll never be able to do that if I don't find a way of earning us some more money.' It came out in one long rush and afterwards he managed to raise his eyes back to Shirley's. The bus was nearing their stop and they shuffled forwards with the other passengers and dismounted to the pavement. They stood for a while whilst the bus pulled away and the other passengers wandered off towards their destinations. Pearson's Palais de Dance was situated close to Cleethorpes promenade and they could hear the sound of the tide breaking against the sea wall behind them. Shirley reached up and placed her hand on the side of Jens' face and said quietly to him.

'You must know how your mother is feeling about this Jens, it will break her heart.'

'I know, I do feel bad,' he confessed, 'but it's something I have to do, not just for me, but also for her and for Frank. I understand why she's upset but fishing isn't the same as it used to be. Dad was sailing on a little coal burning seine netter and it got into trouble in a collision on a big sea. He was unlucky but it was a freak accident. You've seen the Hansen boats Shirl', they're huge, like floating cities. State of the art.' He paused. 'After a while she'll come round, she'll realise why I'm doing it when the money starts to come in and our Frank goes off to university to get his education and really make something of himself.'

She listened, trying to take in the flood of feelings pouring out of him. He continued. 'I'll never be anything special Shirley, I'll never amount to much, but if I can get on the boats, then Frank will get the opportunity to really make her proud. Prouder than I could ever make her.'

'Jens,' she cut in, 'she loves you both so much, you're very different people but she's proud of you both for who you are, not for what you are or what you could be.'

'I know, you're right,' he admitted, 'but I'm serious about this Shirley, I haven't got a brain like Frank's, but I've got the sea in my blood. Dad wasn't much older than me when he came over from Denmark to Grimsby and he'd already seen the world. He was a good fisherman Shirl' and I've always known that one day I would follow in his footsteps.'

'What about me Jens?' Shirley asked. She had so far held back this question. 'Have you thought how I might feel about this?'

He had. He had agonised over this and it had nearly affected his decision, but Jens was so clear in his own mind that this was his destiny and that everything resulting from this would be right, he had managed to convince himself that after some initial resistance his mother and Shirley would soon come around and see things his way.

'Will you do me a favour?' she asked, her voice very serious. 'I want you to tell me that you won't make this decision until we've all had the chance to properly talk about it. Promise me that Jens; promise me that you won't go doing anything rash. It's a big decision and you need some time to think about it. If you really want to go to sea, then you probably should go and I will support you in that, but I just don't think you've thought it through properly. Promise me that you won't do anything straight away, not until we've had a chance to talk it through at least.'

She was holding his face in both hands and tears glistened in her eyes as she made her plea. He caved in, helpless in the face of her solemn appeal and he answered feebly, 'Yes okay, I won't do anything yet.'

With this agreement reached, they began to walk towards the Palais de Dance where they mingled with other young couples milling around the entrance; they paid their way in, checked their coats and stepped immediately together onto the polished wooden dance floor. Once in motion, Shirley's solemn mood soon lifted, she had done enough she thought, enough to buy some time for Gwen and herself to work on Jens. She felt confident that between them, they would keep him ashore. Whilst she knew that his mother lived in fear of losing her son in the same way she had lost her husband, in truth, Shirley did not share Gwen's fear over Jens' safety on the new Hansen boats, they were so big and modern, not at all like the old steamers. Shirley had her own reasons for not wanting him to disappear off to sea for weeks on end.

They moved in time together, fluid and graceful, rising and falling with the cadence of the music, their bodies in close contact, her hand delicately placed on his shoulder, his hand guiding her with slight changes of pressure to the small of her back.

She loved to dance, her small face was raised elegantly, at a slight angle, gazing with a sublime expression at Jens as they glided between the other dancers, whirling together, united and in harmony. She loved to dance, and she loved Jens Peter Thorsen.

CHAPTER FOUR

In the part of town where Grimsby merges into Cleethorpes, nestled between the ranks of terraced homes there is a pleasant, nicely tended Edwardian Park bordered by larger, grander dwellings. Ken Flett was sitting in a comfortable armchair in the well-furnished front room of one of these substantial three storey homes. It was dark outside, too dark to see anything other than the streetlights. The bay window had become a large black mirror reflecting the interior of the room back to him. He watched his reflection, saw his mirror-image holding a tumbler of blended Scotch whisky, toying with it, rolling the glass to make liquid teardrops form and dribble down the inside. He took a sip, savouring the fiery liquid as it slipped down his throat. He admired his reflection. He was twenty-eight years old, in his prime, he thought. His hair was very dark and his eyes astonishingly pale. There was no doubt that Ken was a very handsome man but there was a wolfishness about him that some found disconcerting.

Celia was in the kitchen preparing tea. Three-month-old baby Alice slept in a cradle next to him. They had lived in this house for just over nine months and had been married for just one week longer than that.

Ken was in a contemplative mood and the effect of the whisky was darkening the hue of his introspection. He looked down at the sleeping bundle, his baby daughter Alice, and he thought about his wife. He could hear her in the distance, clanking pots and pans in the kitchen at the end of the downstairs hallway corridor. Celia, with her jet-black hair and her big deep blue, smiling eyes. Celia, with her round face and her apple cheeks. Celia, with her petite but curvaceous figure. Celia, with her melodious voice and lilting Broch accent. It was hardly surprising that he had fallen for her in such a big way.

He recalled the evening they had first met. It was a black tie event and because he did not own one of his own, he'd had to make a trip to Aberdeen especially to hire a monkey suit. He had not expected to be invited, but his boss William Smalley had gone down with flu and Ken had been called upon to take up the spare ticket and represent his company at the Fish Trades Association Christmas Ball. At that time he had been working for William Smalley as a junior manager at the Smalley's family business in Peterhead; they owned lorries, warehouses and cold storage facilities and provided haulage and storage services to the local fishing industry. He had not been looking forward to the evening, he'd felt that he would be out of his depth socially, mixing with the wealthy trawler owners and fish processors – it was a duty call.

But all of that had changed as soon as he'd set eyes on Celia. She had shone and sparkled amongst the over made up, over dressed dowager wives of the industry magnates; so fresh, so appealing, so attractive! Ken may have felt out of his comfort zone mixing in the rarefied social sphere, but he had never lacked confidence in his relationships with women and he soon ensured that an opportunity was created for them to exchange small talk. He discovered that she was called Celia Gibson and that her father was Ralph Gibson, owner of the Gibson Fishing Company, a business that ran a number of whitefish trawlers fishing out of both Fraserburgh and Peterhead. Ralph Gibson was a wealthy man.

By the end of the Fish Trades Association Christmas Ball of nineteen sixty-two, Ken Flett and Celia Gibson had agreed to meet for a date the following weekend. They were to visit the cinema for a matinee performance and have tea together afterwards. At that time, Celia was living at her parent's large house just outside of the town, near the golf course. On the day of the date, her father had dropped her off in the town centre in his big black Vanden Plas Princess, it was clear from the way he had pulled away from the kerb with the vehicle's tyres squealing, that Ralph Gibson was not overly pleased with his daughter's choice of date, but Celia seemed unconcerned by her father's disapproval and she was clearly in a good mood. She was dressed in the latest style and her short dress showed off a pair of shapely legs to well above the knee.

Ken had been captivated by Celia's self assured confidence and her irrepressible good humour, it had occurred to him that she was the personification of what people mean when they say that somebody is 'bubbly.' On meeting her for a second time, it was clear that his first impression was absolutely correct. In fact, she may have been even more attractive than he had originally thought. At the dinner dance, she had been dressed conservatively in formal evening wear but on this day, she looked every bit the modern girl in her clearly expensive, well cut dress and herring bone coat, she wore less make up and looked younger than he had originally thought.

Celia was just twenty-two years old at that time. After finishing her degree in Mediaeval Scottish history at Edinburgh University, she had returned to live with her parents in their large, grey stone home. Uncertain of where her life was taking her, she had decided to take some time out to consider her options and had been helping her father with some light office duties at the Gibson Fishing Company. Quietly, Ralph Gibson was very pleased to have his only child back home after her three years away at university, and to have her flitting around the office, causing a stir with her breezy good humour was an added bonus. He loved her dearly and doted on her. She was his little princess.

Ken and Celia began dating regularly. He was deeply attracted to her and she clearly enjoyed his company. They mostly met at weekends because Ken stayed in Peterhead, only twenty miles away, but in those days he didn't own a car and he worked long hours at Smalley's. At weekends he would either take the bus to Fraserburgh or sometimes borrow a friend's car. Then they would have days out, roaming the Aberdeenshire countryside and exploring the coast, seeking out cafés and pubs where they would have long, light-hearted conversations, teasing each other and giggling like schoolchildren. In truth, Celia did most of the talking, she was incredibly lucid and articulate, her intelligence shone through in the way that she expressed herself and especially in the way that she could find the funny side in almost any situation.

One day he had brought along his box Brownie camera. It was not yet Easter, but the weather was remarkably mild, they had the borrowed car and had ventured along the coast to Cullen. Here, they had parked up and taken a long walk along the beach and around the old port area, looking at the small vessels tied up there. It was very different to the big ports they were used to, everything seemed miniature, so charming and picturesque to the two young lovers. Ken was far from an accomplished photographer but with a subject like Celia, it would have been difficult to take a bad photograph. He took snap after snap that day and took the film into the chemists in Peterhead the very next Monday morning, eager to see the results.

He was not disappointed, the black and white snaps turned out very well, capturing Celia's fresh faced, wind blown beauty. He was particularly pleased with one photograph, a close up. He remembered taking the snap; he had been holding the camera in one hand and trying to slip his other one inside her coat. She had been giggling hysterically, trying to bat away his advances. 'Ken, no!' she had shrieked. 'It's broad daylight, somebody will see.' And then, as she was laughing and tossing her head backwards to try to escape his reach, he had triggered the shutter. It was the perfect distillation of a moment in time.

The same photograph, enlarged from the original negative stood now in a dark wooden frame on the Flett's mantelpiece in the comfortable room that overlooked the park. He looked at it and saw Celia's ecstatic laughing face captured and rendered in silver and pewter tones. He remembered the day, he remembered how he had felt then, right then, at the very instant he had pressed the shutter button. It was taken only last year but it seemed like a lifetime ago to him now. A lot had happened since then, their lives had taken a direction that neither would have guessed on that day just before Easter in nineteen sixty-three. He became aware once again of his dark reflection staring back from the black windowpane, he did not recognise the expression on his own face. He wondered what he had become. He wondered what had happened to the beautiful smiling girl in the photograph?

Ken took another sip of the whisky and stirred a little from his reverie as he became aware of Celia's fluid singsong North Eastern accent calling him to the tea table. Young Alice slept peacefully on. That's a bad sign, he thought, she'll be keeping us awake all night. He put the glass down, placed his palms onto the chair arms and levered himself to his feet; then, on the way out of the room, he kicked the crib ever so lightly but hard enough to startle the baby, who awoke with a mewling cry.

'Oh no,' he called through to his wife. 'Alice has just woken up darling, can you come and get her?'

*

She found herself alone with just her own thoughts for company. Jens had gone out dancing with Shirley, and Frank had secreted himself into the sanctuary of his bedroom at the back of the house, he was doing his homework. Gwen Thorsen could not escape her thoughts, the replayed conversations that could not be silenced, could not be forgotten and could not be denied. She was tired and emotionally drained from the two difficult conversations over tea. Her struggle to dissuade Frank from his university ambitions was effort enough, but then Jens had dropped his massive bombshell! She sat, forlorn and alone in her front parlour, the Light Programme was playing on the wireless, but she didn't hear it, her mind was too full. She was feeling profoundly sad.

For all the years that had passed, it seemed to her like only yesterday when she had sat in this very room, in this very chair and had received the news of her husband's death. He had been a lovely man, the only man for her. It had been a whirlwind romance; they had married quietly and quickly after meeting at the Palais de Dance, then they had lived with her mother and father in Cleethorpes for nearly six months before Kurt had found this home for them. She smiled to herself at the remembrance of those happy days. At first her mother and father had been reticent about her relationship with the Danish fisherman, but Kurt had soon won them over with his excellent manners and charming Scandinavian ways.

She had just turned eighteen years old when she'd married, and Jens had come along less than a year later. By then, they had moved into this house and set up a nice little home together. They were so happy, she remembered that the neighbours used to call them 'the lovebirds' and Kurt was always so kind and attentive when he was back from sea, not like most of the men; out on the raz' then straight back fishing again. Kurt couldn't wait to get home to spend time with her; they'd had some lovely times together in those days.

She recalled the squabbles amongst some of her neighbours. Some of the men badly used their women whilst they were onshore, but then expected everything to be made up just before they went back to the boat. A few trips had been held up over the years whilst the husbands and wives made up their differences at the eleventh hour, even on the quayside sometimes. There was none of that for Kurt and Gwen; he would come straight back from the boat, sleep for hours, then spend the rest of his shore time pottering around the house, tending to his vegetable plot in the little back yard or tinkering with any one of his numerous hobbies in the old Anderson shelter that he used as a garden shed.

When the time did come for him to go back to sea, he always seemed to go willingly but with a heavy heart. He was on a happy boat and the Ophelia was a lucky vessel too, he'd always made good money from the catches. Kurt did love the fishing, but the parting was always painful for both of them, especially for Gwen who was left behind alone. Life on shore for newly wed women could be difficult, it could be lonely and boring, just waiting for the man you love to come back for a few short days before disappearing for days or weeks on end again. Gwen would count the days, storing her news and trying to bottle her excitement about what the future may hold for them and for their as yet, unborn child.

In those early days before Jens was born, she did not know the neighbours on Hope Street very well. On one side there was another fishing family, the Websters; they were always battling and spent most of their time either arguing or getting drunk or more likely, both. They still lived there today although they had settled down a lot over the years. They still argued, but Gwen thought they fought less than before, either that or she'd run out of plates to throw at him. She smiled, briefly, at the thought. On the other side in those days was old mister Reynolds, a World War One veteran, sadly gone now. Next to mister Reynolds was the Coulbecks.

Gwen's friendship with Dolly Coulbeck had started way back then, very soon after she'd moved into the house and whilst she was still carrying Jens. They had recognised each other as neighbours when they'd met one day in the nearby park; Dolly had been out for a walk with her three year old toddler Harry, and Gwen, quite heavily pregnant, was sitting on a bench next to the model boat pond, taking the weight off her swollen feet and enjoying the sunshine and fresh air.

'Hello love,' Dolly had said in a friendly voice. 'Are you the lady who's just moved in a couple of doors down from me?'

They'd got on immediately and had shared a great deal of their histories on that very first meeting in the park. It turned out that Dolly's husband Sid knew Kurt and had even worked with him for a short while on the minesweepers during the war. Sid had a healthy respect for the young Dane who had proved to be a good seaman. The women's friendship had been cemented.

The memories of those days came flooding back to her; how he would return from a fishing trip with a bunch of flowers in his hand for her, those florist shops near the docks must make a fortune every time a boat comes in, she thought. Kurt had always come straight home from the docks with his bouquet, unlike many men who would head straight to the pub. Harry Webster next door used to pop into the florist, buy a bouquet and send it home in a taxi whilst he went off down Freeman Street with his shipmates for a good drink. It used to drive his wife wild and on some occasions she would set off, grim faced to find him and drag him home before he'd had the chance to drink or gamble away all of his settlings.

She recalled the feeling of seeing Kurt walking through the door, the relief of having him safely back in her arms again and listening to the lilt of his soft Danish accent as he told her how much he loved her and how much he missed her whilst he'd been away at sea. And she recalled their nights of love together, gentle but passionate, then sleeping in each other's arms, her head on his shoulder and Kurt's body curved around her growing baby bump.

She missed him so much. She could still hear his voice echoing in her memory, still smiled at his silly, unfunny Danish jokes, still felt the warmth of his breath against her neck. Her heart missed a beat every time she thought of him or heard his name mentioned. She cursed the sea for taking her man, cursed the sea for that ultimate act of betrayal and cruelty, the loss that had sliced into her heart and stolen the joy from her life. She was worn with her grief.

The only thing in her life that gave her the strength to carry on, to bear the loss, was her love for her boys. Jens, so like his father physically, she thought, slender but wiry and strong, with his very fair colouring, whilst Frank favoured more her side of the family, the Padleys. Frank was darker but had more of Kurt's personality, clever and enquiring, always thinking about something, trying to figure out how things work by taking them to pieces and putting them back together again. She smiled at the memory of the eight year old Frank trying to put the living room clock back together after having disassembled it with his penknife. She smiled now, she hadn't then, but she had recognised that innate curiosity in him which had reminded her so much of his late father.

Her boys were all she had now and she rued the thought of Frank's disappointment and Jens being in danger on the sea. It was not possible for them both to be happy, one or the other was destined to be disappointed in their ambitions. But which one of her precious boys was it to be?

*

By half past eight, Shirley, Harry and Jens found themselves standing in the bar area at Pearson's Palais de dance. Shirley wanted to dance again but Jens was talking animatedly to Harry. Bill Osborne was sitting fast asleep on the snug, his head lolled forward onto his chest, his hand still gripping the beer glass in his lap. The house band were playing a waltz. Couples swirled in time to the music, girls in pastel shades, boys in their best suits and Brilliantined hair, the air was pungent with cigarette smoke and perfume. Although the evening was still young, Harry was unsteady on his feet and was swaying slightly from side to side, but not at all in time with the music. Jens was asking him about the trip and life on board the big trawler Apollo.

'She's a good boat,' Harry slurred slightly and belched. 'We caught a shit load of big cod up off Bear Island. Made me a lot of money this trip lad, I will be celebrating in style. Get us another round in Bill!' He flourished a fist full of pound notes but Bill didn't stir.

'When are you out again Harry?' he asked.

'We're sailing on Monday. Norway coast I think. Reckon that could be another big one, we've broken the port record this year already you know, she's the best boat in the fleet.' He paused for a second and added. 'For now anyway.'

'What do you mean for now?' Jens looked puzzled.

'Haven't you heard mate? They're building a new one, the Freya. They reckon she's gonna be something very special.'

'How special?'

'Stern trawler! It's a new design; she pulls the trawl behind her, not over the side like the Apollo. I've even heard that they're gonna fit her out with plate freezers so that she can freeze the catch at sea, that means she can stay out fishing for a lot longer and make even more dosh.'

Harry drained his glass and kicked Bill's foot in the same move. 'Oi, Osborne! Your shout!' Bill awoke with a start, nearly spilling his own pint. He hauled himself unsteadily to his feet and lurched away towards the small but busy bar.

'It's the future Jens.'

'Stern trawling?'

'Yes, but more than that I reckon. I mean, when you think about how our dads fished from those little coal burning seiners, that's history now. It's how they did it in the last century and that's what made this port great, but diesel is the future Jens. But it's not just about putting diesel engines into the old steamers like they are doing over at Croy's yard.' He paused to think and continued. 'The big diesel boats like the Apollo have been breaking records for the last few years and I never thought it could get any better than that. But the Freya will be a totally new way of fishing. It's not just about diesel, it's about technology; that's the future Jens, tech-bloody-nology!'

Shirley was not listening to the boys anymore, she was listening to the house band playing a lovely foxtrot tune, a breathy version of Glenn Miller's Moonlight Serenade, the saxophone player picked out the melody in fluid jazz phrases, the all-important dance beat metered out by the drummer, caressing the skins with his metal brushes and thumping the heartbeat rhythm with the bass pedal. The music was soft and melodic; she soaked it in, although it was not really her type of music, not what she listened to at home on the radiogram. She preferred music from the hit parade and had a small collection of seven-inch 45rpm records, mainly the Beatles but she also liked the Swinging Blue Jeans and the Dave Clark Five. But you couldn't foxtrot to the Beatles. This was proper dance music she thought, losing herself in the classic melody; this was the music of romance, of elegance and sophistication. She closed her eyes and hummed along with the melody. Quietly; just to herself.

Shirley and Jens were amongst the youngest of the regulars at the Palais, but by no means were they unusual. There were a number of good dancers in their age range, although the very best dancers were all about ten years older than them. They were the ones who were the most practiced, their skills becoming more polished and impressive with each passing year. She listened, lost in the jazz music and watching the couples move in harmony. One day she would be as good as the very best of them she decided, all she had to do was practice, and practice and practice. She looked up to see where Jens was, she wanted to dance again, to slide onto the floor and take her place in the flow and eddy of the swaying couples, but seeing him still locked into a deep head to head conversation with Harry, she was a little disappointed and truth be told, a little annoyed with him.

This was Friday night, she thought, dance night! Shirley didn't want to listen to the men talking about trawlers and fishing all night, so she drifted away to talk to Doreen who had just been dancing to the Glenn Miller tune with her boyfriend Colin. They had stepped off the immaculate, shining wooden dance floor and onto the dank, drink-stained and sticky bar carpet. The band was taking a breather and a speaker now piped out music from the record player. It was something by Matt Monro. Plaintive, but hard to hear above the excited Friday night chatter.

Bill Osborne appeared at Harry's elbow with two fresh pints for the fishermen. He gave one to Harry and then offered up his own glass for Jens to take a swig. Despite already having a nearly full glass of his own, Jens took the drink from Bill with pleasure and swigged deeply at it. He returned the half drained glass to Bill who wandered back to his seat and resumed the slumber position. Jens licked the beer foam from his top lip.

'Do you think so Harry?' He was intrigued. The port of Grimsby was thriving and new vessels were being launched almost on a monthly basis. Hansen Group alone ran over sixty inshore, mid-water and distant water trawlers and it seemed that each new boat launched had to be bigger and better than the last. The Apollo was the biggest and best yet, taking that honour from the Zeus which in turn had displaced the Thor. And now the ambitious company was planning something even bigger.

'I can't believe they can build a bigger and better boat than Apollo, she's beautiful.'

'Tech-bloody-nology Jens, that's the secret. Freya won't have to be bigger than Apollo, but she'll be *better* because she'll be more advanced. Apollo isn't a lot more than a giant steam trawler with a diesel engine. Freya will be something new, like nothing we've ever seen before.'

Jens looked impressed.

'Wouldn't mind a go at that Jens mate,' Harry continued, 'I've been getting on well on the Apollo, the skipper likes me and I reckon he'd put in a good word for me if I put me name down for the Freya.'

Jens was fascinated with the news from Harry about the Freya. There had been some rumours in the factory about a new boat but nothing official had leaked out from the management about such an important new vessel coming into the fleet. This was really exciting news, and if what Harry had said was true, Freya would be the most modern and advanced fishing boat in the world. He took a big swig of his beer and seemed lost in thought for a while. He did not notice that Harry's eyes had hardly left

Shirley all evening. He was looking at her now, as she chatted with Doreen, her curls bouncing as she laughed politely at some lame crack that Colin had just made. Harry was hardly even aware of Jens' question.

'If you put your name down for Freya, do you think you could get me a job on her too?'

CHAPTER FIVE

Half past ten on Saturday morning. Harry was just waking up, he was befuddled, dismayed to discover that he was laying prone on the top of his bed, half undressed, his trousers still tangled around one ankle. He hadn't quite made it into bed last night but had slept soundly for nearly ten hours, making up for the sleep deprivation of the fishing trip. It was Dolly's knocking on the door that had roused him and she tentatively pushed it open and peered around into her son's room.

'Oh Harry,' she sighed, seeing him blinking in the late morning daylight, struggling to break the surface of consciousness. 'You must have been in a right state last night.' She tut-tutted as she bustled into the room and put down a big mug of strong tea on his small bedside table.

He rubbed a hand through his tangled hair and tried to smile through the hangover at his mother. 'It was a good night,' was the only defence he could think of. She smiled at her incorrigible son and left him in peace to get back to the world of the living in his own time.

Sitting on his bed with the mug of tea in his hand,

Harry began to piece together the previous evening. After snooker, he had gone to Pearson's Palais and met Shirley and Jens, he recalled. After that, it all got a bit hazy. He remembered drinking beer with Bill in the refreshment room on Cleethorpes railway station; a bag of chips ...somewhere, and a nightcap at the social club before rolling home and hitting the sack around midnight. No fights, he recalled. That was good.

As the tea began to do the job of reviving him, he found himself thinking about the Palais and in particular about Shirley. He remembered her looking adorable in her dancing dress, easily the prettiest girl in the place, by a mile! He was suddenly conscious that he was smiling broadly to himself. Like a grinning loon, he thought and tried to regain his composure. 'What is happening to me?' he said under his breath, shaking his head and rising from the ruffled bed.

A few moments later he was downstairs, finishing his tea in the kitchen where his mother was pottering around, listening to the wireless.

'What you planning today Harry?' she asked.

'Not sure Mum,' he answered. 'Town are playing away, so there's no match this afto. I might go down Freemo for a game of snooker or something though.' Harry was thoughtful for a while and sat silently drinking his second cup of tea whilst Dolly hummed and sang along with the song on the wireless.

'Mum,' he said at last, 'what do you think of Shirley Lofts?'

There was tension in his voice and Dolly knew this question had not come easily to her son. She thought back to his arrival home the previous morning and recalled her sensation, her motherly intuition that there was something on his mind.

'She's a lovely girl' she replied truthfully, 'I've always liked her and her mother Gladys is a nice lady too, I've got a lot of time for Gladys, I have.'

'I didn't ask you about bloody Gladys did I?' he retorted, 'I asked you what you thought about Shirley!' He was jesting, a little uncomfortably to cover his embarrassment at the personal nature of the conversation, but Harry had always trusted his mother's judgment and was keen to understand one thing in particular. She was looking puzzled, not quite knowing what he wanted from her. Eventually, he had to help her, with a more explicit question.

'Do you think there's anything between her and Jens?'

'Well, I'm sure I don't know love' she pondered. 'They're always knocking about together, dancing partners too. But then again, they've always been like that, ever since they was kids. Like brother and sister, joined at the hip they was, as far back as I can remember. At least, since poor Kurt was lost.'

He was looking for more from her. Dolly was cautious now. 'Look darling; if you're interested in Shirley in that way, you'll have to tell her. She's not a mind reader and if you don't say something, she'll never know and neither will you!' She paused for further thought. 'Just bear in mind though love, that she might not feel the same way about you. I mean, I'm sure she thinks very highly of you, and always has done, but I honestly don't know if her and Jens are more than friends. They might be though, so tread carefully.'

She had been as honest as she dare without risking crushing her son's hopes altogether. In truth Dolly felt that Shirley and Jens did share something special, a natural and unselfconscious intimacy that marked them as a pair. She was suddenly worried for Harry.

'Well I didn't say that I felt anything about her at all,' he responded, bluffing wildly. 'I was just asking you what you thought of her. I saw her last night and I thought she'd grown up to be really pretty, that's all.' He got up from the table, draining the mug of tea and headed off back upstairs to get dressed properly.

She smiled at her handsome young son, watching him disappear up the stairs, regretting the advice that she had just given him and hoping against hope that he decided not to take it.

A few moments later he was back downstairs again, dressed casually in an open necked shirt and a sports jacket. 'I'm off for a walk,' he told her, opening the back door and ambling out of her view down the passageway. He had no real idea where he was going, or why. He just knew that he wanted to walk, to clear his head and to try to get a grip on these unsettling new thoughts and feelings.

He walked without purpose, heading vaguely towards Cleethorpes, past the identical rows of terraced houses that spread away from the docks in ordered ranks. He could smell coal fires in the cold air and saw their grey smoke smudges rising from the red clay pots. This was his world, the humble but respectable homes built around the turn of the century to house the thousands of workers drawn to the port to work on the fishing vessels and the shore based industries that serviced them.

They all lived here. The men who went away to sea and the men who stayed on shore; the men who loaded the boats and the men who unloaded the boats, the men who filleted the fish, the men who packed the fish and those who put it onto the trains and the lorries that transported it to the markets all over the country. All of those men, and their wives and their children and their children's children, in fact almost everyone Harry had ever known lived here in one of these houses. He thought about the thousands of them, all living out their private dramas; the minor, the major and the catastrophic events of their lives, all within the walls of these small, faceless red brick homes. He was one of them.

He walked on through the utilitarian streets, losing track of his whereabouts in their sameness until he arrived eventually at the cast iron and latticed steel footbridge that spanned the Grimsby to Cleethorpes railway line.

He crossed the bridge and walked down the steps onto the sandy beach on the other side. The houses were behind him now, beyond the railway lines, not far away but somehow distant. The reverberating echoes of the myriad imagined human dilemmas faded to silence. In front of him, the broad Humber estuary stretched into the distance. He could see the thin, shimmering blue line of the North bank, and stretching away far to his right, in the invisible distance beyond the horizon, the mighty river Humber and the North Sea became one. Pewter clouds heralded rain later, but just for now, they painted a dramatic watercolour skyline as the wan sunlight broke from behind them. He liked this feeling. It's like being at sea, he thought and he moved on once again, his feet sliding now in the slippery fine sand of the high foreshore. Further down, nearer the sea, the sand was darker, harder and easier to walk on as he picked his way past the waist high concrete blocks; tank traps left over from the last war when invasion had threatened. He found better footing closer to the water, the tide was on the way out and the waves rushed and rippled towards him, rhythmic, almost musical to his fisherman's ears. He loved being close to the water; it fascinated him, compelled him and soothed him. He realised he had been drawn here so that he could think clearly, and make a decision.

The retreating tide had left the beach littered with bladder wrack and kelp. Mussel, whelk, oyster and cockleshells, all mixed with jet-black shining nuts of wet coal on the dun sand which was rippled with black veins of coal dust. Harry's feet paddled almost silently over the brown sand, crackled lightly over the black coal dust and crunched over the seashells as he wandered along the tide line, listening to the shrieking seagulls and feeling the chill sea wind on his face. He turned now towards the shore, taking in the panorama as he did so, from the distant latticed wooden structure of the big dipper in Cleethorpes on his left to the stately red brick pinnacle of Grimsby's Victorian dock tower on his right. He liked this perspective, looking towards the land from the tideline.

He was feeling happy now. He knew what he must do. He knew that he had to tell Shirley how he felt about her.

*

Sounds from the street drifted in through the open window, stirring Celia Flett as she dozed on the settee. She was vaguely aware of the distant voices of children playing their Saturday afternoon ball games in the park across the road. Alice slept beside her, swaddled in a soft woolen baby blanket; she was making a soft snuffling noise as she breathed. The clock on the mantelpiece was ticking. Otherwise, the room was silent.

Celia was weary, Alice had been awake for most of the night again, suffering with croup, coughing harsh little barks and struggling to breathe in the cold night bedroom air. Celia had been up and down stairs several times throughout the night, boiling the kettle and carrying hot water upstairs in a selection of kitchen bowls and pans. She had arranged these around the side of Alice's cot in the hope that the steamy vapours would soothe her little lungs.

It was not just the sleeplessness that had tired Celia; it was the worry too. When Alice was having her attacks, she could hardly bear to hear the crackling in her breathing or to see her little rib cage pumping and battling against her constrained airways. She lived in constant fear that one day, baby Alice would not have enough strength for the struggle and would succumb, losing her tortuous fight to keep breathing.

Alice was sleeping soundly now though, and Celia was drifting in and out of consciousness herself. Her tiredness was like an opiate, she could feel it in her bloodstream; her limbs were numbed and she drifted between sleep and wakefulness in a surreal and dreamlike state, anaesthetised. If only Ken would help in the night she thought, maybe she could cope better, maybe she would be less afraid. But they had argued over this so many times that she had given up now. He was insistent that he needed his sleep or else he wouldn't be able to work. She recalled his words.

'Just because your rich father has bought us this house, it doesn't mean that I don't have to work to put food on our plates. You can sleep in the daytime but I can't. I have to get up early to go to work.'

He was adamant that it was her job to look after baby Alice and tend to the house whilst he worked to earn the household money. He was such a strong willed man, she knew she would never win these arguments with him, no matter what logic she used or what appeals she made to his sense of duty as a father and a husband. She had tried coercion, persuasion, bribery and outright confrontation. Nothing had worked.

She looked around at the well-furnished room, her heavy eyes settling on a framed photograph on the mantelpiece. She saw a slightly younger, smiling version of herself in the picture. It had been taken a year ago but it seemed to her now, so much longer than that. A lifetime ago, she thought. She recalled the day it was taken, it was in Cullen on one of her early dates with Ken. She saw herself laughing in the picture and remembered that he had been trying to tickle her, trying to snake his hand inside her coat. He called it 'tickling' but she recalled he had been trying to feel her breast. She'd had to tell him off, it was broad daylight and a number of people had been strolling close by.

Meeting Ken had been exciting. She'd had boyfriends in Edinburgh at university, bookish boys who had fawned over her, some even claiming to have been in love with her. They had followed her around, bought her small gifts and written her long letters, pouring their hearts out in ink onto pale blue Basildon Bond paper. She had enjoyed the company of these boys, but saw them as friends rather than potential lovers. She was at university to learn history, not to fritter away her educational opportunity for the sake of lovesick milksop adolescent boys. They had not really interested her, but Ken Flett had been a different kettle of fish entirely.

From the very first time she had set eyes on him at the Fish Trades Christmas Ball, she had been drawn to him. Whilst most of the men at the ball looked starchy and uncomfortable in their evening suits, Ken had looked dashing and perhaps even a little dangerous. She remembered how handsome he had looked, his dark hair and startlingly pale grey blue eyes had unsettled her, disrupted the nonchalance she had expected to effect for the whole duty bound evening, partnering her father, watching impassively as he held court amongst his contemporaries and admirers. And suddenly, there was Ken.

She had never seen him before and soon learned that whilst he was working just down the road in Peterhead, he was in fact, a Buckie man, coming to Aberdeenshire for the work at Smalley's where he was apparently doing very well. Well enough at least to have gained a very prestigious ticket to the annual fish trades festive bash. He had been polite, attentive and very charming and although she knew that her father would not approve, she could not help herself. She had to get to know more about this handsome newcomer and so when he had asked her for a date, she had readily agreed.

He was a little older than her and very much more mature. She'd had nothing in her experience to compare with her feelings for Ken. The university boys paled in comparison, her mother and father's staid relationship of many years faded to dull and uninteresting shades of grey. He was manly, he exuded strength of character, he knew his own mind and for a while in those early days at least, he seemed to know hers as well. He anticipated her every mood, knew just what to say to make her feel attractive or interesting or funny. She hadn't stood a chance in the face of his relentless battery of charm and flattery.

The 'tickling' had begun quite early in their relationship. Any private moment would usually involve Ken's hand slipping up the inside of her thigh beneath the table or snaking inside her coat or sweater whilst they were walking together. At first, she had been a little surprised by his forwardness and would bat his hand away, ever-so-slightly indignant, but this did not stop him, and perversely, the more he persisted, the less she seemed to mind, until after a while she came to yearn for it; the feel of his manly touch beneath her clothes, caressing her, arousing her. When they kissed goodnight, she would clutch him close to her, pressing herself against his body, feeling him hard against her, her face flushed and burning in the heat of her passion.

But Celia had been brought up in a very religious household, and despite the fact that she thought of herself as a thoroughly modern, liberal and well-educated girl, her Christian values, bred into her from birth, were deeply held. Her father's beliefs permeated everything he did, even the running of his business. His trawlers were not allowed to fish on Sunday, nor would they unload fish, chandle or sail from port. As it was in their home, prayers were to be said before every meal on the boats, even during the heavy work and long days on the grounds. Each vessel sported a plaque, mounted in a prominent position in the mess, bearing a suitable religious homily reminding the men that their Lord constantly watched over them. No profanity had ever been heard in the Gibson household nor was swearing allowed on the boats. Church attendance was mandatory for everyone on Sunday, family members and employees alike. Religion was as natural and habitual to Celia Gibson as waking, sleeping and eating.

Celia had never felt temptation in this way before, the young men she had known before Ken had tried to kiss her and to put their arms around her waist, but she had found them too callow and ludicrous to take seriously as lovers. Throughout her three years at Edinburgh, her chastity had never once been threatened, but suddenly, in

Ken Flett, she had met a man who had inflamed her, and now she faced a constant battle against her base desires every time she saw him. She had tried to fight it, to inure herself against his charming insistence, his beguiling charm and disarming good looks, and she especially fought to steel herself against the power of those unnerving eyes, haunting and penetrating, seeming to see inside her, laying naked her innermost and most secret thoughts. But for all her resistance, she had known the inevitability of it even from the very beginning; that she would one day give herself to him.

And so she had.

And it had been awful, not just for the guilt and the shame she had felt afterwards, but for the terrible repercussions that had followed. She had tried to resist, she had even tried to push Ken away that afternoon on the back seat of the borrowed car. She had at first warmed to his advances, enjoying his kisses and embraces, she had been intoxicated with her desire for him and as usual, he had pushed his luck further and further. His hands were all over her, at first on top of her clothes but increasingly intrusive, artfully undoing buttons and clasps until she could feel him rubbing and touching her most private places. She had thought she'd wanted this but the roughness of his touch panicked her and at the last moment she'd changed her mind and begged him to stop. But it was too late and he would not stop. He said that he *could* not stop, his voice trembling, his breathing shallow and urgent, he would not be denied and she had given in, and Alice had been created, right there in the back seat of a borrowed car, in a lay-by in the Aberdeenshire countryside.

Afterwards, he had been apologetic and tender, cajoling her with affectionate words and loving caresses.

She was wracked with shame and regret but most of all disappointment; she had expected this milestone in her life to be more special, less sordid. Celia believed Ken knew he had gone too far, and his behaviour towards her changed almost immediately afterwards, becoming gentle and respectful. She had agreed to see him again and their meetings had continued as before, although for a short while there was an unspoken and uncomfortable distance between them. It did not happen again, and it was not long before Celia began to look forward to their meetings again, enjoying Ken's charming company, falling once more for his urbane charm and persuasive good humour.

Things were becoming very difficult at home at that time; her father who had never really approved of Ken now seemed to take an even deeper dislike of him, and he had started to take great efforts to discourage her from allowing the relationship to develop. At first, she'd considered her father's interference as plain and simple snobbery. The Gibsons were a prominent family in the community and were very well to do; Celia had assumed her father had higher expectations of her; perhaps he even had plans of marrying her off into another prestigious and moneyed family as part of a business alliance.

She got herself into a terrible state when she first suspected her pregnancy, fighting single-handedly against tumultuous emotions of mortification, shame and fear, which she found sickeningly distressful. But she did not at first share her suspicion with Ken, preferring to carry on as if nothing had happened, denial becoming her strategy for coping. Eventually though, as time went on and she became more and more convinced that she was pregnant, she realised that she could not simply continue in a state of denial. She had to know one way or the other, so she plucked up the courage to make a discrete visit to the family doctor and subsequently, the inescapable fact was indeed confirmed. She decided there was no alternative but to grasp the nettle and to confront first Ken and then her parents with the news.

She wasn't sure how Ken would react, so she had chosen to tell him during a quiet walk together on the second Sunday after she had learned of her condition. He had been very stoic. He did not appear to be angry, nor had he shown any indication of pleasure. He had told her that he loved her and that he would respect her wishes; he said that if she wanted it, he would 'do the honourable thing and make her his wife.' She had laughed out loud at that, at his preposterously outdated turn of phrase, but she was secretly excited and pleased by his ad hoc proposal. She had not accepted him there and then but had told him that she would think about it.

The same evening she assembled her parents in their sumptuous living room and with a shaking voice told them her news. Her mother had lapsed immediately into sniveling tears whilst her father had simmered with barely contained anger at the news. 'I warned you!' he exploded. 'I warned you that he's no good.'

'But I love him Daddy' she had protested. 'I want to be with him.'

'And you're not the only one, or so I've heard,' he'd replied. She hadn't got a clue what he'd meant by that, but he'd continued with hardly a pause. 'I've heard a rumour that he's engaged to Anne Smalley, and that's how he got that job in their office. By romancing the bosses' daughter. He's a gigolo Celia!'

This bolt from the blue had dumbfounded her. How could he be engaged to somebody else? He'd been seeing her for months, they'd spent hours together every weekend. She refused to believe it.

*

It felt good not to have to go to work. It was Saturday and Ken liked to get out for a good long walk on Saturday mornings to fill his lungs with fresh air and take some time out for himself. And he really needed it today. Alice had been awake for much of the night with that cough of hers and Celia had been constantly clattering up and down the stairs, tending to her, boiling the kettle in the kitchen and opening and closing doors all night. He had not slept well and he was tired, but the exercise and the sea air were invigorating. He'd left the house early, leaving Celia and Alice to catch up with their sleep. He had walked into the town of Cleethorpes, strolling along the almost deserted beach, lingering in the out-of-season resort, enjoying the quiet streets and looking into the curiosity shop windows at the strangely unseasonal seaside giftware. He had drunk strong, dark tea from a cracked mug in a café on the promenade before walking on and taking a saunter around the deserted ornamental lake where holidaymakers hired rowing boats in the summer season. He had enjoyed the walk; it had helped him wake up and clear his head.

Finding a wooden bench overlooking the boating lake, he sat and huddled deep into his coat for warmth, enjoying the freshness of the March morning. Geese and ducks clattered onto the water around him, shattering its glassy surface and assaulting his ears with their quacking; it occurred to Ken that their uncouth calls sounded like peels of hoarse, raucous laughter. They swam in small circles, turning their heads to look at him in expectation of scatterings of breadcrumbs, but they were disappointed and after a while they swam away in search of more generous visitors. Ken was thinking about how he had ended up here on the wind-blasted Lincolnshire coast, so far away from his home.

Celia's father had been resolute and uncompromising in his terms. The disgrace that Celia had brought to his door had to be covered up, to be concealed from the community in which he had such standing. He had effectively banished the couple from that corner of North East Scotland. The marriage had been organised by her father and was both swift and quiet, taking place in the registry office in Aberdeen. There had been no guests, no ceremony and no reception. Celia and Ken had celebrated alone in a small hotel close to the city centre where they had stayed for a few days before moving temporarily into a flat on the northern outskirts of the city at Bridge of Don. Ralph Gibson had pulled some strings with his fishing industry magnate friend David Hansen and had arranged for Ken's appointment as filleting hall supervisor at the Hansen factory in Grimsby. An agent of the Gibson's solicitor had been sworn to secrecy and despatched to the Lincolnshire town to find and purchase a suitable house for the couple; the house overlooking the park where Ken now lived with Celia and their baby Alice.

Ralph Gibson's ruling was that Ken and Celia must leave Scotland; Celia was not to show her face in the Fraserburgh area until after the baby was born and Ken had proven himself a worthy and loyal husband, one fit for his daughter. Gibson had told him that he might possibly reconsider the terms sometime in the future, but for now at least they were to disappear so as not to be an embarrassment to the Gibson family in their own community. This had not been what Ken expected when he'd started courting the daughter of one of the richest and most respected men in the area. He had expected to be taken into the fold, to have been given a lucrative position in the family business and the means to provide his new wife with a lovely home and the trappings of comfort expected by a well-to-do family. Instead, he'd found himself living in virtual exile, banished in shame from the family and excluded from the opportunities that he felt should befall him as the husband of Ralph Gibson's only child. He hated his work in the Hansen fish factory; he felt it beneath him, an insult to his intelligence. The only pleasure he found in the position was in baiting and insulting the thick-headed Grimsby fish workers and flirting with the prettier of the girls on the packing lines.

Even though Ralph Gibson had provided him with a reasonably substantial and well-furnished home, and had found him a job that paid enough for a comfortable but modest lifestyle, Ken was haunted by the injustice of it all and was wracked with disappointment in the situation. There had been an ultimatum and Celia, refusing to give him up had accepted her father's terms for their exile. There were no other options available to him. Gibson who had obviously been tittle-tattling with William Smalley had accused him of being secretly engaged to Smalley's daughter Anne. Bill Smalley had called him into his big office and sacked him on the spot, without even listening to his side of the story; that his skinny brat Anne had been pursuing him and had thrown herself at him. So, jobless and without any other options, Ken had acquiesced and had agreed to the terms, making the long train journey south from Aberdeen to the Humber bank with Celia and taking up residence in this strange town.

The birth of Alice had appeased him for a while, she was a beautiful baby and he had been pleased to see Celia so happy with her new daughter. But after the birth Celia seemed to become infatuated with the infant and had lost interest in him. Also, she took less pride in her own appearance. Previously immaculate and stylish, her hair was now often lank and she didn't dress as nicely now that she was a mother. He would often return in the early afternoon from his morning shift to find her still in her dressing gown. Alice's coughing had also proved an annoyance to him, causing Celia and himself to argue, keeping him awake at night and testing his patience and temper during the day.

Ken Flett was a disappointed and angry man.

CHAPTER SIX

By the time that Harry got to Jens' house, it was just after noon. He found him in his shirtsleeves in the back yard; his bicycle was turned upside down and standing on its saddle and handlebars. Jens had removed the front wheel and had the tyre off, he was in the process of testing the inner tube for leaks, holding it immersed in his mother's washing up bowl full of water, squeezing it into sausage sized segments and carefully inspecting it for escaping bubbles. Shirley was sitting on the doorstep watching Jens work; Harry had known that he would find her here.

'Got a blow out mate?' Harry asked cheerfully.

'Yes Harry,' Jens looked up at him with a broad welcoming smile. 'Blast!'

Harry did a pretend drum roll and made the sound of a cymbal crashing. It was a familiar joke, one they had used for many years. Jens continued. 'We was just going to pick up some chips from the chippy but when I got me bike out I saw I'd got a flatty.'

Harry looked down at the much-mended inner tube,

a dozen patches of varying shapes and sizes had been gummed to it. 'Cheer up,' he said, smiling, 'its only flat at the bottom.'

'I don't wish to know that, kindly leave the stage!' Jens called back in his Music Hall voice. The two friends laughed with each other, it was another classic. Shirley looked on impassively, it was clear that her thoughts were somewhere else. Harry caught her eye and wondered if he would have the courage to go through with his plan. He was wondering how he could get her alone for a talk in private, when she turned to him and said.

'Do you fancy walking down the chippy with me then Harry, whilst he gets on and mends that bloomin' puncture?'

Harry couldn't believe his luck. 'Of course I will Shirl, and it'll be my pleasure.' He leaned forward and offered her his arm. Shirley hopped to her feet and linked her arm into the crook of his elbow and led him out of the yard. They walked in silence for a short while until Harry realised that they were heading in the opposite direction, away from the chip shop. 'Where we going Shirl?' he asked gently, realising that she was distant; her mind clearly still elsewhere.

'Oh,' she said, seemingly snapping back to reality. 'I just thought we'd take a bit of a wander if that's okay with you, I'm not that hungry just yet and I thought a walk would give me a bit of an appetite.'

'Fine by me Shirl,' he said, and mustering his courage added, 'there's something I want to tell you anyway, so I'm glad I've got you on your own.'

She turned her face towards him, clearly interested to hear his news. He looked down and met her gaze with difficulty, panicking slightly. He was surprised though, when she said 'I've got something to tell you too Harry, I think we ought to find somewhere to sit down for a bit. Do you fancy the park?'

'I'd rather have a walk down the beach Shirl,' he replied, thinking of the clarity he'd found earlier when he'd been close to the sea.

'Okay,' she replied and they strolled on arm in arm, towards the same metal footbridge that Harry had crossed over earlier in the day. A few minutes later, they were sitting side by side on one of the concrete tank traps; the tide was a long way out, not much more than a thin brown line beyond the expanse of the wet sand flats. They were alone in the vastness of the estuary. Alone, except for the shrieking seagulls.

Harry was struggling to find the right words; he had not lost his resolve, but was nervous about getting this wrong, he knew that he was not a man of words and was suddenly very aware that he may only get one chance to say this. He was hesitating on the verge of babbling out his newly discovered feelings for Shirley when she said.

'Harry, I need your help with something.'

'Anything Shirl, you only have to ask.' He was relieved to have been given a reprieve for a moment and looked enquiringly at her. He noticed the strain in her pretty face but also saw that the wind was playing with her curls, tossing them across her brow. My God she's beautiful, he thought.

'It's Jens,' she continued. 'He says he wants to go to sea and he's going to put his name down at Hansens for a job on the trawlers.'

'I know he's thinking of it Shirl,' Harry replied. 'What of it?'

'I don't want him to go Harry.' She had turned to look directly at him and took hold his big fisherman's hands. She repeated herself, this time with tears just beginning to bud in the corners of her blue eyes. 'I don't want him to go.'

Harry was confused. Taken aback.

'Why's that?' was all he could think of to say.

'Because I love him Harry, I always have and I don't want to lose him, I can't bear the thought of him being away at sea all the time.'

Harry was engulfed with too many emotions at one time to deal with, but Shirley took his dumbfounded silence as a cue for her to continue with her entreaty. 'He respects you so much Harry; you know he does, he loves you like a big brother. You've always looked after him, stuck up for him, and fought his battles. He'll listen to you. You can convince him not to go to sea. Will you help me please?'

Harry was overwhelmed by what he had just heard but fought hard to conquer his emotions and to put on a brave face. The revelation that his two young friends were more than just friends had hit him like a forty-foot wave. He was feeling crushed by disappointment but was at the same time relieved that he had not exposed his own feelings to Shirley, it had been a narrow escape but no damage had been done. He realised in an instant that he had absolutely no resentment that Jens had Shirley's heart, and he kicked himself mentally for his foolishness in allowing himself to believe that this could have been any other way.

'Harry?' He was aware of her voice again as if heard from a great distance. 'Will you help me, please?'

'Er, I'll try,' he mumbled. 'I'll try, but I can't promise anything Shirl, he's got his heart set on it. I think it's all he's ever wanted to do.'

'Well, as long as you try,' she answered, reassured now to have Harry on her side. 'Between you, me and his mother, we'll win him over.' She was smiling again. They sat in silence for a while.

'And anyway,' she said eventually, 'what was it that you wanted to say to me? What's your news Harry?' She leaned towards him, straightened his collar and stroked the side of his face with her small, wind-chilled hand.

'Oh it's nothing much,' he replied. 'Just that I've decided to put in for my mate's ticket. If I get a place, I'll probably be on shore for six weeks after my next trip. I just thought you'd be interested to hear.' She did not see the bravery and massive effort behind his smile. 'Now then,' he continued, hopping off the concrete block and landing on the soft beach sand. 'How about that bag of chips then?' She reached out both of her arms for him to lift her down and as he did, she wrapped them around his neck, burying her face there and saying quietly into his ear.

'Oh Harry, I do love you, you're such a good friend.' He twirled her slowly and placed her gently down onto the beach.

'I love you too Shirley,' he managed in a quiet voice, struggling for composure.

*

They walked together arm in arm again along the deserted beach, over the bridge and back into the town. Conversation had dried up between them but there was no awkwardness, they were simply lost in their own worlds, prepossessed by their own very different thoughts. They queued for a few minutes in the oily warmth of the fish and chip shop and then headed back, Shirley towards Jens' house, and Harry away home to his mother. They had vaguely agreed to meet up on Sunday when Harry would begin his work of convincing Jens that he should not go to sea. He said goodbye to Shirley who reached up to kiss his cheek and headed off towards Jens' house with her hot paper parcels of freshly fried chips.

Soon afterwards, he was sitting in his mother's kitchen where they ate their own portions straight from the newspaper, translucent now with greasy patches of lard from the chips. Dolly had made a pot of tea and buttered some slices of Wonderloaf for them and they ate in silence. She was concerned about her son, he had been quiet since he had come in with their dinner and was clearly brooding over something. She remembered their earlier conversation and especially Harry's question about Shirley and Jens. Knowing his moods so well she had already guessed what must have transpired that afternoon.

'Did you know that Jens wants to go to sea?' Harry asked suddenly, breaking the silence.

'Yes love, of course I did.' Dolly answered, a little surprised by the direction of the conversation. 'Gwen has been worried sick about it for years, ever since she lost Kurt really.'

'Shirley's asked me if I'll try and talk him out of it.' He paused to eat a chip. 'What do you think about that Mum?'

With a mother's instinct, she stifled the impulse of her first thought. She was herself a fisherman's wife and she immediately understood Shirley's reason for not wanting Jens to be away at sea, away for weeks on end, away from her side as life slowly passed her by. And she also saw that Shirley asking for Harry's allegiance in her conspiracy showed not only a trust in her son's friendship and a deep respect for him, but also that Harry was not the object of her true love. She thought quickly and decided on a more tactful answer.

'Well, if you ask me, you've got your work cut out with that. He's a nice boy and he would never want to hurt anybody, but you can tell that going to sea is all he's ever wanted to do. He can't wait for you or your father to get back from your trips and he's round here asking questions about the trip you've had, what you caught, which grounds you were on. It's in his blood Harry, just like it's in yours.'

Harry nodded in agreement. 'I know,' he replied, 'and I'm worried that Shirley will be angry with me if he does go. She might blame me. Maybe she'll think that I didn't try hard enough.' He was clearly perplexed.

'Look Harry,' his mother interjected, seeing her son's plight. 'If Jens puts his name down and gets a job on the boats, it won't be your fault, it will be his choice. Shirley and Gwen will just have to accept it, Jens is a man now and he has to make his own decisions. The best thing that can happen is that he gets on a happy boat and has good men around him whilst he's learning the ropes. There are some nasty pieces of work out there and Jens is too nice for his own good sometimes. If he got on a boat with the wrong sorts, he'd be easy-pickings for them. They'd make his life a misery.'

Harry knew this to be the truth and recalled his own early days at sea as a decky learner, when one of the older hands had tried to take advantage of his inexperience, taunting him with insults about his appearance and playing crude practical jokes. At first, he had tried to ignore the abuse but one day he'd slipped his feet into his deck boots to find one of them soaking inside with a pool of cold urine. He had lost his temper and snapped, he had thrown himself at the man, catching him off balance, knocking him backwards and pinning him to the deck with his knees. He was frantically punching his tormentor around the head and face with a fury of blows when the burly mate, alerted by the commotion had discovered the young decky learner pummeling one of his hardest and most feared deck hands. Harry had been reprimanded and fined out of his wages for the attack, but the jokes had stopped and Harry found that he had gained the respect of the crew. He couldn't imagine Jens coping with a situation like that and felt angry inside that his young friend might have to face something similar on his own.

'Did I tell you that I'm going to go in for me mate's ticket Mum?'

'No love you didn't' she answered, 'but I think it's a good idea, it'll be a nice bit more money and the next step towards being a skipper. You'll make a good skipper one day son.' He was pleased to hear these words of maternal praise. 'Mind you' she added, 'you'll be a lot younger than a lot of the blokes you'll be bossing on the deck, do you think you can handle that?'

'If you're good enough you're old enough Mum' he replied. 'And anyway, I can't be worried about stuff like that or else I'd never get on would I? And there's no way am I going to be a deck hand all me life. The skipper's had his eye on me, or so he says, and he reckons I've got the makings, so I reckon I owe it to myself to have a go.'

Dolly smiled, she knew her son was a good fisherman; he'd learned it from his father who'd learned it from his and so on through all the many generations of Coulbecks who had sailed the North East Atlantic. Reading the currents, observing the colours and the moods of the waters, following its flows and plotting its depths, the sea was as familiar to the Coulbecks as the main road into town was for normal people. She also knew that he was fearless in his dealings with the other men, he could not be bullied or cowed, and given a few years on his back he would have a natural authority about him.

They sat in silence for a while until Dolly asked.

'What you doing tonight Harry?'

'Not sure Mum,' he replied. 'Reckon me and Bill might just go out and have a few beers. Probably go down Freemo.'

'Well just go steady,' she said, concerned. Although he hadn't said very much, she knew he had suffered a disappointment this afternoon and she was worried that he was not in a good state of mind for heavy drinking, especially in the pubs down Freeman Street where a sideward glance could get you into a fight. 'Why don't you go to the pictures or something?' she asked, more in hope than expectation.

'No, I fancy a few beers Mum,' he replied. His voice was solemn now. 'And I really need a drink.' With that he took himself off upstairs for an afternoon's kip before it was time to get ready to go out.

*

'Have you got a minute Mrs Thorsen?' Shirley asked, pushing her face around the back door and peering into the kitchen. Jens had taken his bike for a run to test the newly mended tyre and Shirley was taking advantage of this brief, private moment to talk with his mother.

'For God's sake Shirley, will you stop calling me Mrs Thorsen! You're not a snotty-nosed kid anymore, you should call me Gwen.' She smiled at Shirley of whom she was very fond indeed, her eldest son's very best friend and a lovely, caring girl to boot. Shirley slipped into the room and sat herself down opposite Gwen Thorsen at the kitchen table. Gwen was drinking tea poured into an inexpensive china cup from a large brown ceramic teapot. Without asking, she poured out a cup for Shirley, topping it up with milk straight from the bottle. She took the parcels of chips from Shirley and placed them inside the gas oven on a very low flame to keep warm until Jens got back.

'I suppose you know about Jens,' Shirley began. 'I mean, about his plans to go on the trawlers.'

'Yes I do,' Gwen answered, her voice heavy with sadness at the remembrance of their argument. 'He told me last night before he went round for you. Truth is we had a bit of a fall out over it.'

'He was in ever such a funny mood last night,' Shirley replied. 'He told me about it when we was walking up to the Palais. I asked him not to leap into anything and asked him if he'd give us some time to talk about it.' Gwen looked at Shirley across the table on hearing this. 'He said he would,' she concluded.

'Well that's good news,' she answered. 'At least he's agreed to think about it and talk it over before he does anything rash. The thing is though Shirley,' their eyes met. 'I think he's got his mind made up about this and I can't see that there's much we can do or say to change it.' Gwen's eyes betrayed her sadness as she continued. 'I've been scared stiff this would happen and I've tried to steer him away from it all his life, well, ever since we lost his dad anyway, but deep down I know it's all he's ever wanted to do. His dad loved the sea and he came from a fishing family in Denmark you know. It's in his blood.' There was a tone of resignation in her voice. 'Frank's not like that,' she continued. 'He's not interested in the sea, he's more like my side of the family.'

'Don't give up Mrs Thorsen,' Shirley entreated eagerly. 'There's the two of us and I've asked Harry if he'll help us persuade him not to go. Between us, we can talk him out of it. I'm sure we can.' Her voice had risen and had an urgent tone to it. Gwen looked at the eighteen year old girl sitting opposite her, remembering back to the time when she was a little six year old, comforting her bereaved boy with childish platitudes and small gifts of sweets bought with her own few pennies. She had come to think of Shirley as part of her own family and although nothing had ever been spoken about it, she had simply come to assume, and expect, that Jens and Shirley would always be together. She understood why Shirley didn't want Jens to go on the boats and her heart ached for her because Gwen knew that Jens would not be dissuaded from this.

'Look Shirley,' she said in a kindly tone. 'I'm not sure that Harry is the right person to talk Jens out of going to sea. Don't you see that Jens hero-worships him? His father and Harry Coulbeck have been the two most important men in Jens life. Now, he hardly knew his dad, he was only six when he died, but Harry has always been there, always just that little bit older so he was always doing the things that Jens was dreaming of, and when Harry went to sea I knew that Jens would want to go too. It was in the stars Shirley, Harry was only ever going to be a fisherman, he's from a long line of 'em, his dad, his granddad and even before that – the Coulbecks have always been fishermen, just like the Thorsens, and I think that you and me are going to have to get used to the idea. The sea calls men like that.' She reached over and gave Shirley's small hand a motherly squeeze.

'But I don't want him to go,' Shirley had tears in her eyes now.

'I know you don't darling, and nor do I.' She felt guilty for stealing the hope from the young girl's heart.

'Between us we'll do our best to keep him ashore,' she was still holding Shirley's hand when she said, 'but at the end of the day, if he does go, it doesn't mean that he thinks any the less of us does it?' She smiled warmly. 'He's got his own reasons, and to him, they're good ones. He's the most kind hearted boy you'll ever meet Shirley, he thinks he's doing the right thing; he thinks it's his duty. We've both got our reasons for not wanting him to go.' Shirley's eyes flickered away at this almost overt reference to her feelings and hopes for her life together with Jens. 'But in his mind, this is what he must do; for me, for Frank and for you too darling, for you.'

There was a squealing of brake blocks on wheel rims and Jens' wind reddened face came into view through the kitchen window. He was smiling. The mend to the inner tube had held and he was pleased with his workmanship. He looked through the window, seeing his two favourite girls enjoying a nice cup of tea and a friendly chat together and his smile broadened even further into an outright beam of happiness. He would make them both proud he thought to himself, he would look after these most precious people, he would provide for his mother and his brother and he would make Shirley admire him for the man he wanted to be. A real man! A big earner, and a provider. He knew that he could convince them in time that he was doing the right thing by putting his name down for a better-paid job on the trawlers.

Shirley and Gwen smiled back at this lovable, kind hearted and precious boy. For their different reasons, they both wanted to wrap him up in cotton wool and never let him out of their sight.

CHAPTER SEVEN

Shirley was disappointed that they were not going to go dancing again, but knew that her own love for dancing was not entirely matched by Jens and she realised that she had to accommodate other social activities if she was to keep him happy too. They had decided to go to the pictures, even though there wasn't much on worth watching as far as Jens could see. Having perused the entertainment section of Friday night's Grimsby Evening Telegraph Shirley had opted for Cleopatra with Liz Taylor and Richard Burton at the Odeon, and they had agreed to meet up after tea to walk through to the cinema on Freeman Street in time for the evening performance.

It was already dark when they left the warmth of Shirley's house and walked arm in arm through the evening streets. There were lights on in the rows of terraced houses, making them look cozy and inviting as Shirley and Jens walked past these small havens of family life, each with its own unique story to tell. Other people were out on the street, mostly dressed up, the women in high stiletto heels, the men in suits with overcoats buttoned up against the cold March evening. Shirley and Jens exchanged polite greetings with almost everybody they passed; neighbours and friends out like themselves for a bit of fun on Saturday night. They passed by in swirls of cigarette smoke and fragrant, lingering perfume.

'I'm not sure about this film,' Jens offered. 'It looks like a girl's film to me, a soppy love story.' Shirley laughed and gave him a little dig in the ribs with her elbow.

'Oh Jens,' she said, 'what am I going to do with you? You haven't got a romantic bone in your body.'

'Yes I have,' he defended himself. 'I'll have you know that I'm very romantic.'

Shirley could not believe her ears and let him see her incredulity with a wide-eyed look. 'You're what?' she expostulated. 'You're romantic are you?' There was a pause before she continued. 'Well how come I've never noticed it, or is it just that you're not romantic about me?'

Jens could feel his face burning and cursed his fair complexion for its betrayal of his feelings; for all of his life he had never been able to hide his embarrassment on account of the bright red patches which would flush up from nowhere onto his cheeks.

'Oh give over,' was all he could manage and was thankful to look up and see Harry Coulbeck walking towards them; apparently lost in thought, he hadn't noticed them. 'Whoa Harry!' Jens called, attracting his attention. 'We're off to the flicks, do you fancy coming with us?'

Harry stopped. 'What's on?' he asked, but he didn't really listen when Jens replied.

'Look, I'd love to, but I'm on my way to meet Bill and we're off out for a few pints. You kids go on and enjoy yourselves.' He heard himself sounding more than just three years older than them. He looked at Jens with his fair, boyish looks, so trusting and loyal. He noticed that Shirley had made up her eyes, accentuating their crystal blue qualities and he saw how she was entwined with Jens, coupled like a pair of jigsaw puzzle pieces, a matching picture, perfectly connected. His heart ached but he smiled, clapping Jens on the shoulder and leaning to kiss Shirley's cheek, lingering for a fraction of a second to breathe her in before he strode off towards the Osborne house.

'What's got into Harry?' Shirley asked when he was out of earshot. 'He's been acting a bit strange since he got back from sea yesterday.'

'I haven't noticed,' answered Jens. 'He seems okay to me, they had a good trip and he picked up a good pay packet.'

'There's something going on in his head though,' Shirley added. 'We had a bit of a chat today and he told me he's going to take his mate's ticket, but I sensed there was something else, something he wasn't telling me.'

Jens' ears pricked up at the mention of Harry's plans. He always knew that Harry would prove to be an exceptional trawlerman and expected he would make skipper one day when he was a bit older. But Shirley, realising that Jens' mind had turned to the sea, changed the subject and they gossiped about nothing in particular until they arrived at the cinema and took their place in the queue of people that was beginning to form along the street, waiting for the doors to open for the evening show.

Because they had arrived early they managed to get really good seats, right in the middle of the cinema, taking in the full panorama of the enormous widescreen. The film was lavish and colourful and despite his initial reservations, Jens thoroughly enjoyed the spectacle. They sat wide eyed, following the action from one side of the screen to the other and gazing in awe at the giant projections of the newspapers' favourite couple; Richard Burton and Elizabeth Taylor. Shirley had snaked her small hand into Jens' own and he had held it for most the film, gently caressing it during the tender moments and gripping it perhaps a little too tightly during the more dramatic scenes.

After the film, they flowed with the stream of people out onto the street again, where they stood, buttoning up their coats.

'What do you want to do now Shirl?' Jens asked.

'I don't know, do you want to see if we can find Harry and Bill?' she asked. 'They'll be down here somewhere.' She looked in both directions at the many public house signs hanging over the busy street. She was a little surprised when Jens answered.

'I'm not really in the mood for boozing Shirl; I had a skin full last night at Pearson's. Do you just fancy going for a little walk?'

'Okay then,' she answered, not linking arms this time but placing her hand into his. 'Let's have a wander.'

Almost without realising what she was doing, Shirley led him in the direction away from the docks and they walked together, hand in hand, leaving the bright lights and hubbub of the Saturday night revelry behind them, until they eventually found themselves amongst the rows of larger terraced homes leading towards the more opulent part of town. They were talking animatedly about the film they had just seen, their breath hanging in wisps around them in the cold night air, their footfall perfectly synchronised and their held hands swinging between them in time to the rhythm of their steps.

They came eventually to a broad street that curved in

a continuous arc around a tree-lined Victorian park on their right hand side, and to their left, the grandest homes in town stood stately and huge, washed in the white light of the many streetlights. Large bay windows, decorated gables and porticos embellished their grandeur whilst the most impressive of all had turrets four storeys high like red brick mediaeval castles.

'These are posh houses aren't they,' Shirley said admiringly.

'Our Frank wants to live in one of these one day,' he answered, wondering just how much money you would need to buy one of these mansions. The dream seemed almost too impossible for Shirley to take in and she did not answer.

They walked for a while in silence until out of the blue Shirley asked. 'Shall we go into the park Jens?' He smiled a conspiratorial smile, recognising the impulsiveness he had known for nearly all of his life. It was always Shirley who'd had the ideas that had got them into their childhood scrapes, her curiosity, her sense of mischief and he had grown accustomed to giving in to her. They passed between the avenues of tall elm trees and picked up the path that traced the circumference of the park, following it until it opened into a wider space, a Victorian bandstand at it's centre. They wandered up the steps and onto the podium, a circular space beneath an ornate conical roof supported by embellished cast iron pillars.

It was a cold night but the moonlight was bright, penetrating the bare trees and even illuminating the inside of the bandstand. Jens could see Shirley's face clearly as she turned to him and asked.

'Do you think she's beautiful?'

He was wrong footed by the question. 'Do I think

who's beautiful?' He asked, confused.

'Liz Taylor of course,' she replied, her eyes twinkling in the moonlight, the tip of her nose pink with cold.

'Oh er, of course I do,' he replied. 'She's supposed to be one of the most beautiful women in the world isn't she?'

'Yes, I suppose she is,' Shirley responded, a very slight trace of disappointment in her voice. 'Do you wish that I was Liz Taylor?' she asked.

Jens laughed. 'Not in the slightest little bit,' he replied, smiling broadly. She smiled back at him and stepped towards the centre of the bandstand, lifting the hem of her coat slightly in a curtsey to him, swaying as if in time to imaginary music playing in her head. She hummed, a light melodic tune and began dancing; her coat hem still lifted, her head tilted elegantly to one side as she daintily dipped and twirled before him.

'May I have the pleasure of this dance?' he asked, stepping up, assuming his most gallant pose and offering her his left hand, which she took as they moved smoothly into hold, the fingers of her free hand settling and resting gently on his right shoulder. They glided together in perfect time to the imaginary music, their footsteps on the wooden boards now the only sound as they moved gracefully in small, intricate patterns, their bodies in harmony, moving as one in the dance until at last, Jens led her into a dizzying series of spins and they parted, whirling, laughing joyously and stopping face to face with just a single step between them.

Time is distilled in this single moment.

'Jens.'

'Yes Shirley.'

'I love you.' Her eyes were locked hard into the depths of his.

'And I love you too,' he replied, unflinching in the intensity of her gaze.

'No, I mean I really *love* you,' her resolve wavered and her chin trembled ever so slightly at this.

'I know you do Shirl, and I really love you too.'

'Really?' She asked, but he had taken the single step towards her and wrapping her in his arms, stifled her question with a kiss. After a lifetime of pecks, it was their first true kiss.

They embraced for a long time; kissing tenderly and exchanging words of love for each other until the coldness of the winter's night reminded them of the lateness of the hour, and wrapping themselves even more closely together than ever, they began the slow walk home.

'And to think,' Shirley turned her face towards him as they strolled. 'To think that I thought you never had a romantic bone in your body.'

*

Eleven o'clock on Saturday night, drinking up time had been called in the Lincoln Arms and the pub was beginning to empty. Harry and Bill were leaning against the bar trying to convince Belinda the barmaid to serve them one last shot of whisky each for the road. Belinda was simultaneously tidying up behind the bar; drying glasses and good-naturedly rebuffing the two drunken fishermen who were clearly the worse for wear. Bill was worried about Harry who had been in a strange mood all night and had kept them drinking at pace, draining pint after pint and ensuring their glasses were replenished immediately each time they were emptied.

Eventually, they realised that the experienced

barmaid was not going to fall victim to their slightly slurred charm and they tottered out onto the street. The Lincoln Arms was on one corner of a busy road junction near the main entrance to the docks. Streetlights cast an artificial, almost surreal atmosphere over the area; cars, busses and the occasional cyclist moved slowly past in all directions, their engines revving and their tyres rumbling over the nearby railway crossing, they snaked into the distance in streams of white and red lights. There were a lot of people on the street now, pouring out of the many public houses, shouting and laughing, whooping and cheering, there were bustling groups of drunken men and arm-in-arm couples pouring over the pavements all around them, heading for home or to late night venues.

'Where we going now Bill?' Harry asked, he was still in the mood for drinking and was thinking of hopping into a taxi and heading off towards a nightclub where they could drink into the early hours. He looked to Bill for support of his plan but saw that his friend was struggling to walk straight, rolling as if he were on deck in a rough sea and grasping at the kerbside railings for support.

'I think I've 'ad enough Harry,' he managed, gripping for grim life to the supporting rail. Harry was disappointed to see Bill Osborne struggling with the drink; it was important that a fisherman could take his beer; their time on shore was so brief, they had to get as much down their necks as possible in the limited time available. Bill had been Harry's drinking companion since their first illegally purchased pints when they were still decky learners, but tonight his friend hadn't kept up with the pace and looked shot.

'Just leave me here Harry,' Bill said, concentrating hard on keeping himself upright, breathing heavily and bracing himself against the spinning lights and whirling street noise around him. The fresh air had hit him hard and he was nauseous.

'No chance mate,' Harry answered, he was clearly drunk himself but nowhere near as badly affected by the alcohol as Bill. 'I'm not leaving you here on yer own, this isn't a nice neighbourhood at this time of night you know.' He put his arm around Bill's back and gripping firmly, helped him across the pavement to a shop doorway step, lowering him down into a sitting position there. 'You just take yer time mate,' he said, 'there's no hurry, the clubs don't shut till two, we've got plenty of time.'

Bill slumped into a bundle and rolling sideways onto his hands and knees began retching in the shop doorway.

Harry laughed and wandered back to the street corner where he could see the nightlife milling around him whilst keeping an eye on the spewing Bill at the same time. It's best to let him get it out of his system he thought, looking around at the lively late-night neon-lit tableau. Across the road, two men were fighting whilst a woman screamed at them to stop; their drunken punches whirled ineffectively and inaccurately, connecting only occasionally and inflicting little damage. The fighters danced and dodged unsteadily and warily around each other, both men appearing to regret starting the fight but honour bound now to carry on. Unconcerned passers by detoured around the spectacle.

'Now then handsome, looking for company?' Harry was suddenly aware of the woman standing next to him; she nodded across the road towards the fighting drunks. 'Are you a fighter,' she asked, 'or a lover?'

She was not unattractive but was overly made up. In her thirties, perhaps even early forties Harry thought, she had a good figure but was dressed very much younger than she really should be for her years. Her hair was dyed bottle blonde and steeped into a beehive style, crisp with hairspray that glittered like spider's webs in the streetlights. She had moved closer and was touching him now, gently rubbing the front of his trousers, her face close to his, breathing gin fumes over him. He looked down into the crevice of her exposed cleavage and despite the numbness induced by his stupor he felt a stirring. 'Come on then darling,' he said, leading her into the doorway where Bill was still on his hands and knees. He backed her in, pushing her up against the cold glass of the shop's door and tugging her skirt up around her waist whilst she fumbled with the zipper of his suit trousers.

From his prone position, Bill looked up at the dark silhouettes of his friend and the prostitute, fumbling and humping as pedestrians walked past the doorway just feet away from them. Even though his brain was befuddled with beer, Bill knew it was better that the night should end like this than in a fight. There was something strange about Harry tonight, something dark and unpredictable. Whatever it was, he thought; let's hope that this gets it out of his system.

CHAPTER EIGHT

As was their regular custom, Dolly Coulbeck had popped around for a Sunday afternoon chat with her friend and neighbour Gwen Thorsen. The two were sitting in the Thorsens' front room with their feet up, warming in front of the glowing coals in the grate, drinking tea, nibbling custard creams and talking about their boys.

'Our Harry came home late last night in a hell of a state,' Dolly said. 'He's slept through the morning and still hasn't got up, I tried to wake him up with a cup of tea just now, but he was as grumpy as hell. Just didn't want to know.'

'Jens came in late too,' Gwen replied. 'But he wasn't drunk at all and when I asked him if he'd had a good night, he just grinned at me like a loon.'

'What did he do last night then?' Dolly asked.

'He went to the pictures with Shirley to see that Cleopatra,' she answered.

'Ooh, I'd love to see that film,' Dolly said. They sat in silence for a while, supping their tea until Dolly, feeling that the time was right, decided to ask a more pointed question. 'Your Jens and Shirl have always been very close haven't they Gwen,' she said. 'And, tell me if I'm wrong, but I'm getting the feeling that they're maybe more than just friends now. Am I right?'

Gwen smiled and realising her friend was a little uncomfortable at having asked such a personal question, she replied without hesitation. 'Well the truth is Doll, I don't exactly know. He hasn't said anything to me, but I've got eyes in me head and I reckon they've been getting a lot closer just recently.'

Dolly looked enquiringly at Gwen, urging her to further explanation.

'When they were little, they were like brother and sister,' Gwen was transported back in her mind's eye. 'Shirley was a proper little monkey, always getting him into trouble. Nothing serious mind, just kids scrapes.'

'He was a soft lad, as I remember,' Dolly agreed. 'Up for anything she suggested, he was always putty in her hands.'

'Then, when they got into their teens things started to change, and Shirley stopped being quite such a tomboy. I remember Jens struggled with that for a bit, he thought he'd lost his playmate for a while, but she blossomed Doll, do you remember?'

'Yes I do,' she replied. 'It happened almost overnight. It seemed like one day she was a cheeky little urchin in jeans and T shirts, next day she was a proper young lady, and as pretty as a picture to boot. You just hadn't realised before, never even really thought of her as a girl at all.'

'She's a lovely girl now though,' Gwen said, 'and I'm so grateful to her for looking after our Jens after I lost my Kurt. I love her for that alone. They was only about six then and she's been a big part of his life ever since. If I were to be honest with you Doll, I think I've always hoped that it would grow into something more serious between them as they got older.'

'And?' Dolly prompted.

'And with any luck,' she crossed her fingers on both hands and held them up for Dolly to see. 'With any luck, it looks like they are getting serious.'

'Ooh, am I going to have to buy a hat?' Dolly asked cheekily.

The two women were still smiling and giggling with each other like excitable school children when there was a tap on the living room door and Shirley's face appeared as it opened.

'What's the joke?' She asked smiling, a little confused to find Mrs Thorsen and Mrs Coulbeck in fits of girlish laughter.

The older women momentarily caught each other's eye and burst once more into a round of giggles. 'Come on in Shirl,' Gwen said, indicating with a nod the empty seat on the small settee next to her and reaching for the pot to pour out an extra cup.

'Are your ears burning darling?' asked Dolly.

Shirley was momentarily flustered and realising the import of the question understood that the joke, whatever it may have been, involved her in some way. 'What do you mean?' she entreated.

'Sorry love,' Gwen handed her the cup and saucer, 'you've caught us out so I guess we owe you an explanation.' Shirley waited in anticipation of the confession, hardly daring to take a sip of the tea as Gwen continued. 'We were talking about you and Jens you see, and Dolly and me both agree that you two make a lovely couple and it's about time you stopped messing about and decided whether or not you are ever going to be more than just good friends.'

Shirley's face was crimson now; she had never expected this.

'Mrs Thorsen...' she began, but was stopped in her tracks by Gwen's raised hand.

'Shirley!' she admonished, 'I've told you about that. It's Gwen. You're eighteen now Shirl, you're a woman in your own right and you should call me Gwen and Mrs Coulbeck is Dolly or Doll.'

'Sorry Gwen,' she replied somewhat unnaturally after a lifetime of calling her 'Mrs Thorsen.' It felt awkward in her mouth. 'Sorry,' she repeated, 'but I don't know what you mean.'

'Oh come on,' urged Dolly Coulbeck. 'If you're to be treated like a woman, you have to act like one, and me and Gwen are interested to know if you're going to make an honest man out of her Jens.' Dolly was teasing now, but had seen the look on Shirley's face, a look that betrayed her, and despite her best attempts to conceal the delight, it was plain to see that she was secretly pleased to be discovered.

Gwen reached across and placed a maternal hand on Shirley's knee.

'Look darling, we might be completely wrong, but I don't think we are. You and Jens have always been close, but now that you're all grown up, we've got a feeling that there's something deeper between you.'

Shirley was clearly touched with emotion and struggled to maintain her composure. Gwen placed a finger beneath Shirley's chin and used it to tilt her face towards her own.

'If we're wrong and if we've embarrassed you, then I'm sorry darling, and we won't mention it again. But if we're right, then you might want to get it off your chest, just between us girls.'

Shirley's eyes glittered as they welled up and tears of joy and relief trickled over her flushed cheeks.

'Last night, he told me that he loves me.' She confessed in an excited rush, feeling a glorious release in sharing this news with the two older women, news that had been welling up inside her in surges of deep joyous emotion ever since last night. She saw that they were both smiling broadly at her. 'And I told him that I love him too,' she added.

Gwen's happiness radiated from her and she embraced Shirley, the two sniffling back tears. Dolly was smiling too but her eyes did not glitter quite as brightly as the other two women's. She was genuinely happy for the young couple but her mind was with her troubled son, wondering what impact this news would have on him, how he would cope with seeing their joy in each other paraded, albeit innocently before him.

'There's only one thing spoiling it all,' Shirley admitted, dabbing her cheeks with a tissue. 'It's him talking about going to sea.'

'I know love,' Gwen said, 'but I think we're going to have to get used to that, he's made his mind up and even though it breaks my heart, I can't see him not going.'

'But I don't want him to,' Shirley's voice was small.

'Look Shirley,' Dolly interjected firmly but with compassion. 'Loving a trawlerman isn't easy, but it isn't the end of the world either. The important thing is to find the love of a good man, a man who doesn't use you, and a man who will stay with you and who comes back to you time and time again, not because he has to but because he wants to. Because he loves you.'

Shirley was listening intently now. Dolly continued.

'It isn't easy Shirley and in fact sometimes it can be harder than you think you can bear. When they're in distant waters in the middle of winter, when you're hearing on the shipping forecast that there's gales and snow and you're thinking of them freezing cold out there on the open deck in the middle of the ocean. But you do get used to it eventually. Look at me and Sid! He's out there now, seining in the North Sea, been away since Friday and won't be back until Tuesday. I'm missing him, but I know that when he gets back, he'll have a big smile for me and a nice bunch of flowers and whilst most of his crew will be down Freemo getting drunk as lords, he'll be sitting with me by the fire and everything will be alright.'

As she said this, she felt guilt over her own relative happiness, and for saying this whilst knowing of her friend's persistent grief at her loss. But she felt the need for Shirley to see that a life on the fishing is not necessarily a death sentence and that a trawlerman's wife could still be happy if she had found the right man, a good man.

'And don't forget,' Gwen added, 'that the boats are much safer nowadays too, especially those big new ones that your Hansen company are building, they're like luxury liners they are.' She smiled kindly, but it was an immense effort for her to find the strength to tell the lie, to justify the ambition of her son, an ambition that she so desperately disapproved of and had lived in deep dread of for over a decade. But Shirley's distress was too much for her and she could not bear to see the young woman's newly found happiness blighted in this way.

Although the full glow of joy had not returned, Shirley was at least looking less distressed now, listening to the two older women talk, one a trawlerman's wife, the other a trawlerman's widow. She saw that this was the way of the world, the natural order of things; that the men with the sea in their veins are bound to follow their destiny on the waves and that their women are destined to wait, and to hope. She saw that Dolly was right, it was more important to have a man who loved you properly than to worry about how he earned his living; over the years she had grown up seeing their family friends and neighbours fighting and making up, she had seen women black and blue with the harsh abuse handed out by their hard drinking husbands, seen families living in hardship and hunger whilst their men were at sea because all the money had been blown in two or three days of wild excess. The fishing industry made monsters of some men and victims of some women, but not all men were made the same, and some found their release from the grueling hard work, the severe conditions and the constant danger not in the pubs of Freeman Street but in the love of their families, their wives and their children.

Maybe she could get used to Jens being a trawlerman. She still did not like the idea, she was still fearful for his safety at sea, but if it meant so much to him, if it truly was so deeply in him that he could never be happy doing anything else, if it was the only way she could have him, perhaps she could get used to the idea.

Perhaps.

*

'My God, you look rough Harry!'

Harry looked up from the Sunday newspaper with a grimace at Jens who was standing in the kitchen doorway. He answered with a grunt and put the paper down, his eyes told the tale of a momentous night on the ale and his grey and ashen complexion confirmed the point. 'What did you get up to last night mate?' Jens asked, sitting himself down at the table.

'Don't ask!' Harry's tone had finality about it and so Jens did as he had been told and did not ask. He asked instead about Harry's next trip.

'You ready for the off tomorrow?'

'Aye, I bloody am that.' There was no doubt that the answer was heartfelt, perhaps hinting at an unspoken and compelling reason why Harry would wish himself away from here, back onto the open ocean, many miles away. Jens did not pick up the hidden subtext and saw his motivation simply as a sign of the mariner's calling. They sat in silence for a short while until Harry added, 'it's just a shame I haven't seen Dad this time home. That's the problem when we're both on different boats, it can be months sometimes before we're back at the same time.'

Jens had no answer but looked sympathetically at his friend.

'But I'll be seeing plenty of him in the summer when I'm at the nautical school' he added at last. 'That's six weeks on shore and I'm looking forward to that.' Jens knew that Harry was planning to apply for the qualification but they hadn't yet spoken about it at length – this was the main reason for Jens' visit this afternoon; the women, including his Shirley, were drinking tea, gossiping and giggling in the front room and this was the best chance he'd had all weekend to get Harry on his own to talk about the sea.

'You'll be a skipper one day Harry,' he said, praising his friend but absolutely genuine in the conviction. 'And you'll be a top skipper too, a real big earner I reckon.' Despite his throbbing headache, Harry managed a smile at this. That's two of them had told him that in as many days, he thought, maybe there was something in it.

'Thing is Jens,' Harry answered, 'nobody in this life gets anything for nothing. If you want something, you have to go out there and work for it, but that's the brilliant thing about the fishing Jens.' He was becoming passionate now, forgetting about the hangover. 'If you've got what it takes, if you've got nouse and a bit of a brain in your head and if you've got the courage, you can go out there and make yourself whatever you want to be.' Jens was nodding in absolute agreement as Harry continued with his chain of thought. 'Our parents had it rough mate. Your father paid the ultimate price, and my granddad did too, just the same. But even me father who's still fishing and still a fit, strong bloke has had to live through that bloody war, and then through the shit time after it when boats couldn't turn a profit 'cos of the bloody fixed prices at the market. They worked on crap old boats that were nothing but rust buckets, they had to shovel coal like bloody miners and their families went hungry for years on end. It's been bloody miserable in this country for years Jens, bloody miserable! But things are changing now me old mate and you and me are the lucky ones. We're the ones with a future worth living for.'

'You're right Harry', he agreed. 'With boats like the Hansen Apollo and the even newer one you told us about, we've got opportunities like never before.' He leaned towards Harry to emphasise his next point. 'I want some of that Harry; I want a chance for the big money, I want us to live in a nice house out in Cleethorpes or Humberston, I want a better life for me and Mum and for our Frank.'

'And for Shirley?' the question hurt him but he put on a brave face for his friend who was blushing.

'Yes, of course, for Shirley too,' he added, abashed and suddenly coy. 'But there's only one way I'll ever get the chance to better myself Harry and that's by getting on the boats and working myself up like you're doing. I can't stand the idea of being a bloody filleter all me life Harry, I thought it was what I wanted and it's a step up from tugging pallets about the factory floor and nailing lids onto fish boxes, but if I can get onto a good boat with a good skipper, I can really make something of myself.'

'Do you think you're up to it?' Harry posed the question seriously.

'No Harry, I don't think I am; I know I am.'

Harry smiled at his friend's conviction and admitted. 'Look Jens, I'm probably not supposed to tell you this, but Shirl has asked me to try to talk you out of going to sea, she's worried about you but more than that I think, she'll miss you too much.'

'I know that's how she feels,' he replied, 'and I understand why Mum doesn't want me to go either, but they'll soon change their tune when they see what a difference it will make to our lives. We can have nicer things, I could get us a telly and I could buy Shirley some lovely clothes and other stuff that she likes.' He paused and added at last. 'And our Frank could go off to university and get his qualifications too, he's virtually a bloody genius you know.'

Harry was humbled by his young friend's genuine altruism, recognising that since losing his father, Jens had aspired to fill Kurt's shoes and to adopt the mantle of 'man of the house', and here he was on the threshold of actually being able to do something significant for his family, something which would enrich their lives and open doors of opportunity which may otherwise never exist. He was torn by his divided loyalties; between his promise to Shirley, sweet Shirley, who simply wanted to keep the boy she loved by her side no matter what, and the life changing benefits which may become possible as a result of Jens' unselfish ambition.

Jens continued. 'Look Harry, when you go for your ticket, I'm going to apply for a job on the boats too and do my basic training at the same time. Then, when you go back to sea as a mate, I want to sail with you, I want you to teach me how to be a trawlerman, I want to go fishing with you Harry.'

His mother's words came back to Harry; Jens would really struggle at sea on his own without anyone looking after him. Is it the lesser of two evils, Harry thought, to make sure that when he does go, as he surely will, that Jens goes to sea with him, under his watch, under his wing? And so, with an air of finality, Harry brought this topic to a close with a simple plea to Jens.

'Look mate,' he said. 'Let's not talk about it any more now, let's just say that I hear what you're saying and I'll think about it whilst I'm away. Then, when I get back, if I think it's the best thing all round and if you're still as mad on it as you are now, then I'll do what I can to help you to get a place at the nautical college. And if all goes to plan, we could be sailing together before the end of the year.'

Jens beamed broadly at his best friend, thinking that this weekend had been the best of his life. Suddenly, unexpectedly, all of his dreams seemed to be coming true. Harry tried to smile back but was bitten inside by a deep foreboding over his decision; he was worried about how Shirley would see this apparent betrayal of trust. In Harry's mind though, he was doing the best thing for both of his friends; if he convinced Jens to stay on shore he would never amount to much working in the factory and even Shirley might eventually tire of his lack of ambition and lowly status. On the other hand, by allowing

Jens his way, he was helping him to create the opportunities and the possibilities that could lead to a comfortable life for him and Shirley together. At this moment, it seemed to Harry that he had just made the biggest and hardest sacrifice of his life.

*

The Hansen Apollo was due set to sail on the early Monday morning tide. Harry needed to be on board by five a.m. By Sunday teatime he was beginning to recover from the heavy drinking of Saturday night, but was not in the mood for a big night out on the eve of an early morning sailing. It was not unusual for men to arrive on the boat with a skin full of ale and sleep it off during the long cruise to the distant grounds, and Harry himself had done this many times. But this weekend had been one strange and unsettling experience; he had arrived full of hope and with intentions of opening his heart to Shirley, but he would be leaving tomorrow, a disappointed and saddened man. He had no belly for another big night on the ale, he was jaded and introspective, he wanted to be alone. But before Jens had left to go home for his Sunday tea, he had exhorted him to agree that the three of them would meet up for a quiet drink later at the Corp. He had acquiesced only out of sheer lack of will to resist.

The Corporation did not get overly full early on Sunday evenings and Shirley, Jens and Harry had no problem finding a table where they could sit together. Shirley was drinking orange juice cordial topped up with lemonade whilst Jens and Harry had opted as usual, for pints of draft Bass. They were expecting to see Bill Osborne later on, but for now, the they made an interesting tableau for the Corporation's regulars who were becoming accustomed recently to seeing these three together. Tonight, the three of them were in deep discussion, clearly animated at times, the conversation apparently revolving around the two younger friends, the half-Danish boy and the pretty girl. They were not talking loudly enough to be overheard from the bar and the few other customers on this quiet Sunday evening were enjoying the puzzle over what topic the young folks could be so engaged by.

'Look Shirl, you know I don't want to cut fish in the factory all me life and if I can get on a good boat, I'll be in the money in no time and things could be so different for us then.' Jens was pleading his case with Shirley and turned to Harry for support. 'Isn't that right Harry?' he asked, 'if I got a couple of good trips under me belt, I'd soon start to save a bundle.'

Shirley also looked to Harry who once again felt torn by the division of his loyalties. He thought he had made up his mind on the best course of action to take, but seeing Shirley's face his resolve melted.

'All I can say is that I can see both sides.' They both looked crestfallen at this. 'I can see why Jens wants to go; he's like me, it's in his blood. On the other hand, I can see why you don't want him to Shirl, it's a difficult life for the women when the men are away at sea.' He took a long draught of his Bass and continued. 'I know you both want me to take your side, but I can't do it. It's not up to me and I think too much of both of you to go against one or the other.' Their looks of disappointment softened as they both realised the impossibly difficult situation they had placed Harry in.

'I will tell you this though,' he continued. 'Whatever you do decide between you, I will support you as best as I can.' Shirley and Jens seemed to accept Harry's final word on the matter and there was a slightly awkward silence for a moment before the mood was abruptly changed by the entrance of Bill Osborne, who had breezed into the bar, with a young lady on his arm. Harry, Jens and Shirley all swiveled to see. It was a few moments before Harry recognised Bill's friend as Maureen, the waitress from the café.

'Well, well, well,' he greeted them. 'If it isn't me old mate Bill Osborne and lady muck from the caff,' he teased. 'Come and take the weight off yer dogs and let me get you both a drink in!' Harry got to his feet, feeling inside his trouser pocket for his change. 'Pint of Bass for Ozzy I suppose, and what will you be taking milady?' He was smilingly referring back to their previous encounter when he had teased her for her haughty expression.

'I'll have a gin and it,' she replied, taking the teasing in good humour and settling herself down next to Shirley. 'Hello love, I'm Maureen, but you can call me Mo,' she said. 'And you must be Shirley. I've heard all about you and I've been looking forward to meeting you.' Shirley returned her smile, intrigued by the newcomer and wondering what she could possibly have heard about her.

Harry returned from the bar with the drinks and the conversation immediately turned to the surprise appearance of Maureen with Bill.

'You're a dark horse Osborne,' he said, looking at Mo with an appreciative gaze. She was a fine looking girl he thought, with her strawberry blonde hair and freckled complexion, quite a looker. Bill's done all right for himself here. 'Come on,' he cajoled, 'put us out of our agony and spill the beans!'

Bill was clearly deeply embarrassed, but at the same time was glowing with pride at his new girlfriend. 'Well, I just plucked up me courage and went into the caff on

Saturday morning and asked you out didn't I Mo?' He was looking to her for confirmation but Mo could not repress her giggle.

'Well, it wasn't quite as straight forward as that now was it Billy?' she replied with a twinkling smile and a patronising pat on his knee. 'He came in and ordered a breakfast', she was addressing her story mainly to Shirley, 'and he was sitting there as red as a beetroot and all tongue tied, and I thought, he seems like a nice boy, I'd better put him out of his misery. So I sat down next to you didn't I Billy.'

Bill was mortified but his beaming smile betrayed his joy.

'I just sat down,' Maureen continued, 'and he was so red I thought his head was going to explode, and I said, you come in here a lot don't you, do you live near here?' She looked at Bill with a smile. 'And he said, not really, about ten minutes walk away. So I said, that's a long way to come just for a breakfast, so you ought to make it worth your while and ask me out for a date whilst you're here.'

'And so I did,' chipped in Bill. 'So, it was just like I said, I got up me courage and just asked her out.'

'Aye, with a bit of help,' laughed Harry.

'We couldn't go out last night, 'cos he said he'd already made arrangements,' Maureen continued her story. 'And by the state of him this morning I could tell what kind of arrangements they had been.' She shot a reproachful glance at Harry who smiled back, a little shamed by the memory of the debauched Saturday night, and wondering for just a moment how much she knew, before dismissing the thought. Bill would never be that indiscrete.

'But we've had a lovely day haven't we Mo?' Bill

volunteered, still glowing with pride.

'Yes we have Billy,' she returned. 'We went to Lincoln on the bus, it was really nice, we had a cup of tea in a lovely old café on the hill near the cathedral and we walked around the castle.'

'You certainly know how to treat a girl,' Harry nudged his friend on the shoulder. 'A cup of tea and a walk around a draughty old castle, you really pulled out all the stops didn't you.'

'Don't listen to him, it sounds lovely Mo,' Shirley intervened, looking at Jens who took the hint.

'Yes, really nice, I think me and Shirley might do that one day when the weather's nice.' Shirley smiled, seeing that her hint had hit home.

'Well, he can't have upset you too much during the day Mo,' Harry concluded. ''Cos you're out with him again tonight already.'

'Yes,' she answered, 'I don't want him to think I'm too keen, but he's going away to sea tomorrow and I thought it would be nice to meet his friends proper before he goes off.'

The conversation bubbled along, further drinks were ordered and the new girl was warmly welcomed into the group, especially by Shirley who all too often had found herself the lone female in such gatherings, having to listen to the boys talk about fishing and boats and football and all those boy things which interested her but did not fascinate her to quite the same degree as they seemed to the men. The pub was filling up with more regulars now and becoming louder and even smokier. After a few more beers, it was Jens who suggested that they had a game of darts, and he got up to ask Jim behind the bar for a set of arrows. On his way to the bar, he accidentally nudged a drinker's elbow causing beer to slop over the top of the nearly full glass, it spilled over his fingers and splattered onto the floor.

'Sorry mate,' Jens apologised immediately, seeing what he had done.

'You fucking will be!' He was large, rough looking and unshaven, clearly a fisherman and clearly with a skin full of ale. Harry had seen the incident and called over.

'Everything okay Jens?'

'Oh, Jens is it?' A fucking scrob are we?' He had put the spilled glass down onto the bar and had turned to face Jens. His look was uncompromising and angry, and he was clearly intent on doing some damage to the slight boy who had just caused him to spill his ale.

Without further warning, the fisherman's left hand suddenly snaked out towards Jens' throat, catching him unawares, his large red skinned mauler closing tight around his neck. Jens was startled and felt his airways close as the grip tightened. Dirty fingernails bit into his skin, he was helpless and saw almost in slow motion, his attacker's right hand ball into a fist and draw back in readiness to deliver the blow.

But the blow did not come.

Harry had flown to Jens' side and had managed to get a grip on the man's wrist before the punch could be launched. He was strong, but so was Harry and they stood locked together for seconds before Harry's head tilted backwards and then flashed forwards, his forehead landing hard on the bridge of the fisherman's nose with a sickening crack, spattering droplets of blood across the bar. The grasp on Jens neck was released as Harry manoeuvred fully between his friend and his much bigger assailant, pinning him backwards against the bar, scattering pint glasses and ale as he did so.

'You just picked a fight with the wrong fucking

bloke!' Harry hissed at the now helpless fisherman.

Big Jim Smith behind the bar had seen everything and shouted, loud and commanding.

'That's enough now Harry, leave him to me!' He lifted the bar flap and moved quickly to Harry's side. There was a brief moment of uncertainty as Harry paused, considering whether or not, despite the landlord's orders to batter Jens' attacker. But Jim's big hand, laid quite gently onto his shoulder was enough to bring him back down to earth, the red veil faded and he stepped back, leaving the fisherman to Jim's tender mercies as he was ejected in a bloody bundle onto the street outside.

'Thanks Harry,' Jim said, returning to the bar. 'I'm not counting that one as a strike against you; he was well out of order. You all right mate?' he turned to Jens who was still looking shocked at the speed and the raw aggression of the events which had just happened.

'Yeh, I'm fine. Thanks.' Shirley was at his side now, stroking his face and sniveling. 'I'm okay Shirl,' he said, fingering the red finger marks still emblazoned on his throat. 'Thanks to Harry.'

New drinks were bought and the pub quickly settled down again to the usual buzz of drinker's chatter and laughter. Harry was widely thanked and congratulated by the other regulars for his speedy intervention, which he modestly shrugged off and the rest of the evening passed without significant event. They left at last orders, merry but not drunk and tottered off home, Harry, Shirley and Jens in one direction, Bill and Maureen in the other.

*

It was five o'clock in the morning; freezing cold and still dark, the North Wall of Grimsby's Number Three

Fish Dock was crowded with vessels moored in ranks, side by side like giant sardines, their bows facing the quayside, their steel hulls bobbing and clanking together on the slight rise and fall of the dock's waters, hemp ropes thicker than men's arms creaked under the strain of their restless charges. The harbour side was busy with hundreds of men milling around beneath the electric street lighting, the crews were arriving, chandlers were loading last minute provisions onto the vessels and the mighty ocean-going trawlers were readying for sailing.

Harry Coulbeck had just arrived in a shared taxi with Bill Osborne; his large kit bag freshly packed with clothes laundered by his mother and a few sundry personal items and treats for the voyage. He was a little weary after last night's beers but was ready for the trip. The last three days on shore had been exhausting and he was looking forward to a few days of peace and quiet as the Hansen Apollo made the long trip north up to the distant grounds off the northern coast of Norway.

Harry was just about to mount the ladder and board the Apollo when he heard his name being called. He turned to see Shirley and Jens arriving on their cycles, weaving between the piles of nets, floats, rock hoppers and trawl doors that were randomly stowed on the portside.

'Harry!' It was Shirley who was first off her cycle and by his side, she threw her arms around his neck and gave him a massive and affectionate squeeze. 'Look after yourself Harry, come back safe, please!'

Jens was there now too, grabbing his hand and shaking it with a vigorous pumping action. 'Thanks Harry,' he said. 'Thanks for everything.' He wanted to say more but could not find the right words, tongue tied when there seemed to be so much to say. But he did not need the words as his eyes spoke for him and Harry understood, not hearing but feeling the depth of his friend's gratitude, for his support, his protection and his friendship.

The three of them stood huddled together for a few moments on the cold, wind blasted dockside, a small haven of tranquility in the midst of the hubbub and chaos of activity around them. Each considered their very different experiences of the last three days spent together.

Harry was hurting, smitten by the shortfall between his high hopes when he'd woken with his dream of Shirley still in his veins, and now, with the stark realisation that dream could never come true.

Jens was lost in his own dream. The dream that one day soon it would be himself boarding one of these magnificent vessels and going to sea alongside Harry, for the sake of a brighter future for all of his loved ones, and for the chance of a life together with Shirley.

And Shirley, sad Shirley, was already missing Harry, and wondering how she would ever bear to be able to say goodbye to Jens in this way.

PART TWO

CHAPTER NINE

July 1964.

The sunny days had arrived at last, bringing with them clear, cerulean blue skies and the sweet cacophony of birdsong. Celia Flett, Dolly Coulbeck and Gwen Thorsen were enjoying the sunshine, sitting contentedly on a bench in the park, overlooking the small pond where the local boys sailed their model boats. Celia was gently rocking a pushchair backwards and forwards with one hand, whilst baby Alice slept soundly inside.

'How's Harry getting on at the nautical school?' Celia asked Dolly.

'He's loving it and the teacher has told him that he's doing really well. But he can't wait to get back to sea, it's been nearly five weeks already and he's missing it. Well he's missing the money anyway.'

'And how about your Jens?' Celia asked turning towards Gwen.

'He's enjoying it too love,' she answered. 'I just hope

he gets on Harry's boat, I'll feel better knowing he's got Harry looking after him out there.'

This was the very spot where Dolly and Gwen had first met so many years before, and coincidentally where the two older women had bumped into the young Scottish girl with her baby just two months previously. It had been a lovely spring morning and Dolly Coulbeck and Gwen Thorsen had decided to take a detour through the park on their way back from the shops. Here, they had seen the young mother, also out for a walk, pushing her pram in the spring sunshine. As is the way with mothers, intrigued by the small bundle in the pram, they had stopped to coo over the baby. They had immediately taken a shine to the polite young Scottish woman, and after a long chat about baby Alice, they had invited Celia to join them for a nice cup of tea in the park café. It was an offer that she had accepted with evident pleasure.

Now, the summer had come and over the intervening months the three women had become firm friends. The younger woman taking pleasure in company and conversation, the elder two enjoying the baby talk and taking their turns cradling and caring for the infant Alice. Dolly and Gwen had taken Celia Flett under their wing, first through their frequent meetings for tea in the park café, and more recently they had welcomed her into their homes as a guest to share tea, biscuits and friendly chats.

'Jens is such a nice boy,' Celia said. 'I just love to see the way he is around Shirley, it's so sweet.'

'Yes, they're made for each other,' Gwen replied. Despite her reservations about her eldest boy's insistence on signing up for the fishing vessels, she was deeply happy to see his lifelong friendship with Shirley Lofts blossoming into a full blown romance.

'I'm jealous,' admitted Celia, thinking about the happy young couple she had so recently met. She was a little wistful, still rocking the pushchair but gazing into the distance, the shadow of a remorseful look played across her pretty face.

A discrete glance passed between Gwen and Dolly at this. They had their suspicions that Celia's marriage was not a happy one, not that she has shared this confidence with them, but there had been little unspoken hints that she had inadvertently let slip in the way that she had described her husband Ken and his ways. Dolly and Gwen had gradually pieced together Celia's story and had developed a deal of sympathy for the plight of this well brought up, clever Scottish girl.

'How's Alice's croup been?' Gwen tactfully changed the subject.

'Oh she's a lot better in this weather and with the warmer nights, we've hardly had a wheeze have we darling?' She peered into the pushchair at the still sleeping, peaceful baby. 'And Daddy's been in a much better mood now that he's getting his sleep isn't he.'

'Will we ever meet your hubby?' Dolly asked.

Whilst Gwen and Dolly had sincere sympathy for their new friend's apparently less than blissful marital situation, they were nevertheless intrigued by the tales they had heard about her man Kenneth, and they both shared a deep curiosity and a yearning to meet him; it was like an unscratched itch for them. Shirley and her friend Doreen had both said that he was a really handsome man. 'Like a film star,' Doreen had testified, although Shirley would not be drawn quite that far, perhaps mindful that Jens might hear of it and feel unnecessary jealousy.

'Oh I don't know,' Celia replied. 'He's a bit of a loner, especially since we moved down to Grimsby from the North East.'

'You should get out more and make some friends and have a bit of fun, it might take him out of himself and it will be a tonic for you too. You're still young Celia, why you're only a few years older than Shirley,' Gwen said in a kindly tone. Celia smiled at this, the age gap between Shirley Lofts and herself was five years, perhaps not a major difference on paper she thought, but she felt a generation older.

'We can't really go out together at all, what with baby Alice here,' Celia replied. 'Ken sometimes goes down the pub at night on his own, but we haven't been out together at night since she was born. Not once.'

'Look darling,' Gwen continued, 'if you did want to get out, you could always leave Alice with one of us to babysit, she knows us now and you know that we'd look after her like one of our own.'

Celia was pensive but clearly excited by the proposition being put to her by Gwen Thorsen. Her life had changed so dramatically after Alice's birth that she hardly recognised herself. She knew that she was no longer the vibrant, modern girl she used to be, and Ken had become moody and remote, disappearing for hours on end in the evenings and weekends, clearly preferring his own company to Alice's and hers. Perhaps this was the answer; if they could get out together as a couple, have some fun and rediscover what they had originally seen in each other, then maybe the quality of their life together would improve. Instead of virtually ignoring her for most of the time, maybe Ken would look at her once again, really look at her with those pale blue grey eyes of his and make her feel interesting and funny and desirable again.

'That's a really good idea, and so kind of you to

'offer,' she said to her two friends. 'If you really don't mind, and if it really isn't any trouble to you, now that Alice's coughing is better, I might just take you up on that offer.'

*

Every day for the past five weeks Harry had cycled with his knapsack heavy with books, to Grimsby's new Technical College at Nunn's Corner to attend his course. As a child, he had never been very fond of school and in truth he had not been looking forward to what he had come to think of as 'the necessary evil' of classroom learning. In his mind it was something only undertaken because it was an essential step for his improvement and progression to the position of mate. But, instead of being something to be endured, his return to the classroom had been an entirely new and surprisingly enjoyable experience. The new Technical College building was a large, modern, red brick and plate glass cube, set back from the arc of one of the main arterial roads into Grimsby town, sitting behind broad green lawns and comprising three storeys of well appointed, bright and airy classrooms.

After feeling intimidated by the scale and modernity of the place for the first few days, Harry soon overcame his inhibitions about book learning and studying, largely because the lessons themselves had proven so interesting and relevant to his life on the trawlers. The main course teacher was a local man from one of the oldest fishing families in the port; Bob Lawson, a man with over twenty years experience at the helms of fishing boats and also the author of the course's main text book 'The Principles of Trawl Fishing, A Practical Handbook.' Bob Lawson had become a hero to Harry and the book was rarely far from his side, even in the evenings when, to his mother's amazement, he had forsaken going to the pub in order to finish his studies.

Being at home from sea for weeks on end had also allowed Harry to spend more time with his father Sid. Sid had been supportive of Harry furthering his career at sea, he skippered a seine netter himself and whilst Morning Glory was a mere snibby in comparison to the super trawlers that Harry worked on, he was a skilled fisherman and had been a good earner. His boat had a good reputation and Ray Harley, the ship's husband had never had any problems finding men willing to sail on her. Sid's only reservation about Harry studying for his ticket was that the lessons took place at the Technical College, over two miles away from the docks!

In Sid's day, the nautical school was sited on the docks. He remembered that you could see the masts of the ships from the school windows and in his opinion, it just didn't seem right to learn about fishing so far away from the boats. But there was nothing Harry could do about that, and after settling in for a day or so; he was more than happy to learn the more advanced skills of his trade in this modern facility. The bright new school concurred with his private view that the future of the industry, of all industry for that matter, was in technical advancement, and that the future lay not in the traditions of the past but in the innovations of the future.

Today, Harry and Jens were cycling home together after attending their lessons at the nautical school; the weather was fine as they sped side by side through the broad, tree-lined streets of Grimsby's most affluent residential area and past the grand Victorian park where Shirley had first declared her love for Jens. Jens looked across and caught fleeting glimpses of the bandstand through the trees, bringing a smile to his face as the memory of that cold winter night came back to him.

The town was basking in early evening sunlight; well-dressed couples and families with children were strolling in the park and around the well-to-do streets surrounding it. Like Harry and Jens, they were enjoying the lovely weather, feeling carefree, their lives illuminated by the amber light. Harry's cycle was newer and sportier than Jens' machine; he had a five speed Sturmey Archer hub gear compared to Jens fixed wheel model and consequently, when Harry looked over at his friend he saw him working much harder on the pedals than he was.

Despite the effort of the pedaling, Jens was still smiling to himself, buoyant with happy thoughts of Shirley and the knowledge that his longed for life at sea was very close now. It's almost too good to be true he thought, he hadn't been surprised that Harry had succeeded in getting himself a place as second mate on the new trawler, the Hansen Freya, but he could hardly credit it, Harry had been as good as his word and had actually managed to get him a job on the boat too.

The Freya was not just a fishing boat; it was also a floating fish processing factory with fish washers, plate freezers and a cold store on board so that fish could be processed and frozen whilst she was still at sea. Harry had been interviewed for his job by Captain Taylor, the Head of Fishing Operations in Hansen House, the new Group head office building. He had worn a smart shirt and tie for the interview but still felt out of place in the sleek office block with its crew of stolid, greying senior executives and immaculately groomed, pretty secretaries. The interview had gone well though; Harry's previous good record at sea on Hansen Group boats along with his evident passion for modernity and technical advancement in the industry had impressed Captain Taylor; he was exactly the kind of man they were looking for to crew their next generation boats and so, despite his youth and relative inexperience, Harry had been given a place on the company's newest boat, their showpiece of fishing technology, the Hansen Freya.

One of the first things Harry did on receiving the news of his appointment by post a few days after the interview was to visit the Freya. She was in port having the final finishing works completed before her maiden voyage. He particularly wanted to meet with her skipper who turned out to be a Scot called Jim Cunningham who Harry had found on the aft deck supervising some engineering work on one of the winches. The two men had greeted each other and Harry soon found the opportunity to mention his friend Jens, and to explain that he had worked in the Hansen fish factory, that he knew his fish and would be a useful hand in the fishroom seeing as he already had experience working on plate freezers and in cold stores. It was not difficult for Harry to convince Cunningham that he had an eye for a good seaman and the deal was done. And as easy as that, Jens was in too.

Jens had pinched himself once or twice to ensure that this wasn't all a dream, he had actually nipped the flesh of his forearm between his finger and thumb and then asked Shirley to do the same; so difficult was it for him to believe his good fortune.

'You'll be able to dump that penny farthing and get yourself a decent bike soon.' Harry laughed across to Jens, seeing his exertions at the pedals.

'You bet.' Jens replied breathlessly. 'I can't wait!'

'Tell you what,' Harry replied; 'before we go to sea,

we ought to have a special day out with all our mates, a sort of celebration for us passing our courses.'

'If we do,' Jens interjected.

'We will,' Harry answered self-assuredly. 'What do you think of a nice bike ride and a picnic next weekend after we finish?'

'It's a great idea,' Jens agreed. 'You and me and Shirl and our Frank, and if Bill is back he could bring Mo. It will be fun, where shall we go?'

'How about Hubbard's Hills?' Harry replied.

'Well, it's a long way, must be about fifteen or sixteen miles, but if we set off early I reckon we could do it.'

'Easy!' Harry was as confident as ever.

'Might be for you on that speedster, but we haven't all got state of the art bikes have we?' Jens replied, laughing. They pedaled on together towards home, enthused and lifted by the glorious summer evening, excited by the prospects of their future working together on board the finest trawler in the world, bringing home the big money and building good lives on shore for their loved ones; thinking that all was well with the world, thinking that they were the bee's knees.

*

Shirley and Doreen were drinking tea in the Hansen factory canteen. Work had seemed a hollow experience for Shirley these past few weeks since Jens had left the factory to attend the nautical school. Knowing that there was no chance of glancing him at his work on the factory floor, no chance of sharing a cuppa with him at tea break, no shared bike ride home, no after work gossip about their experiences of the day, had made her shifts seem so much longer and unbearably tedious. She felt his absence from the factory like an ache; the whole place had been rendered joyless and empty simply by the absence of one boy.

Doreen did her best to cheer Shirley up. She had noticed that her mood perked up whenever they talked about Jens, so Doreen talked about him often, asking Shirley how his training was going and indulging her flights of fancy as she fantasised about their prospects of a good life together once he started earning the big money. The two girls also gossiped about their other friends; Bill Osborne's new girlfriend Mo had been quite a hit with them, she was clever, confident and quick witted. The only girl they had ever known who could give Harry Coulbeck a run for his money with the lip. But their favourite topic at the moment was Shirley's new acquaintance, Ken Flett's wife Celia.

It had been a surprise for Shirley to meet the Scottish girl and her baby daughter at Jens' mother's house one day just a couple of months ago, and an even bigger surprise to discover once they began to chat, that she was married to Ken Flett, the enigmatic overseer. Shirley and Doreen were puzzled by the apparent mismatch between the surly and aggressive overseer and his delightful, intelligent wife, and they wondered what such a nice girl saw in such a surly man.

Today they were in the very act of talking about Celia and her enigma of a husband over their tea, when Ken himself came into the canteen and after getting himself a mug of tea poured at the serving hatch, he turned to look for somewhere to sit. The canteen was not full, there were a number of empty tables available but he set off towards the two girls.

'Is he coming over here?' Doreen whispered through

clenched teeth as he wended his way between the empty tables and chairs towards them. There was no chance nor indeed any need for Shirley to answer her as Ken arrived, and swivelling a chair around to face backwards, he straddled it like a cowboy mounting a horse, putting his mug onto the table between Shirley's and Doreen's.

'Hello girls,' he opened in his Scottish accent. 'Mind if I join you?'

They looked at him, a little taken aback but they did not make any objection to him joining them. That would not be appropriate, he was a supervisor and they were just packers.

'Hello mister Flett,' Doreen began. 'What can we do for you?'

'Now that,' he answered with a wry smile, 'is a very good question indeed.' The smile played across his lips as he eyed both girls simultaneously, they realised the innuendo in his reply and both girls coloured slightly at this.

'Ooh mister Flett,' Doreen replied. 'If I didn't know better, I would suspect you of being a little bit naughty.'

'Just a little bit? You obviously don't know me all that well.' He winked at Doreen.

'Mister Flett, I'll have you know that we're nice girls!' Doreen responded, feisty and good-humoured, rising to his flirtatious teasing.

'That's a shame,' he came back with a playful glint in his eye. Doreen couldn't help herself and she giggled out loud, provoking Shirley to a slightly uncomfortable smile.

'I'm sorry pet,' he turned towards Shirley now, giving her the full focus of his pale eyes. 'I'm not embarrassing you am I?' His eyes did not leave hers as he continued; 'I'm only having a laugh, just breaking the ice if you know what I mean.'

'S'all right mister Flett,' she answered. 'We can take a joke can't we Dorrie?'

'Now what's all this mister Flett business?' he said. 'You two can call me Ken.' They were confused by his attention.

'So what *can* we do for you, Ken?' Doreen asked.

'I'm just checking,' he replied, 'but I think that my wife has taken up with some women who you two both know, is that right?'

It was Shirley who answered. 'Yes Ken, she's made friends with Jens' mother Gwen and her friend Dolly. I've met her once or twice at Gwen's house and she's absolutely gorgeous.'

'You're right about that,' Ken replied. 'She's a little belter and I'm pleased she's found some friends here at last, I was beginning to get worried about her not settling. And she tells me that she's got an offer of a babysitter too, so we can go out together, and I was wondering if you two girls about town could give me some tips on where to take her.'

'Course we can,' both girls answered together, and then Doreen continued solo.

'There's some really good dances round here if you like dancing.'

'Yes,' Shirley picked up, energised and engaged by the mention of dancing. 'The best one is Pearson's Palais de Dance in Meggies on Friday night. Do you dance?' she asked.

'I've been known to,' he replied with a laugh. 'But where the hell is Meggies?'

'Cleethorpes!' both girls answered in unison again, giggling and hooking their little fingers together in the tradition of two people who had said exactly the same thing at exactly the same time.

Ken looked on, bemused and smiling broadly at the two friends. 'Look girls,' he said, 'thanks for the tip, I guess we might be seeing more of each other now that my missus has fallen in with your crowd, so I thought we ought to treat each other a bit more friendly like. D'ya ken?'

They giggled again, this time at the quaintness of his Scottish turn of phrase. The atmosphere at the table had become jovial and relaxed. Doreen saw that Shirley was smiling more now than she had done for some weeks previously, she also realised that there was something about Ken's presence that made her feel special and she wondered if Shirley felt the same way too. She had never seen anybody else favoured in this way by the man whose reputation was more typically one of bad tempered brutality. He picked up his drink, swivelled the chair back into place with a deft movement and moved to leave.

'Thanks girls,' he said, 'I'll be seeing you around.'

'Bye Ken,' they chorused, watching him walk away before turning to each other; mouths open in wonderment.

'Who would have thought it?' said Doreen. 'He's not like we thought he was at all is he?' Ken Flett had made a very favourable impression on the two young women; he had been charming, funny, affable and very friendly. Doreen looked over at Shirley who was still gazing at the retreating Ken, now leaving the canteen.

'He's good looking isn't he Shirl?' Doreen said, fanning her flushed cheeks with a wafted hand.

'Yes he is,' Shirley replied, turning now to face her friend. 'You've got to admit it, he is a very attractive man.'

*

In recent months Celia had found great solace in the company of the Thorsen, Lofts and Coulbeck families. They had been generous with their friendship and had shown her genuine kindness - but most importantly of all, they had thrown her a social lifeline just at the point in her life when she had been suffering the keenest agonies of isolation. Since her hasty marriage to Ken and their ignominious departure from Scotland soon thereafter she had been effectively ostracized from her own family and even more worryingly, recently she had been feeling an increasing remoteness, even from her own husband.

She very much enjoyed these visits with her new friends and although her feelings of friendship for her new acquaintances were genuine, Celia also enjoyed the secret thrill of observing them; their relationships and interactions intrigued her, and whilst she baulked at her own half-conceived notion that her superior education raised her above them, she could not help but feel that the perspective afforded by social distance enabled her to see them more objectively. She certainly felt that she was able to unpick the mesh of their interweaved relationships and their unspoken triangles, to see them more clearly than they did themselves.

She thought of Jens and Shirley as a delightful tableau of teenage intimacy in this new era of post war optimism - they were both just eighteen years old, sweet and innocent and to Celia's mind, oblivious of the sexual tensions and dynamics that crackled around them like a massive, undischarged electrical potential. Jens was a simple boy, so obviously and single-mindedly besotted with his sweetheart, he was a guileless young man whose ambitions knew boundaries set by simple aspirations of modest domesticity. But Shirley, so vivacious, so full of energy and so-far unfulfilled promise, appeared to be oblivious of her beauty and her feminine powers, of the compelling magnetism of her attractiveness and the insidious extent of her beguiling influence over the small circle of devoted men in her life.

And Celia's delight in her new friendships was absolutely reciprocated. Her arrival had been a welcome surprise and during his five weeks on shore, Harry had become accustomed to seeing Celia around, either at Gwen Thorsen's house or at his own home, visiting with his mother. Her visits had become regular, almost daily, appearing in the afternoon with her pushchair and baby and stopping for an hour or so for a cup of tea and a chat with the women. Harry liked Celia; she was pretty, polite and engaging with her singsong Scottish accent and breezy, affable ways. If she weren't married he would have been even more interested in her and although it had been something of a struggle for him, he had managed to curb his natural inclination and had so far maintained a respectable friendship with her. His mother had something to do with this state of affairs. Seeing the almost predatory look in her son's eyes on first meeting Celia, she had taken great pains to point out to him that Celia was a lovely, well brought up young lady and because she was her friend and therefore someone she didn't want to see hurt, she was out of bounds to him.

In truth, Harry was not looking for a relationship, he was still hurting inside from the Shirley Lofts situation and despite steeling himself against the deep disappointment of his unrequited feelings for her, he could not help but lapse occasionally, in his quiet moments, into periods of despondency. His nautical school course had been an effective distraction for some of the time, but when alone at night or when he saw Jens and Shirley's relationship flourishing and becoming yet more overtly demonstrative, he was saddened and hurt. To this end, the young Scottish lass had been a Godsend to him. She was a delightful and harmless distraction, he thought. He knew that nothing could happen between them, partly because of her marital status and her baby, and partly because he dare not risk the wrath of his mother; but seeing her around somehow lifted his clouds and brightened up his days a little.

In looks, Celia was very different to Shirley, whilst Shirley was fair, Celia was dark, they both had blue eyes but Shirley's twinkled and flashed whilst Celia's were deep and dark, soaking up light and locking it into the depths of her liquid black pupils. Harry liked Celia's round face with its high cheekbones and had noticed that the sun had brought out a flush of freckles, peppering her forehead and nose and giving her a girlish look. He liked these differences between the two, there was something about Celia that was unique; she was intriguing, an exotic summer visitor to his life.

Whilst Harry was most definitely attracted to Celia's looks, he also liked to talk to her about the fishing industry, and had found her remarkably knowledgeable on the subject. At first he couldn't believe his ears when she'd told him that her father was Ralph Gibson. Harry had of course heard of Celia's father and had seen his numerous boats on the sea and in the harbour at Peterhead, a port that he had visited a number of times whilst fishing on smaller boats before his days on the Apollo. From her work in her father's office, Celia had gleaned a good understanding of the fish catching sector, the different types of fishing vessels, their gears, their ranges and their catches, and because she had worked mainly on her father's profit and loss ledgers, she also understood about the various markets and values for fish.

This was a topic that they did not always agree on, and Celia did not share Harry's optimism for the future of the fish catching industry. In fact, she held quite the opposite view, formed from snippets she had heard of her father's business conversations and from being an intelligent observer around a major fishing company's office. Whilst Harry believed that the future of the fishing industry in Grimsby lay in the technical developments of fish capture technology, Celia believed that businesses trading in fish must diversify their commercial interests into other areas to offset future declines in the fishing industry. They argued about this for hours on end, Celia citing the company that Harry worked for as an example of this diversification in action.

'Look at Hansen's', she'd said to him. 'They're moving out of fish into other things like vegetables and chickens, why do you think they're doing that?'

'I don't know,' Harry had replied, genuinely wrong-footed.

'It's because David Hansen is a very clever man,' she'd continued. 'Dad knows him really well and says he's a shrewd cookie. He's told Dad that he sees problems coming with the boundary disputes with the Faroes and Iceland and if that goes on, we could lose access to those grounds altogether. Then Norway and Russia will follow and we'll have nothing left to fish but the North Sea and then there'll be way too many boats going after too few fish.'

Harry did not agree but found it hard to take Celia on in an argument involving politics.

'There's always been fishing at Grimsby,' he said. 'And there always will be. Hansen is a clever man, and that's why he's putting his money into these new boats. He wouldn't be doing that if he thought there wasn't a future for the industry would he? The Freya is the most advanced boat in the world, and I've heard that there's another one, even better than her being built right now for him over in Hull.'

Despite the conflict of their opinions, Harry and Celia both enjoyed their fishing conversations; for her, it was a reminder of her family and the life she had left behind, a life she was missing terribly now. For Harry it was quite simply a double pleasure to be able to talk about his favourite subject whilst enjoying the company of a delightful and wickedly attractive young woman.

This evening, Harry had arrived back from nautical school in a good mood, the cycle ride home with Jens had been a pleasure and they had enjoyed concocting a scheme to celebrate their finishing nautical school and embarking on what would undoubtedly be a profitable and enjoyable future for them both on the world's most advanced fishing vessel. Harry came into the house with his bike clips still in his hand to find his mother and Celia drinking tea in the kitchen. Baby Alice was sleeping in her pushchair.

'Hello Mum, hello Celia,' he said, then looking into the pushchair he silently mouthed, 'hello Alice,' to comic effect, making his mother smile.

'You're in a good mood Harry,' she said. 'Had a good day at school?'

'Yes Mum, the course is nearly finished and I'm looking forward to getting back to sea. It's going to be great.'

'Are you having a graduation party?' Celia asked, not quite sure whether this was appropriate terminology for the course that Harry had been taking. He laughed at the grandeur of her phrase.

'Not exactly a graduation ceremony,' he replied, 'but

we are thinking of having a bit of a special day out next weekend before we go off to sea.'

'Oh,' she said, 'what kind of special day out?'

'There'll be a gang of us go for a picnic on our bikes. Probably head off to Hubbard's Hills and make a day of it.'

Celia had never heard of Hubbard's Hills but replied politely. 'That sounds really nice Harry.'

She was taken by surprise when he said. 'I've got a brilliant idea Celia, why don't you come with us? It will be fun, there'll be Jens and Shirley and Frank and I think Bill and Mo will make it too.'

'No Harry, that's really kind of you, but I can't.'

'Yes you can,' he was insistent. 'What's the problem, why can't you?'

'Well for a start, there's baby Alice here, I can't leave her all day.'

'Well, you could darling if you really wanted to,' Dolly answered. 'It's only for a day and me and Gwen would be dead happy to take care of her, she's no bother at all, just look a her now, she's as good as gold.'

Celia was reticent to agree and followed up with another good reason why she couldn't go on the bicycle ride.

'I haven't got a bike Harry, so I can't go can I?"

'Course you can,' he replied instantly. 'You can borrow Mum's. It's in the shed, just needs a quick look over and a pump up and she'll be good to go.'

'Well, the thing is,' she replied more seriously now, 'it's Ken that I'm worried about. He doesn't mind me coming round here visiting in the week when he's at work, but I don't think he'd be keen on me going off on my own at weekends, he likes me in the house.'

'There's a simple solution to that Celia love,' Dolly

chipped in. 'Invite him too, he can borrow Sid's bike if he hasn't got one and it will be good for you two young'uns to get out together for a change. It will do you both the world of good!'

Celia pondered this for a moment and then replied. 'You know what, I think you just might be right Dolly. It's really nice of you to offer Harry, you're so kind and I think, yes I think I will take you up on it.'

She smiled gratefully at Dolly for her thoughtfulness. Her relationship with Ken had been strained of late and if he did agree to accompany her and these nice young people, her new friends, on this expedition it might just perk him up and take him out of himself. She turned now to Harry and said. 'Harry, you're the best. I'm really looking forward to it now. I'll ask Ken tonight and I do hope he says yes.'

Harry smiled at her, conflicted by contrasting emotions; pleased that she had consented to join the friends on their bike ride, but not at all happy that her allegedly irascible husband was now going to accompany them on their big day out.

*

Ken Flett was sitting alone in his kitchen, thinking about Celia. He was wondering why she had allowed herself to become dowdy, why she had lost interest in her appearance after the birth of their baby. There was no doubt that she was a beauty he thought, but she ought to make more of herself and she could do with losing a few more pounds too. When they were courting she would turn heads wherever they went. When she walked into a room, men would visibly pause from whatever they were doing in order to look at her. Somehow she had lost her sparkle. Maybe it's because we've stopped doing fun things together, he thought. So, when Celia had mentioned that her new friends would be happy to offer their services as babysitters, he had immediately been interested in the idea. Perhaps a good night out would do them both good.

Ken was still thinking about Celia when she arrived home. He heard the front door open and the pushchair being trundled down the hallway. He looked down the corridor from the kitchen and saw Celia lifting baby Alice out of the chair and carrying her through into the kitchen. Alice was ten months old now, quite a bundle, alert and attentive. She had seen him and was wiggling her little arms towards him. He smiled at her and made a childish gurgling noise, but he did not take her from his wife. Instead he stood up and lifted the kettle with an enquiring gesture.

'Cuppa?' he asked.

'Aye, go on,' she answered, sitting down and cradling the baby on her lap. Ken boiled the kettle and spooned tealeaves into the teapot. It was late evening but still warm, his shirt was undone by three buttons at the neck and his sleeves were rolled up above his elbows. She watched the lithe muscles flex in his forearm as he poured the boiling water from the heavy kettle into the large brown ceramic pot.

'Ken,' she began, a little hesitantly. 'I've got something to ask you.' He looked at her, puzzled a little by her hesitancy and her tone. 'We've been invited,' she continued, 'to go for a day out on a bike ride and a picnic with the Coulbecks and the Thorsens on Saturday.' She suddenly lost her conviction and added. 'Of course, we don't have to go, and it's probably a silly idea anyway.' He noticed that she was suddenly crestfallen and her voice was faltering. She was apparently talking herself out of something that she clearly wanted to do. He felt a pang of compassion seeing the disappointment in her large, sad eyes.

'Well doll,' he answered, 'it is a bit strange you have to admit, and you haven't even got a bike for a start. And anyway, I don't even know these people.'

'They're going to lend me a bike,' she answered. 'There won't be many of them, just Harry and Frank and Jens and Shirley. And you do know Jens Thorsen and Shirley Lofts,' she reminded him.

'Where are they going?' he asked.

'Somewhere called Hubbard's Hills apparently,' she replied.

'How far is it?'

'No idea.'

He was thoughtful for a little while. He did indeed know the young Danish boy, who until about a month ago was one of his trainee filleters. And as for Shirley Lofts, well he certainly knew her. He had in fact noticed Shirley very early on, soon after he had started his job at the Hansen factory, he'd noticed her fresh, pretty face, her shapely legs and her wiggling way of walking.

'Look, I'll make you a deal,' he said at last. 'I'll go on this picnic with you, on this bike ride, if you can arrange for a babysitter for us on Friday night so we can go out together.'

She looked surprised and puzzled at the same time.

'You see,' he continued, 'when you said the other day that those wifeys you've got friends with want to babysit for us, I got to thinking that it would be good for us to get out together and have a bit of fun.' Her face was suddenly illuminated with pleasure. 'So I've been doing a bit of asking around and it seems that your little friends all go out dancing on Friday nights. If you fancy it, we could go along too, it could be fun and it will be a good chance for me to get to know them all a bit better before I have to spend a full day with them.'

Celia was overjoyed. She promptly sat baby Alice down onto the kitchen floor and threw her arms around her husband's neck with a squeal.

'Oh Ken, that's brilliant!' she said. 'I'll ask Gwen and Dolly tomorrow, I'm sure one of them will be able to babysit.'

CHAPTER TEN

Celia did not have an awful lot of her clothes with her in Grimsby. The departure from Fraserburgh to Aberdeen and then from Aberdeen to Grimsby after their hurried wedding had left her with but the bare essentials, and what new clothes she had bought since her move had largely been maternity wear or simple comfortable clothes for housework. As soon as Gwen Thorsen and Dolly Coulbeck had agreed to share the child minding for baby Alice on both the Friday night and Saturday daytime, Celia had rushed off to the shops in Grimsby's old town to buy something nice to wear at the dance on Friday night. She had asked whether Shirley would mind accompanying her as she was a little out of touch with the current trends in fashion and felt the need for some young female company to help her choose.

Shirley was eager to help, but because it was Thursday, she had to come straight from her shift at the factory. Celia had arranged for them to meet outside Neilson and Appleyard's, the big department store on the main shopping street, at half past two in the afternoon.

When Shirley arrived, she was flustered from the cycle ride but was smartly dressed albeit with the feint odour of fish about her. Celia ignored this and embraced her friend, pleased for the company.

'Right, what we looking for then?' Shirley asked, clearly excited at the prospect of clothes shopping with her elegant new friend.

'Oh I'm not sure,' Celia admitted. 'It's ages since I've been out socially and I've no idea what's in nowadays.'

'Are you a good dancer?' Shirley asked.

'No, I'm afraid not,' she replied. Shirley was a little disappointed; she would have loved to have another friend to share her enthusiasm with.

'Never mind, I can always teach you,' she replied. 'And at least it helps us choose something for you to wear. Most of the dancers wear very flared skirts or dresses, it gives you freedom for the steps and a nice full skirt always looks lovely when you twirl doesn't it!' Celia was amused and delighted by Shirley's enthusiasm at this simple pleasure. 'But you're not going to be dancing much,' Shirley continued, 'so we'd better choose you a nice dress that you can use for other occasions too. There's some lovely dresses in now and I really like them, but I have to make sure that anything I buy is good for dancing in.'

They headed off towards the ladies' department, Celia pushing baby Alice ahead of her in her pushchair. Within moments of arriving, Shirley had directed her to a very nice range of evening dresses. She seemed to know the store inside out and she attacked the clothes rails with a fury, rifling them, looking for that perfect little dress for her friend. Celia was looking on a little bemused at the frenzy taking place in front of her, but was happy to put herself in Shirley's capable hands. With very little money to spend, Shirley was always immaculately turned out she thought, if this girl can't find me a nice dress, then no one can!

'Here!' Shirley exclaimed. 'Look at this one, and this!' She was pulling dresses from the racks and holding them up against herself on their hangers. 'And this one is lovely too, it would really suit you. And this one! This midnight blue one is the perfect colour for you Ceel, it goes with your eyes.'

'Calm down Shirley.' Celia laughed at her over excited companion and taking the blue dress from her, she turned it to the light, smiling at the iridescence of the fabric and the rainbow sheen that shimmered over the blue satin material under the bright store lighting. 'It is lovely,' she said, looking at the size tag. 'Do you think it will fit me, I've put a few pound on since I had Alice?'

'Course it will,' Shirley answered. 'You should try it on Ceel.'

'Do you think so?' she looked at Shirley.

'I know so,' she replied. 'I'll keep an eye on Alice; you pop into the changing room and slip it on. Go on!'

Moments later, Celia emerged from the changing cubicle wearing the dress. She stood in front of the full-length mirror admiring the highly tailored design, cut just above the knee with short sleeves and a smart if slightly plunged square neckline. Shirley was looking on, brimming with joy at her choice.

'Blooming heck Celia, you look absolutely blooming gorgeous.' She was not lying; the dress was perfect for Celia and it was purchased without further ado. With the dress in the bag, the girls headed off to seek out the vital accessories, and soon; a pair of high-heeled shoes, a clutch bag and a pair of long gloves in a perfectly matching fabric had also been purchased. Celia was enjoying this short shopping expedition more than almost anything she had done in the last year. Shirley was a charming friend and because of her incredibly good nature she was easy company, her vitality and energy were a tonic for Celia and simply being in her company made her feel invigorated. Years fell from her in those few moments, and for the first time in a long time, she felt young.

*

The floor of the Palais de Dance was crowded with the usual melee of Friday night dancers; they milled and swirled around each other like the colourful dodgems at Wonderland. Shirley and Jens were in their very midst, weaving intricate, dizzying patterns but never once faltering or colliding with the many other dancers. A fairground atmosphere pervaded the Palais on Friday nights, for most, the week's work was done and this night heralded the liberty and infinite exciting possibilities that the weekend could bring. Shirley was a little distracted as they danced and Jens noticed her far away look.

'What's up Shirl?' he asked, although he already knew the answer.

'I'm just thinking,' she said. 'This will be our last dance for a long time.'

'Well, for a couple of weeks,' he replied. 'This first trip is a short one; we're just testing the fishing gear and the factory equipment. I'll be back in no time.'

She smiled at this. 'Yes, I'm already looking forward to you getting back.'

'I haven't even gone yet!' He laughed as they danced, he spun her in a heel turn and they glided away together.

'You're getting good at that,' she commented. 'It's a

pity we won't be able to show it off at any competitions now. By the way, I've cancelled us from that trip to Lincoln next week.' Despite her good nature, Shirley found it hard to disguise her disappointment, it was not just Jens she would miss, there was the dancing too. Jens knew this and had no answer for her. In his mind the sacrifices they were both making would be worthwhile in the long run and he believed that Shirley would also realise this once their lives started to change. He was planning a surprise for her tomorrow when they went for the picnic, and felt sure she would come to see that he had been right all along.

The music ended and the bandleader announced a short break. Music from the speaker system kicked in with the crackle of the stylus hitting the record, and arm in arm, Shirley and Jens stepped off the floor into the bar room area where they saw Harry, pint in hand, talking to Bill and Mo.

'Bill,' Jens shouted, leaping forward and pumping Bill Osborne's hand in a vigorous shake. 'You alright mate, good trip, where did you go?' Shirley went to Mo and they greeted each other with smiles and hugs.

'Steady on Jens, you'll shake it off,' Bill laughed. 'The answers to your questions are; yes, yes and the White Sea, in that order. Okay?'

'Sure,' Jens answered, and then in the same breath, 'has Harry told you about our picnic tomorrow? We're going to Hubbard's Hills on our bikes.'

'Yes, we were just talking about it,' he said. 'Sounds like a cracking idea, there's just one thing though.'

'What's that?'

'There's no bloody way you're going to get me to bike all the way to Louth and back! It's alright for you load of landlubbers, but I've been at sea for three weeks and I'm knackered!'

Jens' disappointment was evident, he had worked out that Bill would probably be home from his trip and had hoped for his company along with Mo for his and Harry's big celebration day.

'Don't fret young'un,' Bill relented, seeing Jens looking downcast. 'Me and Mo are going to meet you there, we're going on the train aren't we Mo?'

'Brilliant!' Jens exploded. 'It's going to be a fantastic day.'

A round of drinks was bought and the group of friends chattered about their forthcoming day out. Harry was chided by Shirley for his drinking, warned to be on his best behaviour and told that he was definitely not permitted to get kaylied tonight, or else he would spoil tomorrow. Harry acted suitably contrite at his telling off, but still took a swig of his beer. They continued to talk about the picnic arrangements when Ken and Celia Flett arrived, entering the bar arm in arm. There was a moment's hush as heads were turned to see who the new couple were, and there was an almost audible drawing of breath as the two newcomers to Pearson's Palais de Dance strolled over to where Harry and the group of friends were standing.

Ken was wearing a dark lounge suit and Celia the midnight blue ensemble purchased with Shirley's help the day before. Her hair was pinned up in the Audrey Hepburn style, her face immaculately made-up. Dressed up like this they were an unbelievably glamorous pair, the handsome Scot and his beautiful wife. The bar was just beginning to revert to its normal hubbub of conversation and laughter when Ken and Celia arrived at the small group. A good deal of that hubbub was obviously directed at the two newcomers, speculating about who they were, admiring their good looks and elegance.

'Hello Shirley,' Celia went straight to her with a friendly embrace, kissing her lightly on the cheek, careful though not to smudge it with her lipstick.

'Ooh Ceel,' Shirley gasped. 'I told you that dress would suit you didn't I!' She turned to her friends. 'Doesn't Celia look lovely in that dress?'

Mo was nodding vehemently but Harry, Bill and Jens were simply staring at Celia, smiling inanely in agreement at Shirley's question but unable to find any words until Harry managed.

'Hi Ceels, you scrub up nice don't ya!'

'And this is my husband Ken.' Celia announced to the small group, moving on from Harry's clumsy compliment with aplomb. Ken nodded to the ladies and offered his hand in turn to Harry, then Bill and finally to Jens who took it somewhat reservedly, thinking back to the times when he had been abused by Ken on the factory floor.

'Now then Snowy,' Ken said to him, taking his limply offered hand and giving it a firm squeeze. 'Now you're off the factory floor, you and me can be friends,' he was talking to Jens but he was thinking about the impression his words would have on Shirley. 'I want you to forget all that nonsense from the factory. I didn't mean a word of it; it's just what I have to do. I can't be mister nice guy on the factory floor, the men would take the piss.'

'Okay mister Flett,' Jens answered, still unsure of what was being said to him.

'Ken, please!' He answered. 'I hope you understand what I'm saying Snowy,' he continued. 'I'm not the bad guy you probably think I am, it's all just a show for the men. They're a rough bunch and I can't have 'em thinking

I'm a soft touch can I? I've always thought you were a good kid and I'm sorry if I ever upset you at all. Can we put the past behind us and be friends from now on?' He raised a brow in a genial expression of conciliation.

'Okay Ken,' Jens answered. 'On just one condition.'

'And what's that Snowy?'

'You stop bloody calling me Snowy. Me name's Jens!'

They all laughed at this and Ken offered up a round of drinks, an idea readily agreed to by the friends.

'Come on then Jens,' he called over, 'come and give me a hand with this round,' and the two of them went off to the bar together.

When Ken and Jens returned with two trays of drinks, the girls had their heads together, admiring Celia's finery and generally gossiping. Harry and Bill were ostensibly talking about fishing but scarcely managing to disguise their covert admiration of Celia.

'Right then,' Ken said, raising his glass. 'Here's to our two young graduates, and to a very successful new adventure for them. Cheers!'

'Cheers!' Everyone reprised, raising and chinking their glasses in the toast to Harry and Jens.

'And just one other thing,' Ken continued. He was confident in their company and did not shrink from dominating proceedings. 'What's all this I hear about you lot talking my Celia into a thirty odd mile bike ride?' He had asked around at work and discovered that Hubbard's Hills was a wooded park on the outskirts of Louth, a Lincolnshire market town over fifteen miles away from Grimsby. He looked around accusingly. 'You do realise that she hasn't been on a bike since she was a bairn. I doubt if she could make it to the end of our road, let alone to Hubbard's bloody Hills whatever that is.'

There was a consensus that what had appeared to be

a good idea at the time was probably not the wisest idea for a novice cyclist, and the group looked perplexed at the potential loss of the popular and now glamorous Celia from their party. They stood in their circle, speechless until Bill piped up.

'Me and Mo are going on the train, why don't you come with us?' There were nods of consent at the idea and he added. 'You can even take your bikes if you want to bike around a bit at the other end. But Ken's right Celia, you shouldn't try to bike all the way there and back. Not in that dress anyway!' he added with a cheeky grin, provoking a nudge in the ribs from Mo.

And so it was agreed. Harry, Jens, Shirley and Frank would cycle all the way and Bill, Mo, Ken and Celia would go on the train and meet them there, bringing most of the picnic things with them to lighten the cyclist's loads. Celia liked the idea of taking the bicycles on the train, so that is what was agreed for Ken and her, although Bill was still adamant that he and Mo would not be doing any cycling this weekend at all.

The whole group were happy with the arrangements and the conversation soon turned to other topics, with the girls and boys dividing into two separate groups. Celia was enjoying the company of the slightly younger women and felt cheerful and a little giddy with the alcohol. She was savouring the attention and the compliments of her friends, and she was also aware of the many admiring glances she was receiving from the other men in the bar. The house band had returned and dancers were once again taking to the floor, Shirley was enjoying the camaraderie of the girls, nattering about clothes and hair, but she was also itching to get back onto the dance floor again.

'Jens,' she called, 'can we dance?'

'Just a minute Shirl,' he called back, 'we're just talking at the moment. I'll be with you in a sec.'

She turned back to the girls, disgruntled at this off-hand dismissal.

'He blooming gets on my wick sometimes,' she said. 'I love this tune, it's a lovely waltz and we'll miss it now he's gabbing on about his blooming fishing.' The band was playing Moon River in their hallmark jazz style; breathy, with achingly tender saxophone flourishes. Shirley was clearly pining to dance, already losing herself in the sultry music, her eyes closed, her head swaying in time, and so she was startled a little when Celia put her gloved hand on her forearm.

'Why don't you dance with one of the other boys then Shirl? There's plenty of young men in here who would be more than happy to dance with a lovely young lady like yourself, I'm sure.'

'Well, Harry can't dance for toffee and Bill is even worse. And I don't really like dancing with men who I don't know,' she said flatly. 'I guess I'll just have to wait for them to finish with their hot air.' She was resigned and a little grumpy. Celia noticed this, she was enjoying everything about the evening; she was happy and she wanted her friend to be happy too, she didn't want anything to spoil the mood.

'I know!' she exclaimed. 'You can dance with my Ken.' She was triumphant at her brainwave.

'But you two can't dance.' Shirley responded, puzzled.

'No Shirley, I said that *I* can't dance, not that Ken can't. He's quite a good dancer actually; he did some medals or something back in Scotland before he met me. Do you want me to ask him for you?'

Shirley did not really want to dance with Ken, she

wanted to dance with Jens, but she was annoyed with him and she wanted to make him realise that he couldn't take her for granted. She also didn't wish to appear churlish to Celia who had so generously offered the services of her own husband as a partner. 'Okay then,' she consented decidedly. Celia reached over and pulled her husband towards her by his arm. He moved willingly into the girl's group with a smile.

'Will you dance with Shirley please darling?' Celia asked him. 'She loves this waltz and Jens is so involved with his discussion that Shirl thinks she'll miss it.' Without another word, Ken turned his pale blue eyes immediately towards Shirley and raised his arm to her.

'May I have the pleasure?' he asked, holding her eyes with his own disarming gaze, and almost without realising what she was doing she felt herself take it and be led without resistance onto the floor, almost as if her will had been suspended. They moved into hold, pausing for a second to find the tempo, and in that brief moment she realised that Ken was bigger than Jens, somehow more substantial, more solid. And then they were away, moving in time with the steady three beats to the bar punctuated for them by the throb of the bass drum. They danced, a little stiffly at first she thought, but very quickly she adjusted to the feel of her new partner and surrendered herself to his lead, allowing herself to be guided. Ken was a good dancer, strong in the hold, firm in his direction but light on his feet, moving with stealth rather than grace perhaps, he was clearly very accomplished, and although a little rusty, he nevertheless danced with a high level of proficiency.

'You're good,' she said in the turn. He smiled his disarming smile at her but said nothing; his chin was raised and tipped slightly to one side. She could see his handsome profile out of the corner of her eye. She could feel his body moving against hers wherever they touched, which was intimately, from their hips upward to where her breasts pressed against his chest. She was reminded once again of the difference between Jens with his slight touch, and the manly way that Ken was holding her now. She had danced only with Jens for so long now that she found herself surprised by Ken's dominance, his strong arm cradled into the small of her back, pulling her into him, leaning into her. And then, with a lingering tenor saxophone note that dwindled eventually into nothingness, the song was over and the dance had ended. She allowed herself to be led by the hand back to her friends where Ken turned fully towards her and with a small bow of his head said. 'Thank you Shirley, it was an honour,' and with that, he released her fingers and turned to re-join the men and their fishy conversation.

Celia was smiling with pride at her gallant husband, and although Shirley returned her smiles with thanks and small talk, she didn't quite know what had just happened; she didn't dislike Ken Flett but she didn't particularly like him either. He was certainly charming, but he was also arrogant with it she thought, and whilst she had been thankful to Celia for giving her the opportunity to show Jens the error of his ways and to give him his comeuppance for ignoring her, she hadn't expected it to be the best, most graceful and most accomplished dance she'd had in years.

Perhaps ever.

CHAPTER ELEVEN

It was just after eight o'clock when Harry, Jens and Frank straddled their bicycles and headed off together to pick up Shirley for the ride to Louth. They had been lucky with the weather and it promised to be a sunny day for their picnic. The boys were wearing open necked shirts with their sleeves rolled up and when Shirley emerged, wheeling her bike around from the rear of her house, they saw that she had opted for blue slacks and a blue and white T-shirt with hoops like a French matelot; she was also sporting a broad brimmed straw sun hat to keep the sun off her fair skin. The team mounted up and they set off in single file through the streets towards the southern outskirts of the town. Only Harry was slightly hung over from the night before and he wore a pair of round-rimmed sunglasses to shade his light-sensitive eyes. It did not take them long to clear the town and within half an hour, they were riding in a cluster through empty country roads. Frank had plotted their course to avoid the traffic of the main Grimsby to Louth road and they found themselves pedaling easily over the flat coastal plain of

Lincolnshire with the soft, green, rolling hills of the Wolds rising to their right hand side and a clear blue summer sky above their heads. It was a lovely morning, they were lighthearted and enjoying the liberating feeling of being in the countryside.

Celia Flett had picked up Gwen Thorsen's bicycle; it had been serviced and the tyres had been pumped up by Harry in readiness and she was now riding a wobbling course towards Grimsby Town railway station with her husband Ken wheeling easily beside her on his racing cycle, his arms resting on top of the curved, dropped handlebars. He was smiling at her efforts and thanking God that she had not agreed to the full ride to Louth. Her face was locked in a serious expression, she was biting her bottom lip and frowning as she struggled to come to terms with the unfamiliar cycle, but she was enjoying the experience and was looking forward very much to the day out and to meeting her friends in the local beauty spot of Hubbard's Hills.

After a lovely night out last night, she felt at last that her prospects were beginning to look a little brighter; Ken had been charming all evening, chatting to the men about fishing and making the girls giggle with his silly jokes. Later on, after he had danced two or three times with Shirley Lofts, he had even tried to teach her a simple dance, a waltz, but it had not been a great success and after a few squashed toes they had settled for simply walking together in hold and in time with the music. She had felt vital and attractive for the first time in months, perhaps even in years. When they'd got home they'd found Gwen Thorsen dozing lightly in the comfortable arm chair in their front room and baby Alice safe and sound, fast asleep in her cot upstairs. Ken had walked Gwen home and returned within a quarter of an hour.

She had waited up for him but on his return he had been very tired and they had turned the light off.

At the station Celia and Ken saw that Bill and Mo had already arrived. Bags full of food surrounded them and Bill had a crate of Worthingtons by his feet. The two couples greeted each other warmly and waited together for the Louth train to arrive.

'That looks like a lot of snap,' Ken commented to Bill, nodding at the paper carrier bags.

'Yes, we picked most of it up this morning from Gwen and Dolly. And Shirley's mother Gladys had some more,' he answered. Ken and Celia had brought a knapsack with their own sandwiches and drinks, which they added to the pile. 'And this lot,' Bill added, kicking the crate with the tip of his toe, 'is all mine!' They smiled at the joke and stood back as the diesel train approached the platform. The bicycles were wheeled into the guard's van and the two couples found seats together in the same compartment.

'Wasn't it a lovely night last night?' Celia asked, directing the question mainly at Mo.

'Yes it was,' she agreed with a smile, 'and you looked lovely, didn't she Bill?'

Bill agreed but tried not to sound overly enthusiastic, fearing that Mo would not wish him to be too gushing about the loveliness of another girl. 'I see you decided not to wear the dress today then,' he joked.

'No, not today,' Celia answered. I thought that slacks and a blouse would be more appropriate for cycling.' She liked Bill Osborne, he was a kindly lad and had a good sense of humour. She could see why Mo liked him so much as a boyfriend. Celia looked at the young couple now, her hand clutched in his and the both resting on his thigh, his thumb stroking the back of hers in gentle, massaging circles. Maureen was a sweet girl, her red hair glowed brassy gold when the morning sun broke through the gaps between the houses and illuminated their carriage; they would be happy together she thought, you can just tell sometimes.

The train trundled steadily along, snaking past the long rows of houses that overlooked the track, and before many minutes had passed, they emerged into the light and space of the open fields beyond the edge of town. They passed through a number of small villages and rattled over level crossings where the white barred gates had been drawn across the roads to halt the non-existent traffic. The journey ended when they pulled into Louth station, just less than half an hour after they had left Grimsby Town.

They disembarked and stood on the station platform, Ken and Celia with their bicycles, Bill and Mo with the paper carrier bags. The crate was still full, Mo having succeeded in deterring Bill from opening a bottle for the train ride.

'Do you know where to go?' Bill asked Ken, who had pulled a map out of his knapsack.

'No problem,' he replied. 'See you later, how are you getting there?'

'I'm a fisherman,' Bill replied as if no further explanation was required. And after a pause, and a blank look from Ken. 'I'll get a taxi.'

Ken and Celia headed off on their cycles, Ken pedaling smoothly and easily but Celia, still a little wobbly at his side. Neither had ever visited the Lincolnshire market town of Louth before and once out of the industrial area that surrounded the railway station, they became impressed with the historic town and in particular with the distinctive Gothic steeple of St. James church.

Their journey took them out of the small town and into some hilly territory; testing Celia's cycling skills to the limit and making her legs ache with the effort of pedaling up the steep inclines. It was a flushed Celia, who eventually free wheeled with relief down the long hill, the final drop towards the entrance to Hubbard's Hills, where she found Bill and Mo standing already with their bags and Bill's crate, waiting for them.

'No sign yet?' Celia asked, breathless from the ride.

'Not that we can see, and this is where we agreed to meet them, so I suggest that we just go in a bit and find a nice spot by the river and have a sit down until they get here,' Bill answered, indicating that they should push on through the open wooden gate and into the sunny parkland beyond.

*

The roads from Grimsby to Louth were mostly flat and the cycling was easy for the four friends. They made good time, pausing only occasionally to take in the pastoral views across the rich agricultural land of Lincolnshire. Despite being the youngest member of the group, Frank had clearly put himself in charge and cycled at the head of the pack, his Ordnance Survey map folded open at the relevant section and tucked into his belt. The spire of St. James church served as a constant guide, rendering the map virtually unnecessary, but he was enjoying the job of navigator and made frequent comments and observations along the route.

'There she is,' he said as they approached the town. 'The noblest spire in Christendom as Alfred, Lord Tennyson put it.' The others smiled at the school lesson they were being dished up, but he had not finished yet.

'It's the tallest spire of any Anglican parish church in England,' he added. 'Two hundred and ninety five feet high.' Frank was pleased with this useful piece of general knowledge; he turned to look over his shoulder at his companions and wondered why they were all giggling.

It was just before eleven o'clock when Harry, Jens, Shirley and Frank free-wheeled down the last incline to Hubbard's Hills, dismounted and pushed their cycles through the gate onto the broad, tree lined path inside. It did not take long for them to locate Bill, Mo, Celia and Ken lounging on the grass in the sunshine just across a small wooden footbridge that spanned the river.

'Been here long?' Harry shouted, wheeling his bike across the bridge.

'About seven hours,' Bill shouted back, smiling at his own joke.

The bicycles were laid to the ground and the friends greeted each other, pleased to be here together on this sunny morning in such a pretty spot.

'Get the snap out then,' said Harry. 'I'm famished.'

'Hold your horses Coulbeck,' Shirley chided him. 'Let's just get settled and cool down a bit before you go eating all the food. I want to relax after that ride, my legs are blooming aching, especially after that last hilly bit.'

Celia, whose face had lost its deep red hue but retained a healthy pink glow, agreed with Shirley and the girls took charge of the food parcels to keep them out of the hands of the hungry Harry. But by now Harry had spotted the crate of beer that Bill had thoughtfully placed into the edge of the river to keep cool. He was smiling broadly at his friend's good thinking.

'Well, if I can't have me snap, at least I can wet me whistle eh Bill?'

Four glistening brown bottles of beer were pulled

from the water, one each for Harry, Ken, Bill and Jens, whilst Frank and the girls shared lemonade poured into paper cups from a stoppered Bellamy's bottle that had also been nestling in the shallows of the stream beside the crate. The friends stretched out on the warm grass, drinking their refreshments and sharing tales of their respective journeys. Harry took a long refreshing swig of the Worthingtons and looked around at the group.

Shirley, Celia and Mo had gravitated to each other, daintily sipping lemonade and chatting. Three beauties there, Harry thought, each one very different; there was pretty Shirley with her blonde hair, flashing eyes and twinkling smile, flame haired Mo, pale skinned but full of vitality and then there was the dark haired, beautiful Celia, a little older than the others and more womanly. That Ken was a lucky man to share his bed with a woman like her he thought.

Ken was still the dark horse of the group and although he had been affable enough at the dance last night, Harry was still a little unsure about him. He did not for instance, like the way that he monopolised Shirley on the dance floor. Poor Jens had never got a look in once they'd got going.

And there was Jens. Young, eager and full of optimism for a future that he could see so clearly for himself and his loved ones. Even now, he was sharing his ideas and plans with good-natured Bill Osborne.

And of course, not forgetting young Frank. Frank the brainbox. He had pulled out a book and was in a world of his own now, thinking God knows what thoughts in that little professor's head of his. It occurred to Harry for the first time, seeing him laid out there on the grass, between the men and the women of the group, that Frank was virtually grown up now. He'll be getting himself a girl of his own soon, Harry thought, remembering his own burgeoning interest in the opposite sex when he was the same age.

They lounged on the grass, enjoying the sunshine and the views across the steep, wooded valley of Hubbard's Hills, listening to the summer birdsong and the gurgling of the little river Ludd as it meandered past them. This was just what Harry had hoped for; all of his closest friends together for one lovely, memorable day out. It had been some months since his disappointment with Shirley and although he still longed for her, he had become accustomed to the situation and had tempered his feelings for her with a large dose of reality and his total immersion in the lessons at nautical school.

As predicted, he had passed the course with flying colours and a new life on board the world's finest fishing vessel beckoned him. He had committed himself to his ambitions at sea; he would be a skipper one day and then he would have money to burn. Then, and only then would he think of settling down, if he could find somebody who would have him. But for now, if he couldn't have Shirley Lofts, then he wouldn't have anybody.

To Harry's left Celia was sitting half listening to Mo and Shirley talk about dancing and half taking in the beautiful natural surroundings of the wooded valley, she had plucked a long stalk of grass and she twirled the end of it absent mindedly between her lips.

'I thought you looked beautiful last night Ceel,' Harry said to her, quietly.

'Why thank you Harry,' she replied, turning to him, her reverie completely shaken off now.

'I'm sorry I didn't tell you properly last night,' he continued. 'I was like every other man in the room. A bit tongue tied when I saw you.' Celia's cheeks flushed again at this, not from the rigors of cycling this time, but from the heat of Harry's compliment. Somehow, without a baby on her knee or a pushchair at the end of her arms, Celia seemed different to Harry. It was almost as if last night had been the first time he had really seen her for who she was. And today, in her casual summer clothes and in the context of this group of young friends, she had become more wonderful than he had ever imagined. No longer the dowdy, careworn mother, he saw her now as a vivacious and beautiful woman.

Refreshed by their drinks, the girls decided eventually to serve up the food, laying out a paper tablecloth from one of the bags and arranging the sandwiches on paper plates. Everyone dug in to the feast, especially the cyclists who had built up a hunger from their ride. As he was tucking into his sandwich, Harry noticed that Ken appeared to give him a look, one that he immediately interpreted as unfriendly. He wondered if he was mistaken when he saw Ken smiling and laughing with the rest of the company, it had been just a fleeting impression and perhaps he had misread the glance. After they had finished eating, the group broke up to pursue different activities.

Celia's legs were still feeling a little weak, so she opted to stay and watch over the picnic site by the little river, along with Frank who had attached himself to her and was busy telling her interesting facts about Hubbard's Hills; how it was formed at the end of the ice age by a melt-water lake from a glacier and the history of the public park, a gift to the people of Louth from a philanthropist in remembrance of his beloved wife. It was a romantic tale and he relished telling it to her. She lay in the sun, her eyes closed but her lips forming a small smile to show to him that she was listening.

Shirley and Jens had wandered away from the main group along the riverside, following the grassy bank to where the waters widened and passed more quickly over pebbly shallows, coming eventually to an area where children were playing in bathing costumes, paddling in the cold ankle-deep water.

Bill and Mo had rather more adventurously headed up a narrow, winding path through dense deciduous woodland towards the rim of the valley. Ken Flett was standing underneath a willow tree by the water's edge, smoking a cigarette and looking after Jens and Shirley, following their progress with his wolf-grey eyes.

Shirley had stopped at the riverside near the stepping-stones and had removed her sandals, rolling up the soft, elasticated fabric of her trousers to above her knees. She stepped into the water and hopped around with the shock of the cold, laughing and calling to Jens and stooping to scoop arcs of glittering water towards him as he stood laughing at her on the bank. They were some distance away, just out of earshot, but Ken's keen eyes could still make out the delicious white curve of her calves and the shape of her bottom in the tight slacks. He felt the surreptitious thrill of watching her young body bristling with it's youthful energy.

Harry hopped to his feet and strolled towards Ken, hoping to get to know him a little better and perhaps put his mind at rest over that fleeting impression of animosity. On arriving at his side he too looked towards Jens and Shirley messing around in the shallow water.

'They make a smashing couple don't they?' He said to Ken.

'Aye they do that,' he replied. 'He's a lucky boy to have a lovely girl like that.' There was something about

Ken's reply that unsettled Harry. Was it because of the coincidence that he had so very recently been thinking something very similar about Ken's own good fortune to be married to Celia? Or was it something deeper, something in the tone of his voice or in the way that his eyes were dwelling on Shirley? 'I mean, just look at that body,' Ken continued. 'She's a little cracker and no mistake.'

'Steady on Ken!' Harry replied, trying to keep the tone of his voice friendly whilst reproving the older man for his unwarranted attentions towards Shirley. 'She's only a baby, just eighteen and as innocent as a lamb.'

'She wouldn't stay innocent for too long if I ever got my hands on her.' Ken was more thinking aloud rather than talking to Harry, but Harry heard him clearly enough.

'I'm not having that Ken,' he answered back more strongly now. 'She's like a little sister to me and I'm not having you talking like that about her. Not when you've got a lovely wife like Celia back there.'

'Aye, I've seen you eyeing up my missus,' he turned to Harry now, confident and unabashed. 'Can't keep your eyes off her can you?' Harry was confused and momentarily unsure of what to do. His instinct was to grab Ken Flett by the throat and to pin him against the tree trunk, but the truth of his comments about his feelings towards Celia had wrong-footed him and instead, he just stood there, gaping, his hands flapping ineffectually by his side.

'Look Coulbeck,' Ken said. 'Maybe I just overstepped the mark there, and you're right, I had no call for talking about a sweet kid like Shirley like that and I shouldn't have said what I said.' His voice was steady and reasonable now. 'Look, we're both just red blooded blokes you and me, we're cut from the same cloth, we can't help what we are, can we?' He looked to Harry who did not want to agree with him, but could find no rational reason not to accept Ken's apology. He took Ken's hand when it was offered and they shook. On the surface, Harry and Ken had just made up but despite their smiles and handshakes, Harry could not help but continue to harbor distrust and a dislike for the Scot. Despite the fact that he had been discovered in his desires for the man's wife, he felt that he needed to keep an eye on this one. He's dangerous, he thought.

*

At the top of the valley, on a bench beside a quiet stretch of pathway, Bill and Mo were kissing, making up for lost time whilst he had been at sea. They were deeply engrossed in each other, but in between kisses they peered through the trees to the distant valley floor beneath them. To their left, they could see Celia Flett sprawled lazily on the grass, her arms outstretched beside her and young Frank Thorsen lying on his tummy close by. To their right, they could see Jens and Shirley, their shoes in their hands, paddling shin deep in the little river. Harry and Ken were not in view.

Also deeply engrossed in each other, Jens and Shirley climbed onto the river bank and laid down on the grass in the sun together, holding hands and waiting for the sun to dry their feet for them.

'Isn't this lovely?' Shirley said to him, sighing with contentment.

'Yes Shirl, it's a perfect day,' he replied, squeezing her hand. 'We'll be able to do this sort of thing all the time when I'm earning, I've got all sorts of plans you know!'

'What sort of plans?' she asked, wanting to hear his stories, to find strength in his plans of their future life together.

'Well for a start,' he began, 'I could learn to drive and we could get a little car.'

'That would be nice.'

'And after I've saved up a bit, I'd like to put a deposit down on one of those nice bungalows they're building out at Humberston.'

'For your mother and Frank and you?' she asked.

'No Shirl, not for them,' he sat up so that he could look down on her pretty face from above, placing his head so that his shadow shielded her eyes from the bright sunshine. She opened them fully, looking up at him. He leaned over her and planted a single, tender kiss on her lips.

'You know, I said this was the perfect day?'

'Yes Jens.'

'Well it's not quite, but there is something that would make it absolutely perfect.'

'What's that Jens?'

He took both of her hands and pulled her upright into a seated position, swiveling himself onto one knee at the same time and producing a small packet from his trouser back pocket. 'Shirley Lofts,' he continued, his voice trembling with nerves. 'Will you do me the honour of marrying me?' He opened the packet and produced a ring, which he offered to her.

'Jens!' It was a shriek more than anything, and suddenly her arms were around his neck, forcing him off balance and they both tumbled in a heap onto the grass. 'Yes, yes, yes, yes!' she sang in excited, joyous gasps, interspersing each yes with a loud kiss.

Bill and Mo looked down at Shirley and Jens from their vantage point and watched them as they tumbled in an embrace on the grass. 'Look at them two,' Mo said. 'Isn't it sweet, they're just made for each other them two are!' She gazed down at the couple, the smile freezing on her face when she saw that Shirley had leaped to her feet and was now running and skipping back towards the picnic site, she was waving her arms in the air and Mo could just hear her excited voice shouting.

'Harry, Harry, where's Harry?'

'Come on Bill!' Mo said. 'We'd better get back down there, something's going on.' They got up from the bench and began to scramble hand in hand for safety, down the steep valley side.

Harry, who was sitting on a fallen tree trunk relaxing and watching the river bubble by heard his name being called and got up to see what was causing the commotion. Before he knew it, Shirley was on him, her arms wrapped around his neck, her legs wiggling wildly in the air behind her.

'Jens has asked me to marry him, I wanted you to be the first to know,' she squealed.

Harry spun her round and around, until they were both giddy and he had to put her back down onto the ground. By now, Celia, Frank and Ken were also on their feet and congratulating Jens who had just arrived, with slaps on the back, vigorous hand shakes and kisses on the cheek from Celia.

Bill and Mo arrived seconds later, Bill looking confused but Mo running straight to Shirley shouting.

'Congratulations darling, I'm so happy for you!' The girls embraced whilst Harry explained about the good news to Bill, who on hearing it called for a toast. Bottles of beer were pulled from the crate, their crown caps flipped off with Bill's bottle opener to a series of gassy fizzing pops and beer was poured into paper cups for everyone, even young Frank. As Jens and Shirley's oldest friend, Harry felt it incumbent on him to make the toast.

'Ladies and gentlemen,' he began. 'May I ask you to raise your glasses, er, well, paper cups, and drink the health of our very good friends Jens Peter Thorsen and Shirley Lofts on the occasion of their engagement.' He paused and called out. 'Jens Peter Thorsen and Shirley Lofts!'

'Jens Peter Thorsen and Shirley Lofts!' Everybody chanted in unison, raising their paper cups and swigging the river-cooled beer.

'And now it is a perfect day,' Jens said to Shirley, taking her in his arms and giving her a long kiss. Celia and Mo made gooey 'aah' noises at this, Frank and Bill slapped each other on the back, but Ken stood a little separated from the main group, a smile on his lips but not in his eyes. And Harry was watching Ken.

The remainder of the beer was drunk and the unanimous decision made, that the whole group would return to Grimsby together on the train. So, in time they headed off walking, most of them pushing bicycles to Louth railway station to catch the train back home. Once the cycles had been stowed in the guard's wagon and the group had settled into their carriage, an air of contentment descended as they relaxed into the coarse, dusty upholstery, feeling tired from the exercise, the sun, the beer and the emotional excitement of the proposal. They all agreed it had been a perfect day, a perfect send off for Harry and Jens and the perfect start for Jens and Shirley's life together.

CHAPTER TWELVE

Harry had found the Hansen Freya moored in rank, side by side with the other trawlers on the North Wall; a ladder extended some twenty feet from the dockside to her prow where it was lashed for safety with a short length of rope. It was Sunday morning and he was visiting the vessel to ensure that everything was in order prior to her departure on tomorrow's early morning tide. He scrambled up the precarious ladder and dropped to the deck. Shore crew were working to ready the new vessel but he did not see the skipper Jim Cunningham amongst them. He climbed the steel steps up to the bridge; he tapped and pushed open the steel door and put his head around.

'Skipper, you here?'

'Come in Harry,' he heard, and stepping into the bridge house saw the skipper sitting in his chair at the command console, surrounded by banks of the most modern electronic equipment that Harry had ever seen. From the latest Marconi radio equipment to Decca sonar and radar, Freya had it all. Jim Cunningham was an experienced skipper, one of the best in the port, he had skippered a number of Hansen's biggest boats in the past and this appointment was the company's recognition of his quality. He had a big mug of tea in his hand and seeing Harry step into the bridge, he piped up. 'Wasn't expecting to see you today Coulbeck, ain't you got a home to go to or some nice little tart who needs a cuddle before you disappear from her life for a couple of weeks?'

'I just thought I'd come and have a look around if that's okay skipper,' he replied smiling. 'It's been six weeks since I've been at sea and I'm itching to get back out.'

'Aye, I've heard you're a good lad Coulbeck,' the skipper said, 'that's how you got the job. Your old skipper's a big mate of a neighbour of mine and he put in a very good word for you. Truth is, you're a lucky bugger to get on this boat, Hansen wanted a handpicked crew of experienced men for this beauty. My bosun is a qualified mate you know, and the first mate, your boss, has already got his skipper's ticket. There aren't any decky learners on board so the only rookies we're taking on is you as second mate and your little chum in the factory.'

'Yes, I know we're lucky skipper and we won't let you down, you have my word on that' Harry replied earnestly.

Cunningham took a gulp of his tea and asked, 'Do you want a look around her then?' Harry nodded and the two men headed back down the companionway to the metal steps and then down to the top deck below.

'This is where the action happens,' he said taking in the ribbed metal working deck with a sweep of his hand. Harry could see the two powerful winches that pulled the steel trawl warp cables, there were over a mile of warp rolled onto each of the huge drums. The deck tapered away at a steep forty-five degree incline at the stern of the vessel, plunging right down almost to the water's edge to form a huge ramp where the trawl net would be hauled out of the sea, right up onto the working deck. That all looks fine in the millpond calm of Grimsby docks Harry thought, but out on the open ocean in a big sea, this could get hairy. He noted without comfort, the single safety chain strung about waist height across the opening of the ramp.

Turning away from the vertiginous opening to face the working deck and bridge, Cunningham pointed at the deck below their feet. 'This hatch is controlled by pneumatics,' he said proudly, indicating that where they were standing was in fact a moveable section of deck. 'When we've got the bag on board, I open this up from the bridge and we can winch the net up with the Gilsons and empty the catch down here, straight into the holding pounds in the factory below.'

'Now come and look at this,' he said excitedly, swinging his body through a smaller hatch and sliding down a steel ladder into the factory area below. Harry followed and once inside the claustrophobic lower deck he saw that there were engineers still working, putting the final touches to the fish handling equipment. Blue sparks scattered in arcs from a welding rod nearby, where a workman was kneeling to weld a supporting bracket for one of the stainless steel fish washer tanks.

'Nearly done Roy?' Cunningham asked the welder.

'Yes skipper,' he returned, flipping his mask to the top of his head. 'I've just about finished fitting the fish washers now, should have been done yesterday but it turned out to be a tricky job. They were too big to bring down here in one piece, so I had to make them in sections in the shop and weld them up down here.'

'Good job Roy.' Cunningham slapped him on the shoulder and moved down the line to show Harry the plate freezers. The metal ceiling was just a foot above his head and he could imagine the engine noise reverberating between the metal walls, floor and ceiling. 'See these Harry?' he said, pointing at the ten rectangular metal machines, each with a large slotted compartment in the top. 'These are the vertical plate freezers. We'll load the fish into these cavities and then freeze them into solid blocks; it should take about four hours if they work like they should. Then, when we pop them out, they'll be rock solid, like paving slabs and the lads will slide them down this chute here into the cold store below. She takes four hundred tons to fill her up and when the hold is full, we come home. Easy as that!'

'Easy as that!' Harry echoed. He thought about Jens and the six weeks he had just spent at nautical school learning the basic aspects of fishing, from learning about the component parts of trawl gear and how to mend damaged nets, to first aid and even a bit of cooking in case he was needed to help out in the galley. He should by now have a good grounding in the rudimentary skills needed to be a fisherman, and with his willingness to learn, he should be a useful addition to the crew. 'So what will Jens Thorsen be doing then?' he asked.

'Well Harry, we don't really want him on deck to start with. As I said, this is an experienced crew but it's a new type of trawling and we'll need good men who know what they're doing. There's twenty-five of us in total and all are good, experienced fishermen apart from him. He'll be down here mostly, gutting and doing the livers and unloading the plate freezers. It will take time to work through a catch because of the freezing cycle, so if we get it right, your mate will have just about finished loading up the frozen blocks and we should have another haul for him to start on.'

'Don't worry skipper,' Harry said, 'he's a good worker is Jens.'

'He'll need to be,' Cunningham replied. 'I plan to make this a happy boat, but it will be hard work, twelve hours on, six hours off, seven days a week. We're going after big catches Coulbeck and that means hard work and fat pay packets. After we've tested everything out on this short trip to the Faroes, we'll mainly be fishing the West Atlantic, off Labrador and the Grand Banks.'

'Bloody 'ell skipper!' Harry ejaculated. 'Long trips then, two thousand miles at least, that must be six to eight days steaming just to get to the grounds, then the fishing and the return trip on top of that. Best part of a five thousand mile round trip I reckon!'

'Aye lad, we could be away anything between four to ten weeks, depends how good the fishing is.'

'Not a problem for me skipper,' Harry said. 'I'm used to it and I love it.' But secretly he was worried for Jens; the long trips across the Atlantic plus the fact that Freya was an all-freezer vessel which meant she wouldn't need to return to port until the hold was crammed full with four hundred tons of fish, meant very long trips and that could very well put a strain on his new relationship with Shirley. He had seen it before. It was not easy being married to a fisherman at the best of times, because a distant water fisherman's life was not his own, he had a wife and a mistress; one who he spent most of his time with and the other who waited around for him, waiting for her fleeting share of his days – and it was not the woman who was the wife, it was the trawler.

*

'This is our last night together for ages.' Shirley was sad; she was curled possessively around Jens, trying to enfold him with her limbs. They were sitting on the Thorsen's little settee in the front room; Gwen and Frank were discretely giving them some private moments together on Jens' last night at home before his first trip to sea. Shirley was tenderly stroking his face and repeatedly kissing his cheek and neck. Her heart was breaking.

'I'll be back in a couple of weeks,' he answered her, trying to force light heartedness into his tone, whilst inside he was fighting his own sadness at their imminent parting.

'That's what I said,' she replied. 'It'll be ages!' Her eyes, normally bright and full of vitality were red rimmed, their whites shot with pink. She had been crying.

'I know,' he conceded. 'I'm sad too Shirl,' but you have to remember why I'm doing this. It's all for us darling, for our future.'

'Tell me again what it's going to be like,' she asked, needing his optimism.

'We're going to miss each other when I'm away, that's a fact,' he admitted, 'but when I'm home it will be fantastic and it will all be worthwhile. I get a day off for every week I spend at sea and with my holidays on top of that I'll be home loads, I've been working it out Shirl and I reckon it will be about seventy days every year.'

'Seventy days,' she said, 'that will be lovely. We'll make every one of them extra special.'

'And I'll be on good money Shirl, really good money.' She smiled at this. 'I'll start saving up straight away, I want to put some money aside for our Frank so I'm going to open a bank account for him at the TSB on Fiveways and I'll open another one for us. In about a year, I reckon we'll have saved up enough for a deposit on a nice little bungalow and then, when we've got somewhere of our own sorted out, we can actually get married.'

'Oh Jens, it sounds wonderful.' She could see herself in the future, happy and settled, living away from the grimy brown brick terraces of Grimsby town, out in Cleethorpes or Humberston where the air was cleaner and where the skies were bigger. It was a happy dream, the only thing that would possibly make it any better would be if Jens could spend more time with her to share it, to be at home with her instead of being out at sea all the time.

Her own father had worked hard all his life on the docks to put a roof over his family's heads and good food on their dinner table and he had struggled to do that through the very hard times after the war when men laboured just to keep body and soul together. The plans that Jens talked of now would have been an impossible dream for her father, but the world was changing very quickly now, this was a new, modern era and Shirley believed in their dream. She couldn't see why young folks like themselves shouldn't dream of a better life, of a good education if you've got the brains like Frank had, of a nice modern home, of clean, fresh air and big skies.

'I'm going to do what Harry is doing,' Jens continued. 'After a bit, I'll do my mate's ticket, then I'll go for bosun and who knows? One day, I could even be a skipper myself and have me own boat.' Shirley smiled at her enthused fiancée.

'Look at you,' she said, smiling, 'you haven't even done your first trip yet and you've already got yourself promoted to skipper!' He laughed with her; they cuddled and kissed, feeling the restorative energy of the laughter momentarily taking the keen edge off their sadness.

*

It was barely light, a pink sky glowed over the river to the east, but landward the sky was still veiled in darkness. It was five o'clock in the morning and the Hansen Freya was already preparing to sail on the early tide. Jens and Harry had been on board since four o'clock, having shared a taxi down to the North Wall. Shirley had not come with them. All twenty-five hands were on board and the chief engineer had started the two big diesel engines that drove Freya, their enormous power constrained in the dock to a low, throbbing hum that reverberated through the hull and made the steel decks vibrate.

Skipper Jim Cunningham was in his captain's chair, barking orders to the crew over the crackling tannoy as they cast off and Hansen's new super trawler backed slowly away from the quayside. Despite the early hour, a collection of wives and children thronged on the dockside, waving and hoping for a last glance of their loved ones, they were calling messages of love and luck to each other. Shirley was not amongst them.

Without any formal duties to perform, Jens stood amongst a small group of unoccupied hands on the fore deck, enjoying the momentous occasion of his first sea trip and trying to contain his nervous energy. He was looking around at his crewmates, wondering whether he would get on with them, when he was suddenly surprised to see a familiar face amongst them. It was Percy Bennett.

'Hello mister Bennett,' he said, genuinely pleased to see his old supervisor on board. 'I didn't know you were part of Freya's crew.'

'I'm not son,' Percy replied, turning to Jens with a big smile. 'Hansen wanted someone with factory management experience on board, just for the first couple of trips to sort out the shift patterns and manning levels. Don't forget Thorsen, Freya isn't just a fishing boat, she's a floating factory too, the first of her type and a new venture for the company.'

'It's great to have you on board though mister Bennett,' Jens replied.

'I wasn't first choice for the job son.' He held up a mutilated hand. Jens had forgotten that his old factory supervisor had lost half of his left hand in a winch accident when he had been a trawlerman himself. Not wishing to lose the services of a good man but knowing that his fishing days were over, the company had found him a new job supervising the filleting lines in one of their factories.

'But a willing volunteer is better than a pressed man, so here I am.' Percy pressed on. 'I'm happy to be here and to be back at sea again, even if it is only for a couple of trips.' He looked around at the dockside scene. 'I miss this though,' he added in wistful tone.

Although he tried not to, Jens could not help looking into the crowd in the vain hope of a glimpse of Shirley. They had agreed last night that she would not come, it would be too painful, but nevertheless, he looked. Just in case.

Skipper Jim Cunningham took the vessel out of the rank towards the centre of Grimsby's Fish Dock Number Three before engaging forward engines and with a slight increase in revs, moved her slowly towards the lock gates. The crowd of wives and girlfriends followed the progress of the trawler; they aggregated at the side of the lock pit, waiting for one last glance of their loved ones. The children though were waiting for the copper coins that the fishermen would throw ashore for good luck.

And then he saw her. She was pedalling like fury towards the lock pit down the North Wall road, her head was down but somehow she managed to avoid the many obstacles and people in her way. She was nearer now and looking up, calling his name.

'Jens, Jens darling, I had to come. I had to tell you that I love you. Good luck,' she shouted, hoarse with the effort. 'Come home soon, and please, please come home safe!' She was wild eyed with her passion. He waved frantically back at her, she was on the lock jetty now, still astride her bicycle, still waving and shouting to him.

The Hansen Freya slipped slowly, smoothly out of the lock pit and into the open River Humber beyond. To her left was the looming brown brick edifice of the dock tower, to her right the throng of well-wishers on the wooden pier, but Jens saw only Shirley, he watched her diminish as the distance between them grew, watching until he had to guess which one of the tiny figures was hers. Watching until he could see her no more.

And Harry was by his side, his immediate duties completed now that the trawler had reached the open water.

'There's nothing like it Jens,' he said. 'Nothing like this feeling of setting sail, watching the land get further away until all you can see is sea and sky. It's one of the best feelings in the world.' He breathed deeply of the sea air, his eyes closed, luxuriating in the ozone.

Jens was almost overwhelmed by the confusing and conflicting rush of feelings coursing through him; there was the excitement of his first sea voyage, his nervousness of this major new challenge, the exultation of finally achieving his life's ambition and yet somehow, sitting behind all of this, at his core, he was bereft at his separation from Shirley, his Shirley. Harry saw the mixed emotions in his friend's face and gave him a hearty slap on the back as a shake up.

'Now we'll find out if you're a sailor or not,' he declared with a laugh.

'What do you mean Harry?' Jens asked.

'We'll know soon enough mate, when you start to throw up.'

'You mean seasickness?' he asked.

'Aye Jens, seasickness, most of us get it, even the old hands. Don't worry about it when it comes over you, just let it go, it's better out than in.'

'I'm feeling alright though,' he protested proudly.

'Yes mate, but we're still in the Humber aren't we?'

They both looked around and saw the green hills of the Lincolnshire Wolds rising on their starboard side, the seaside town of Cleethorpes appearing to nestle in their foothills. Jens who had never seen the town from this perspective before had not realised just how steeply the Wolds rose behind the coastal plain. And on their port side he saw the patchwork fields and distant church spires of East Yorkshire, tapering to the spit of dun sand that was Spurn Point with its distinctive white lighthouse.

'Once we get past Spurn and out into the North Sea proper, things will get a bit choppy and then we'll see,' Harry added, with a knowing look and a big smile at his rookie friend.

The Freya was a powerful vessel, fitted with two mighty Ruston-Paxman diesel electric turbines, she had both power and grace and she cut through the muddy estuarial waters with ease, leaving a wake of caramel coloured foam on the surface behind her. The weather was fine now, just a light south-westerly breeze and a clear, now pearl grey early morning sky to light her on her way. In only minutes it seemed, skipper Jim Cunningham had taken her around Spurn and was turning his charge north eastwards into the heaving currents and bigger waters of the North Sea. She rolled as she encountered the swell but he gunned the engines and her bow lifted with the surge of power and they were truly on their way. The coast of Yorkshire's East Riding grew increasingly distant until it was just a feint brown line on the horizon. And then it was no more, and there was only the sea and the sky and the seagulls and Freya and Jens Thorsen, heaving his guts over the starboard rail.

*

Shirley had stood on the pier looking after the Freya until she had disappeared out of view. She felt the invisible string between her heart and his drawn tighter with every passing second, and then at last, when she could see the boat no more, she had turned and cycled slowly back to the factory. It had taken her just two minutes, she was still early for work and she found herself sitting alone in the staff canteen, dabbing at her eyes with a tissue, trying to stop crying.

'Shirley, are you okay?' She was startled because she thought that she was alone. She recognised his accent. The tone of the voice was tender. She turned to face Ken Flett, who, passing the canteen on his way to the factory had noticed the lone figure sitting by the window gazing out over the dock to the river beyond.

'Oh, hello Ken,' she said, 'I've just been to see Jens off.' Her voice broke as she struggled to stifle a sob. But no further words were necessary. Ken pulled out the chair beside her, he sat down and took her small hand gently in his.

'Aah baby,' he said, 'you must be feeling heartbroken right now.' She nodded; her eyes brimming with unshed tears. 'Why don't you pop around to ours later and have a nice chat with Celia?'

'Yes, I might just do that,' she said.

*

After a few hours of nausea during which he had cursed his decision to come to sea and vowed never to return, his seasickness had abated and he had at last found his sea legs. The journey to the Faroe plateau had been uneventful, Jens had spent some time in the plant, familiarising himself with the machinery and the cold storage facilities, otherwise, he had spent hours laying on his bunk, daydreaming and missing Shirley.

The Hansen Freya had performed admirably during the passage north, the steady growl of her twin diesel engines driving her with speed through the waves. The sea hadn't been too bad so far, although they had encountered stronger currents and bigger seas funnelling through the Pentland Firth and Jens had felt the pitch of the engines increase as the skipper once again gunned the vessel, driving her harder into the more powerful waves. He had slept little, feeling the swell of the vessel rocking him and rousing him in his uneasy slumbers. He had eventually discovered that by pulling his knees up to his chest he could brace himself against the walls of his small bunk and reduce the rocking and rolling. But then he found it was the sound of the ocean waves slapping against the small round porthole that kept him awake.

'You'll get used to it,' Harry had assured him. 'After a while you won't be able to sleep on shore without someone throwing a bucket of water at your bedroom window every thirty seconds.'

Once he had taken Freya through the Pentland Firth, Jim Cunningham had turned her northwards and they had steamed directly to the rich fishing grounds of the undersea plateau to the South West of the Faroe Islands, one of the Hansen Group trawler fleet's richest hunting grounds for cod fish.

They had arrived on the grounds in the late evening of their fourth day out of Grimsby and given that he still had no formal duties to perform, Harry had allowed Jens to watch the crew shoot the net for their first trawl, taking him to stand on the stern platform above the bay where the starboard trawl door was stowed.

From this vantage point, Jens looked down, watching the crew organise the net on the deck below, getting it ready to shoot. He knew from his lessons at nautical school that what looked like a disorganised tangle of floats, rubber wheels and nylon mesh was in fact, the carefully laid out trawl gear, ready to slide into the sea behind the vessel. He looked towards the bridge and could see Jim Cunningham overseeing the operation from the rear bridge house windows overlooking the stern deck. Harry was mobile on the deck below him, giving orders to the men in his charge; Jens was filled with pride at his best friend's competence and assurance on the job.

The small metal gate, which closed off the ramp during steaming, was unbolted and kicked aside and the safety chain unhooked to give the net unimpeded access to the sea. The winch men drew the cod end onto the incline of the ramp where it slipped down into the water and was pulled by the forward motion of the trawler and the drag of the waves into the sea. The body of the trawl followed, sliding en masse along the flat steel deck, the men hopping precariously between the moving warps, bobbins and floats as it slid unstoppably into the ocean.

The net was dragged visibly behind the vessel for a while just beneath the surface until two of the more experienced members of the deck team released the trawl doors from their stowage points, feeding them out slowly until they hit the sea and almost immediately hydroplaned outwards on both sides. Jens could hear the two winches playing out the steel warps and he watched the net disappear beneath the dark green surface of the Atlantic Ocean. He imagined it just minutes later, two hundred fathoms down and a full mile behind Freya. The heavy rubber wheels of the baseline hopping along the flat seabed, rolling the gear over any rocks that may stand in the path of the sweep, the floats on the headline opening up the trawl, and with any luck, shoals of big fat cod would soon be herded into that insatiable, gaping mouth.

It was just a matter of time now. It would be up to the skipper to decide how long to run the trawl. It was entirely down to his experience and judgement, too long and the net could overfill and tear, losing the catch entirely, too short and the trawl could be hauled up half empty, wasting time and effort.

Jens was thrilled at seeing the gear shoot over the stern of Freya and took deep pride in his friend's role in supervising the operation. It was his first time shooting trawl gear from a stern trawler, but Jens thought, you would never have known it, he had seemed to instinctively know just what to do.

'Oi Thorsen!' Harry was yelling up to him from the deck. 'Get your arse down into that factory and make sure everything is ready for the fish, it won't be long now!'

*

Celia had been a great comfort to Shirley. From her first visit to the Flett's home on the day of the Hansen Freya's maiden voyage, the elder woman's council had been reassuring to her, focussing her thoughts on the positive benefits of Jens becoming a trawlerman and trying to distract her from her more negative pre-occupations, her sense of loss and loneliness. The two women were becoming ever-closer friends through this shared experience, and a visit to the Flett's home after her shift in the factory had quickly became an important part of Shirley's daily routine.

'Just think Shirley,' Celia said to her whilst she poured out a nice cup of tea from the brown teapot, 'when you have your babies, they'll be brought up in a lovely new bungalow and when they get old enough they'll be able to play in fields, not on these grubby streets.' She lifted the strainer from the rim of Shirley's cup, letting the drops fall before moving it to her own. 'And they'll go to that lovely little village school and have nice friends to play with.' Their minds were racing ahead and they were already imagining Shirley and Jens married and with a family of their own. Celia knew that this diversion made Shirley happy, and gave her hope for the future, distracting her from her immediate feelings of missing Jens. They had even chosen names for the yet to be born children, Steven for the boy and Karen for the girl.

'I can't wait,' she said, her eyes distant with the dreaming of her golden future. 'And when Jens is home, we'll have nice days out as a family, and holidays away.' She tried to imagine what it would be like to have a proper holiday, 'I've always fancied Butlins at Skeggy,' she added, 'it's brilliant at Butlins, they've got amusements for the kids and shows and competitions and a great big swimming pool with fountains.' Celia was smiling at her friend's enthusiasm, seeing that the sparkle had returned to her eyes.

'You know what Shirley?' Celia said to her, smiling ruefully. 'I really envy you.'

'Envy me, why on earth?' It was beyond Shirley's comprehension that her clever, beautiful, married friend with her lovely baby could ever be envious of anything in her own simple and unspectacular life.

'Yes I do, you've got everything before you, and your life can be anything you want it to be.' Shirley was looking at her now, intense with interest, wanting to hear more. 'You've got a good man who loves the bones of you, and you two are so perfect together, it's as if you're two halves of the same person.' Shirley was beaming with joy at hearing this. 'You won't ever have to worry about whether Jens is the right man for you; you know he is and he will be forever. You will be happy together, you will grow old together and you will bring up a loving family.'

'Oh Celia, you say the loveliest things,' a tear had squeezed out from the corner of her eye and it trickled down her cheek, 'talking to you always makes me feel so much better. I still miss Jens like mad, but you're the only one who ever makes me feel like this, like all this pain will be worthwhile.'

Celia smiled her acceptance of the compliment, knowing that her comforting words were largely premised on simply telling Shirley the things that she wanted to hear, but she also knew there was some truth in these platitudes and in so doing, she saw her own relationship with Ken in stark contrast to the way that Shirley and Jens were together. Celia believed completely that Shirley and Jens were perfectly matched; they were similar and complimentary to each other in so many ways; in their even, caring, fun-loving temperaments, in their shared interests and in the way that their love had incubated for over a decade from its embryonic beginnings as a childhood friendship.

Shirley and Jens couldn't be more different to her and Ken, she thought. Her own temperament was so very different to his; she knew herself to be generally even-tempered and optimistic whilst Ken tended towards mood swings and pessimism. They also had few shared interests; Ken was something of a loner, spending many hours in the evenings and at weekends out of the house on his own. She knew that their relationship had been a whirlwind affair; since meeting him just over a year and a half ago she had been swept along on a tide of events; the pregnancy, the marriage and then Alice's birth, bringing with it all the burdening responsibilities and worries of parenthood.

'That's why I'm envious of you Shirley,' she recalled herself to the task in hand, the task of helping Shirley cope with her distress at her fiancée being a thousand miles away in the middle of the Atlantic Ocean on a fishing boat for the first time. 'I'm envious because you've got a rare relationship, I'm envious because of the way that your family and friends are loving, protective and supporting of you and I'm envious because your future is in your own hands, that you and Jens can build your life together and make it whatever you want it to be.' The words were heartfelt and Shirley accepted them, fortified and sustained by them but she did not realise the pain they evoked in her friend's own heart.

*

After two hours of trawling, skipper Jim Cunningham decided that the time was right and he gave the barked command over the crackly tannoy to the men on the deck to begin the haul. The two winch men immediately and simultaneously heaved their weight onto the two large wheels, disengaging the drum brakes and setting the winches rolling, slowly drawing in the thrumming steel cables, drawing the trawl on its mile long journey from the sea bed. It took twenty minutes before it came into sight beneath the Freya's wake to the stern of the vessel and the deck crew could already see that it was bulging with fish. They began to whoop and cheer at the prospects of a good catch.

The winches were slowed and the net began to slide up the ramp towards them and onto the aft deck. It was a good catch of cod, their fat mottled green bodies bulging against the mesh of the cod end. Harry set his deck crew to work; they fastened long straps around the gear just in front of the bulging mass of fish and linked them up to lines drawn by the Gilson deck winches through pulleys on the foremost of the two giant steel superstructures that spanned the deck some twenty feet above their heads. From the bridge, Cunningham triggered the opening of the watertight hatch and a section of the deck moved upwards under the power of pneumatic pistons. Rising towards the stern, the opening hatchway exposed the chute down to the fish pounds in the deck below, and closed off the open access to the ramp, forming a solid barrier to prevent the fish from spilling back into the sea.

The bosun untied the short length of rope that closed off the cod end, leaving the end of the trawl open and ready to be emptied. On Harry's command, the winch man drew up the line attached around the middle of the trawl and the massive mesh bag of fish was raised slowly into the air, causing the cod to gush outwards and downwards into the chute, thundering against the raised steel hatch and dropping into the pounds below. In this manner, the entire catch was disgorged from the suspended trawl.

'Can't believe how easy that was,' one of the deckies commented to Harry. 'All that hand hauling to get the net in off the sidewinders was back breaking, this is gonna be a breeze.'

'Tech-bloody-nology!' Harry replied, laughing out loud. 'Tech-bloody-nology, it's the future!'

Straight away, the factory crew began to work on the catch whilst the deck crew under Harry's supervision began inspecting the trawl for damage and relaying it for the next shoot. Jens was suddenly thrust into action in the factory, working alongside a dozen others they were standing knee deep in fish in the four feet high compound that held the entire catch. Most of the fish were already dead but many still flipped and thrashed and squirmed around them, their gill covers gasping wildly as they suffocated in the air. Each fish was hand gutted by the team, with a single slit with a sharp knife blade inserted into the anus and ripped swiftly and deftly along the belly towards the throat. Percy Bennett was central to proceedings, allocating the men specific tasks, shouting his orders to be heard over the drone of the engines.

Jens had done gutting work before in the factory and was working as quickly as he could; picking up a fish, slipping the knife in, slicing upwards, pushing his hand into the cavity, pulling out the guts and then slipping the liver free and flipping it into a barrel before throwing the gutted fish through the air into one of the waiting fish washers. The large stainless steel baths filled now with seawater were soon running vivid red with the blood from the bleeding fish. He was working as fast as he could but he noticed that some of the men were doing five or six fish to his four. This was a skill that they had developed over many hours of the repetitive work on their past voyages. He would get faster he thought to himself, he knew he would, with more practice.

The washed fish were being discharged from the washers on a network of conveyor belts and Jens was called out by Percy Bennett to be one of the crew to load the vertical plate freezers. He was pleased, this was easier work, easier than working at breakneck speed with a razor sharp knife on a trawler that was pitching and rolling in a heavy North Atlantic swell anyway. He loaded each gutted and washed fish into the rectangular box compartments, pressing them down to eliminate as many air pockets as possible and only when all of the deep, rectangular chambers of the plate freezer were full did he lock down the lid and start the freezing cycle with a twist of the dial.

It was now a waiting game for the fish to freeze down fully and Bennett called Jens back to the gutting, helping to prepare the rest of the catch for the next cycle in the freezers. It was hard work but he loved every moment of it and a broad smile was on his face as he grafted alongside his more experienced crewmates and under the watchful eye of Percy.

In time, the plate freezers were discharged by push rods that automatically extended and slid out the solid paving slab sized blocks of frozen fish. Jens was sent down into the pine wood lined cold store and was given a heavy jacket to protect him against the cold. But after just a few minutes he was sweating with the effort of the heavy work. The frozen blocks came thundering one after another down the stainless steel channels from the factory deck above. Now three decks down, he was deep in the belly of the trawler. His job was to take the blocks as they slid into the store and stack them in a solid wall from floor to ceiling. He knew that on a full voyage, they would not turn for home until this store was so full that they couldn't get another single block into it, and as he began stacking the first of the slabs he looked around the huge wood lined cold room with its refrigeration pipes running in patterns along the ceiling, and he wondered how many trawls, how many hours of toil it would take to fill it's four hundred ton capacity.

CHAPTER THIRTEEN

Although he struggled to fight it, Ken knew that he was becoming increasingly preoccupied with Shirley Lofts. The temptation to daydream about her was strong. In unguarded moments his mind returned to her constantly and she was never far from the surface of his troubled thoughts. He was sitting now in the factory canteen, in the chair where he had found her five days before, when she had been crying for her boyfriend on the day he had gone to sea. He recalled that her eyes were pink and swollen from the stinging tears; he could remember her anguished expression, the blotches on her cheeks, flushed from the battle with her emotions and the redness at the tip of her small nose. She had looked beautiful.

He thought fleetingly about her relationship with Jens. She's wasted on that boy he thought, dismissing their romance, thinking it a teenage infatuation. Just puppy love that won't last, not now that he's away at sea for weeks on end. He smiled outwardly at this, savouring the idea that Shirley's devotion to Jens would soon fade, that she would get bored waiting for him. And whilst the stupid boy was a thousand miles away in the middle of the Atlantic, he would be here, lavishing her with the attention and compliments that she deserved, making her feel special. In time, he knew she would come to realise what a real man could do for her.

He felt a flutter of excitement when he thought of the possibility of seeing her later that afternoon, in his own home. She would be there he hoped, visiting Celia, and although she would not stay for long after he arrived, he was looking forward to seeing her outside of work. Their meetings somehow seemed more personal, more intimate outside of the factory environment, and these regular afternoon visits had become something he cherished. Maybe today she would give him a little cuddle he thought, or a kiss on his cheek as she departed.

*

Jens had been gone since Monday and by Friday afternoon Shirley was just beginning to acclimatise to the dull ache of his absence. She had finished her last shift of the week and was walking with Doreen from the factory towards the ladies' changing room to get their coats.

'What you gonna do tonight Shirl?' Doreen asked, feeling a little awkward but wanting to know what Shirley had got planned for this, her first Friday night without Jens. 'You coming up the Palais? Me and Col will be there, we'll keep you company.'

'I don't know Dorrie,' she answered, 'it's nice of you to ask but it will seem odd, I've never been to the Palais without Jens.' Doreen understood but didn't know what else to say except to repeat her invitation.

'Well, if you do fancy it, it will be nice to see you. You know we'd look after you.'

'Yes Dorrie, I know that.'

They were just about to enter the ladies' changing room when they bumped into Ken coming from the opposite direction. He winked at Doreen. 'Hello gorgeous,' he said to her, with a cheeky smile. She blushed. 'Ah Shirley,' he added, almost as an afterthought, 'I'm glad I bumped into you. Are you popping around this afternoon?'

'I thought I might,' she answered. 'Why? Is that a problem?'

'Not really hen,' he answered. 'Just don't keep my Celia talking too long will you, we're going out tonight and she'll need plenty of time to make herself look beautiful.'

'You're going out tonight?' Shirley was incredulous. 'She didn't mention it yesterday afternoon.'

'I know she didn't, we only decided last night. She was going to pop round to see Gwen this morning and ask her if she'll babysit for us.' Shirley was still taking this in when he added. 'Look Shirl, I know its been tough for you this week, but why don't you come along with us? It'll take you out of yerself and you could do with that I'm sure.'

'Oh Shirley, that's such a good idea,' Doreen chipped in. 'Please come out, it will be fun, much better than sitting at home with your mum and dad just watching the telly and moping. Please come!'

'I'll think about it,' she said, tempted now she knew that Celia would be there. 'I'll think about it.'

'Aye, do that,' Ken added as he began to walk on. 'And remember doll, life goes on!'

*

And so Jens Peter Thorsen's life at sea has begun. He had stacked all of the frozen fish slabs and had been called back upstairs to help gut the next haul that had already thundered from above into the fish pound. When he arrived, he saw that fish were already being thrown through the air, landing with splashes in the washers. Splashes that could be seen but not heard above the background throb of the big diesel engines reverberating around the metal plant room. He worked solidly at his tasks until he was relieved again and staggered exhausted, to the accommodation deck, falling fully clothed into his bunk. Six hours later he was back in the plant, loading the plate freezers again, bleary eyed and with aching muscles. The pattern of his life for the next three weeks had been established. Working twelve hours on and six hours off, day and night, seven days a week. And this was just a short voyage to test the equipment.

*

Shirley and Gwen arrived together at the Flett's house and were ushered into the spacious living room by an immaculately groomed and suited Ken. He offered them a sherry. Shirley accepted the offer but Gwen declined, preferring a cup of tea instead. Ken had already popped out to the telephone box and ordered a taxi so that they could arrive at the Palais in style; it was a little treat for Shirley, to make her feel special.

Shirley enjoyed the car ride into Cleethorpes, whizzing past the many bus stops that would normally have punctuated this, her regular Friday evening journey. She sat in the back of the vehicle with Celia whilst Ken occupied the front seat next to the driver. The warm July evening had brought many people onto the streets and the last mile, which took them along the resort's sea front, saw hundreds of people still out strolling, enjoying the last of the day's sunshine. There were families with children, and couples old and young, all spilling from the pavements and spreading over the grassy areas and benches of the pier gardens. They were eating chips from newspaper parcels, wearing novelty hats, carrying polythene bags full of pink and yellow candyfloss as light as air; the holiday atmosphere lifted Shirley's spirits. She found herself looking forward to her evening at the Palais more than she had ever thought possible without Jens being there with her.

Once inside, they soon meet up with Doreen and Colin who had also just arrived, although not by taxi, they had taken the more traditional method of the bus. Although everyone was being very attentive to her, once she was inside the Palais, a place so very familiar to her, Shirley could not help but miss Jens. Their normal Friday night routine would have been to go straight onto the dance floor to enjoy the early freedom of space before the crowds arrive later. Somehow, it didn't feel right for her to be just standing there watching other couples dance, she realised that it was not just Jens that was missing from her evening, it was also the liberating joy of the dancing.

'What's up Shirley?' Celia had noticed that Shirley had become remote and a little forlorn.

'Nothing Ceel,' she answered untruthfully. 'I'm just fine.'

'No you're not,' Celia persisted.

'Well, I've just realised,' she answered, 'here we all are at a dance and I won't be doing any dancing myself. Don't get me wrong, it's really nice of you all to look after me, but there just doesn't seem much point in coming to a dance if I'm not going to dance.'

'Ah Shirley, don't worry about that,' you can have some dances with my Colin can't she?' Doreen flashed a meaningful look at the unsuspecting Colin.

'Yes Dorrie, of course she can. I'll dance with you Shirley,' he offered dutifully.

'And my Ken will dance with you too,' Celia added.

'It would be my pleasure,' added Ken. 'Shall we begin right now?' He raised his arm as an invitation. Shirley looked at Celia who nodded encouragement and she was whisked away to the dance floor. Celia looked at her husband and friend moving lightly and elegantly together around the half empty dance floor, noticing as they flashed by, that Shirley's pretty face was illuminated with delight.

*

Most days, in Celia's front room, they drank tea together, talked and played with baby Alice. Shirley and Celia's friendship had continued to grow and with the passing of time, Shirley's need to talk constantly about Jens had abated a little. She still felt his absence as keenly as the day that he had gone away, but she was adapting to a new way of life on shore without him. Even to the extent that after three consecutive solo Friday nights at the Palais, she was beginning to look forward to them nearly as much as she had before. Colin had not proven to be a very reliable dance partner, but Ken was really a marvellous dancer and Celia didn't mind lending him to her at all. It really was quite a convenient arrangement.

Shirley had also developed a strong emotional bond with baby Alice, intrigued by her and constantly entranced by her little ways. She would hold out two extended forefingers and let Alice grip onto them with her tiny, pink hands and raise herself onto a pair of chubby but unsteady legs.

'Aah look Ceels, she's really strong!'

'Yes, it won't be long until she's walking, I reckon,' Celia answered. 'And then there'll be no stopping her.' Shirley smiled with delight at the baby girl.

'Are you sad that your mum and dad aren't seeing her grow up?'

'Yes, I am Shirley,' Celia answered. 'I write to them about once a month, just to let them know how she's getting on. You know, how her croup has been, that kind of thing. I usually send them a photo too but I hardly ever hear back and never from my father, although Mummy sometimes drops me a quick line. I think she regrets the way things have worked out and would like to see her, but Daddy is so very stubborn.'

'It's their loss,' Shirley said. 'They're the ones who are missing out on magic moments like this. But at least your mother is getting your letters, I reckon that they'll mean the world to her Ceels.'

'I do hope so,' Celia answered ruefully.

Shirley was deeply saddened by her friend's unfortunate situation with her parents and was still thinking about it when she arrived at her own home. 'Hello Shirl,' her mother called out as she entered the kitchen from the back yard. 'There's a letter come for you this afto, it's in the living room. I took it in for you from Hansen's message boy.'

She could hardly believe the coincidence. She had only been talking about letters with Celia half an hour before and now one had arrived for her. She rushed into the parlour full of hope and just as her mother had said, there it was, waiting for her, propped up on the mantelpiece, lodged behind the savings clock. She recognised Jens' spidery hand immediately and took the small blue envelope in her trembling fingers. She could barely contain her eagerness, barely stop herself from ripping it open right there and then, but she ran upstairs, threw herself down on her bed and tearing open the envelope began to read.

Dear Shirl,

I'm missing you like mad. The work is dead hard much harder than I thought it was going to be but I'm getting on just fine and have made some mates. I've shown them your photo and they can't wait to meet you when we get back. I look at it every time I go to bed which can be any time night or day because we are fishing round the clock I look at it and give it a little kiss to remind me what I'm doing this for. I've mainly been working below deck in the plant, gutting cod and putting it into the freezers then stacking the blocks up in the cold store. Harry says that he'll get me some deck duties when I've proved that I can hack it to the skipper. His name is mister Cunningham but I don't see much of him and we're not allowed to talk to him unless he speaks to us first but we never see him anyway so that doesn't matter. Harry says that he's telling him that I'm getting on fine. I wasn't sea sick much and some of the crew who have been coming to sea for years have been sicker than me so I guess it is in my blood after all just like I always knew it was. I've bought you a tin of Quality Street from the bond stores and can't wait to get back to see you again. The skipper told us if we wanted to write home he would pass the letters to another Hansen boat that is just finished fishing and is heading back to Grimsby, so I hope you get this. I'm thinking about you all the time, even when I'm gutting fish and I can't wait to get back, I keep thinking about our plans and that gives me the strength to do this, it will all be worthwhile, believe me. It's funny but even though I'm out here in the middle of the ocean I still feel connected to you, it's like there's a bond between us that can be stretched but can never break. I love you to bits.

All my love,

Jens Peter xxx

PS I hope that you haven't been moping and are getting out and having a bit of fun, there's no need to mope, I'll be back soon.

PPS I'm also getting bigger muscles, you'll be surprised when you see me xxx

A teardrop fell onto the page. It smudged the ink of his signature. She wiped it away with the side of her hand, leaving an inky smear on the pale blue, faintly fishy smelling letter paper. He would be home soon. The Hansen Avenger had carried the letter back to port and Shirley calculated that Freya would only be two or three days behind her. With any luck, he would be back by Thursday night, and then they would have three or four days together before he went away again. She would make every second perfect.

A timid knock rattled the door; it opened a few inches to reveal the face of her younger sister Sally.

'Come in Sal,' Shirley called to her.

'What does he say, can I read it?' She asked, excitedly.

'No, you can't read it,' Shirley clasped the letter to her breast. 'It's private.'

'What does he say though Shirl?' She pounced onto the bed next to her big sister. 'Is it all lovey-dovey and stuff?'

'Well,' Shirley said, looking at the letter once more and scanning it line by line. 'He says he misses me and that it's hard work.'

'What else?'

'That he hasn't been sick much.' Sally screwed her nose up at this. 'And that he's bought me some Quality Street.'

'Is that all Shirl? Didn't he say that he loves you to the end of the earth?'

'Sort of.' Sally's enquiring look at this encouraged Shirley to further disclosures. 'He says that our hearts are joined together and that they can never be separated.'

'Aaah,' Sally smiled, 'how romantic!' Shirley was enjoying this small moment of intimacy with her little sister, and perhaps she's not such a little sister nowadays either, she thought, fifteen going on twenty. 'I wonder if all the Thorsen boys are that romantic.' Sally added, shooting Shirley a coy but meaningful look.

'Don't say you've got your eyes on Frank!' Shirley exclaimed with a laugh. Sally looked a little abashed.

'Might have,' she answered, 'he's a handsome boy.'

'Well you'd better clear off and get on with your homework then. He won't be interested in any old thicko.

He's like a blooming genius or something.'

'Even geniuses like a pretty face.' Sally laughed, interlinking her fingertips and holding them beneath her chin in an affectation of a Hollywood smile. Shirley giggled with her.

'You know what Sal,' she said, 'you just might be right. If you find the right person, everything else just seems to fit.' She thought again of Jens' letter. She was energised and inspired by the simple, honest words he had written down especially for her. 'If your love is strong enough it can conquer anything. Like me and Jens, our hearts are joined together in an inseparable bond that can never be broken.'

CHAPTER FOURTEEN

It was seven o'clock on a sunny Thursday evening and a large crowd of girlfriends, wives and children had accumulated to welcome their menfolk back from the sea. Shirley was waiting for Jens at the same familiar dockside where she had waited for Harry so many times before. But this time it felt very different. The Hansen Freya had berthed alongside the factory on the South Quay and a metal gantry had been placed across the gap between shore and boat. One by one, the trawlermen crossed the wobbling bridge, carrying their kit bags over their shoulders. They all looked tired, but most were cleanly shaven and some were already wearing suits, ready for an evening out down Freeman Street.

Jens was one of the last to appear, stepping up onto the gantry wearing an open necked shirt and his jeans. She felt the excitement boil over inside her and she rushed towards him, throwing her arms around his neck and kissing his face and lips repeatedly, tears were streaming down her face. He took her into his arms and they folded into each other, lost entirely in their reunion. Other couples variously embraced or just exchanged pecks on cheeks; this was not a new experience for them.

But Shirley and Jens were overwhelmed, he had been away and he had returned and nothing else in the world could possibly feel better than this.

They were still lost in the depths of their embrace when a gentle hand placed firmly on each of their shoulders brought them both back to reality. Looking up, they saw Harry's smiling face. 'Steady on you two,' he said, 'you're making me blush.' They laughed and Shirley reached an arm around his neck, pulling him towards her, and placing her lips on his cheek she gave him a big kiss.

'It's so good to have you both back,' she said and the three of them stood motionless, joined together in a three-way embrace. United once again.

*

It was a glorious Friday afternoon with hardly a cloud in the sky. Shirley and Jens were riding their bicycles side by side; they had pedalled through Cleethorpes, along the busy promenade and beyond the resort, past the boating lakes, they had rumbled over the wooden deck of the Bailey bridge that crossed Buck Beck and onto the narrow cinder road that led towards the village of Humberston. He had been waiting for her at the factory cycle sheds when she'd finished her shift, a shift that could not pass quickly enough for her, knowing that an afternoon with Jens awaited. A shift during which an ever patient Doreen had listened over and over again to Shirley's ecstatic description of the homecoming and of their plans for the afternoon.

Jens glanced across at Shirley as she cycled confidently alongside him. She was chattering about something or other, animated, radiant, and smiling; she appeared to glow in the sunshine. His golden girl he thought. She looked up and saw him gazing at her and realised that his bicycle was drifting towards hers, trapping her against the grassy verge. She braked hard, narrowly avoiding the collision.

'Keep yer eyes on the road Jens!' she shrieked, laughing as he wobbled so much that he nearly lost control of his own bicycle.

'Sorry Shirl,' he called back over his shoulder. 'I was just looking at you.'

'I know you was, you nearly knocked me off. Why was you looking at me?'

'Cos you're the most beautiful girl I've ever seen,' he replied.

'You great soft 'apeth,' she replied, rising up onto her pedals and setting off after him again.

They wheeled on towards the village, which was a village no more, growing as it had in the last ten years to meet the housing demands of Grimsby and Cleethorpes. When they reached the new estate roads that conjoined with the old main road to the sea, they turned off into unknown territory. They were pedalling now on dark, freshly laid tarmac roads with bright, new concrete kerb stones and wide grass verges; they saw newly built bungalows standing far back from the roadside, behind low wooden picket fences and carefully tended front gardens. Everything was new; everything was modern. To Jens and Shirley, born and raised in the Victorian terraces of old Grimsby, these new detached and semi-detached bungalows seemed to give the sky space to breathe above their low rooftops, and in the wide open spaces between them.

'Oh Jens,' Shirley said, her eyes wide with wonder at the lovely new homes. 'This is amazing, but it can't ever be for the likes of us can it? We're from the town, this is for posh people.'

'No Shirley,' he disagreed, 'we could have one of these darling. It's what I want for us, it's what you deserve.'

'Do you really think so?'

'I'm sure of it,' he answered with confidence. 'It's what's kept me going when I was falling asleep on me feet in that bloody plant on the boat. It's why I'm doing this at all, it's to give you and me a better life, better than our mothers and fathers could ever have had.' They had reached an area where there were no completed homes; just part built, windowless and roofless shells and flat, grey concrete foundations. They pulled up their bicycles and hopped off, picking their way carefully between piles of brand new bricks and stacks of unpainted wooden window frames. They made their way to one of the building plots and stepped gingerly onto a newly laid concrete base. It formed the footprint of what would soon be a pair of semi-detached bungalows. They tested it with their toes first, to ensure that the cement was set hard enough to bear their weight.

'Just think Shirl,' Jens said, taking both of her hands in his and swinging them from side to side. 'This one could even be ours; we could actually be standing in our own living room right now. This could be our home.'

'Don't be daft,' she answered him, dismissive but nevertheless beguiled by his dream.

'No, seriously Shirl,' he continued. 'When you were at work this morning I picked up my settlings from the trip. It was more than I was expecting, and loads more than I would have earned in the factory. I was made up. And then I popped to Fiveways and did what I said I would. I opened a bank account for us.'

'Really?'

'Yes, and it's really going to mount up fast Shirl. I'm giving Mum a bit extra but I won't spend anything at all when I'm at sea will I?'

'Jens, it would be marvellous,' she answered, beginning to believe in the dream. 'And what a lovely place to bring up Steven and Karen.' She let go of his hands and spun in slow circles, her arms raised at her sides, taking it all in as she turned; the smart suburban surroundings of the new bungalow estate.

'Who the heck is Steven and Karen?' he asked, looking puzzled. She laughed and putting her arms around his neck gave him a kiss.

They cycled back towards the town with their minds buzzing, filled with their daydreams of a dazzling new life together. A future far away from the drab ranks of soot blackened brown brick town terraces, away from the crumbling Victorian homes built for long dead Victorian trawlermen, and away from the narrow strips of sky and no horizon. It all seemed so possible, so real.

'We going to the Palais tonight Shirl?' Jens asked eventually, shattering the reverie.

'Er, I don't know,' she answered. She thought about her recent visits to Pearson's Palais and her many dances with Kenneth Flett. She knew that her dancing had improved. She had progressed since she had been dancing with her friend's husband who really had turned out to be a very accomplished dancer. He had taught her some new tricks and they have even discussed entering a competition soon. It would seem strange dancing with Jens again she thought, and she wasn't sure how it would make her feel knowing that she would be dancing at a lower level again, not fulfilling her full potential as a dancer. After a long time thinking, she eventually answered him.

'You know what Jens,' she said with a sunny smile, 'I don't fancy dancing tonight. I'd rather you and me do something nice together. Just the two of us.'

'Fine by me,' he smiled back, a little surprised but nevertheless happy to be getting her all to himself for a change. They hardly ever had the chance to be properly alone, just the two of them.

*

Harry and his father Sid were in the bridge house of the seine netter Morning Glory. Sid was at the wheel, manoeuvring the vessel beneath the ice funnels of Grimsby's Number Two Fish Dock. Sid was taking Morning Glory out on the evening tide for a two-week trip to the Dogger Bank and was stocking up on crushed ice for the voyage. He had just filled up with coal from the coaling jetties in Number Three Fish Dock and once the ice was on board too, he would be heading for the lock gates and then away to sea. Harry was grabbing these last few moments with his father, knowing that their paths may not cross again for many weeks. Sid slid the boat expertly against the quayside into the icing berth. They left the bridge by the deck ladder and hopped across onto the quayside.

'Alright Ernie?' Sid greeted the Ice House man. 'Fill her up mate.' Ernie laughed, waiting for Morning Glory's deck crew to open up the hatches before releasing the crushed ice which thundered down the metal chute and out of the funnel end into the vessel's hold where the rest of the crew were waiting to shovel it into the fish pounds and build up the wooden planking barriers to keep it in place for the voyage.

'Now then Harry,' Sid said as they stood together

watching the icing operation. 'How did Jens get on at sea?'

'He did fine Dad,' Harry answered. 'He was down in the plant most of the time, gutting and freezing but he wants deck duties. I've told him he's got to earn his stripes first.'

'Just watch him Harry,' Sid added. 'He wants to do it all at once. You know what he's like, so eager, so keen to please. You'll have to keep him in check Harry.'

'Aye, I know that Dad, but he'll make a good deck hand in time, he's a good sailor and a hard worker.'

'And what about Shirl? Your mother tells me them two have got themselves engaged.'

'That's true.'

'And how do you feel about that son?'

'I'm happy for them Dad.' Sid looked at his son and saw the brave face he was clearly putting on.

'Look Harry, I know you carried a bit of a candle for her yourself.' Harry looked reprovingly at him. 'Don't deny it lad, your mother told me all about it and to be honest, it's bloody obvious from the way you moon about after her.' Harry coloured up and they stood for a short while in silence, watching the white flow of steaming ice pour from the chute.

'I only raise it because Jens is in your crew now, which means you're responsible for him, for his well-being and his safety. I'm just checking that there aren't any ill feelings between you two over this girl. It doesn't pay to take those kinds of problems to sea lad!'

'No need to worry Dad,' Harry replied. 'I can't say that I was over the moon when they got together and you're right, I do think the world of Shirley,' he suddenly became very awkward at this. It was not easy for him to talk about his feelings with his father. 'In fact, I'm in love with her.' He paused to recover from the effort of the admission. 'But they're both very special to me Dad and I love them both, Jens is like the brother I never had and I'd give my life to protect him.'

'That's good to hear son,' Sid answered. 'I just had to ask you that, I just needed to be sure.'

Ernie was locking off the ice supply, halting the conveyor that spanned the road between the huge red-brick Victorian Ice House where it was made and the funnels of the icing jetty where it was dispensed to the vessels.

'All done Sid,' he called over. 'Have a good trip, see you when you get back.'

'Sure thing,' Sid called back. 'There'll be a nice little fry for you. I'll drop it round when I get back.' The two men waved as Ernie headed back to the Ice House and Sid turned once again to his son.

'Well, that's us off then,' he said, offering a hand which Harry took and pumped vigorously. They exchanged a last look and Sid hopped back onto the deck of his beloved Morning Glory whilst Harry turned towards the beery delights of Freeman Street.

*

It was late evening and the sunshine of the afternoon had faded to a rosy pink glow. Shirley and Jens were walking hand in hand along the beach, they were carrying their shoes in their free hands and Jens' trouser legs had been rolled up to just above his knees. Sand covered their wet legs and feet; they had been paddling in the caramel coloured waters of the Humber.

'Just look at the town,' Jens said to her, pulling her to a halt by the hand and turning her towards the promenade. They saw the coloured lights of the amusement arcades that were just beginning to twinkle and the neon signs and the welcoming illuminated windows of the many hotels and pubs on the foreshore. 'Doesn't it look lovely from here.'

'It looks a lot better from here than it does when you're actually in it,' she answered with a smile, surveying the glittering panorama as she spoke. She could see Pearson's Palais de Dance quite clearly and she turned to Jens, squeezing his fingers. 'I'm glad we didn't go dancing Jens,' she said, 'I'm glad we decided to spend some time together, just the two of us.'

'Me too,' he added, 'it was a lovely afternoon and this is the perfect way to end the day.' They embraced and kissed before walking on, his arm around her shoulders, hers around his waist, not dancing but walking in harmony instead. They walked at the tide's edge beyond the end of the pleasure beach promenade and around the high fencing that marked the perimeter of Cleethorpes' seawater bathing pool. They strolled on into the fading evening light to where the wind blown drifts of sand formed undulating dunes, topped with hardy gorse bushes and marram grass. The dunes rose above head height on the landward side from the level plain of the tidal edge on their left.

'Fancy a sit down?' Jens asked, nodding towards the now shadowy dunes. They laboured up the incline together, their feet slipping on the still warm dune sand until they found a comfortable nesting place between two grassy hummocks. They sat with their bare feet drying in the warm evening air, looking out across the broad mouth of the mighty Humber estuary. They could see the lights of fishing vessels twinkling in the distance as boats arrived and left the two major fishing ports of the river;

Grimsby and Hull.

'Just think,' she said dreamily, nestling her head into his shoulder. 'You'll be on one of those boats in a couple of day's time, leaving me again.' He plucked a stalk of the sharp edged grass and creased it between his fingers, careful not to cut himself on its serrations. He looked at the river.

'One of those boats will be Morning Glory,' he said. 'Sid Coulbeck will be out there, and soon he'll be back again. That's just the way it is Shirl. I will go and I'll come back again and every time I come back, I'll have a big pay packet and that will go in the bank. And every time I go, we'll get more and more money and then soon,' he paused for effect, 'we'll have enough for a nice bungalow for Steven and Karen to grow up in.' They laughed together, he looked deeply into her pretty blue eyes. Somehow, they seemed a deeper, darker blue in the evening light he thought, and then they kissed.

'I love you so much Jens,' she said, pulling her face back to look at him again, her hands caressing his shoulders and chest. 'And you were right, your muscles are harder now,' she was lost in the moment, her hands stroking him, feeling him beneath the thin cotton fabric of his summer shirt. He swallowed hard, his mouth was dry and she felt him tremble, a shiver that seemed to come from his very core.

'I love you too Shirley, more than you could ever know.' There were tears in his eyes and he was unable to control his voice, to stop it from trembling. They laid back together, enveloped in each other's arms and rolled a few feet down the inside incline of the dune into a sheltered, secret hollow. It was pitch dark when they eventually stumbled, sandy and happy from the dunes back onto the tarmac footpath leading back towards the lights of the town.

*

Harry had popped into the café for a cappuccino coffee and a chat with Mo. It was half past ten in the morning, just after the breakfast rush and just before the dinnertime crush. Mo was taking advantage of the quiet period and was taking her tea break, sitting at the red Formica table opposite Harry.

'You all right Harry?' she asked, concerned about him. He seemed a bit down she thought.

'I'm just fine Mo,' he answered with forced jollity. 'How are you pet, are you missing Bill?'

'Yes I am,' she answered immediately. 'I miss him like mad.'

'So do I Mo, it doesn't seem the same being on shore without that little bugger around. We'll have to see if we can get back on the same boat soon.'

'He'd like that,' she answered. 'But that's not all is it?'

'What d'you mean?'

'You're not yourself Harry, and there's no use pretending that you are, I can see it in your face. Is it because of Jens and Shirley?' She took a sip of her tea, and watched him closely over the rim of her cup, noting the involuntary reaction to her question, seeing his eyes flicker downwards, suddenly seeming to find the inside of his half empty coffee cup fascinating. He was momentarily exposed. He didn't answer straight away, weighing up whether or not to disclose his feelings to Maureen but before he made up his mind she continued. 'You can talk to me Harry. If you want to.'

'Ignore me Mo,' he eventually answered, 'I'm feeling a bit sorry for myself, that's all. I'm missing my old mate

Bill of course and it's true that since Jens and Shirley took up together, I've not seen much of them either.'

'Well it was bound to happen wasn't it darling,' she reached over and squeezed his forearm tenderly. 'It's only natural, they're a couple now and just like me and Bill, they will want to spend their precious shore time together.' She was painfully aware of what she was saying to him, that his three best friends were now in relationships and that his role in their lives would necessarily change. 'You'll have to find yourself a nice girlfriend Harry,' she continued, deliberately injecting a tone of optimism into her voice. 'Just imagine how brilliant that would be! We could all go about together; Shirley and Jens, me and Bill and you and your sweetheart!'

'I can't see that happening,' he said, quite downhearted now.

'Surely there's someone you fancy,' she answered. 'A good looking boy like you should have them queuing up.'

'I'm not that interested at the moment Mo,' he answered. 'There are only a couple of birds I could even begin to imagine myself with, and believe me, it could never happen with either of them.'

'Never say never,' she replied, puzzled by the confession. 'You never know, it *could* happen.'

'Trust me Mo,' he replied earnestly, thinking fleetingly about sweet, precious, engaged Shirley and clever, alluring, married Celia. 'It could never happen with either of them. Believe me, I know what I'm talking about!' She sensed that he was reaching the limits of what he was prepared to share with her and so she tactfully changed the subject.

'What you planning for later then?'

'Oh I don't know,' he answered, 'I don't fancy the

boozers, not in the mood see? I'd only end up getting into trouble and I just can't be bothered with that. Reckon I'll just go for a nice long walk. Stretch me legs.' He got up from the table, and bending over, gave her a kiss on her cheek. 'Thanks for the chat though,' he said with genuine gratitude, 'and don't you go telling anyone what I've told you will you.' She smiled as he left, wondering what it is that he thought he had told her.

*

Ken and Celia Flett were taking a walk together along the promenade at Cleethorpes. She was pushing Alice's pushchair whilst he strolled alongside her, his hands thrust deep into his trouser pockets. As usual for a Saturday morning, he had made to go off on his own, but Celia had been quite insistent that she and Alice should join him today. They had not been to the dance last night because he had not wanted to go, and given that it was a lovely sunny morning, Celia had seen this as an opportunity for them to make up for the missed night out and at least spend some time together as a family. He had agreed at length, but after half an hour of walking, she had began to think that this had been a mistake, Ken was taciturn and not good company and they walked now almost in silence.

The fine weather had brought out the usual crowds of holiday makers and day trippers and Celia and Ken moved slowly through them, pausing for a moment at a concrete slipway to look out at the waves that were breaking some distance away on the brown sand flats. Children had walked out the two hundred yards or so to the waves and could be seen bobbing up and down in the water, splashing and jumping over the breakers, their coloured swimming costumes bright in the sunshine. A solitary figure, an adult male was also standing at the water's edge, his back towards the sea, looking towards the promenade.

Ken had very keen eyes and taking Celia's arm he pointed out towards the figure. 'Look Celia,' he said, 'there's that bloke who fancies you, isn't that Harry Coulbeck?' She was puzzled and a little annoyed at what was clearly intended as a sleight, but she shielded her eyes against the glare of the sun on the water and looked hard.

'Why yes I think it is, and don't be daft Ken, he doesn't fancy me.' She raised her arm in a wave. Ken continued to scan the beach for other familiar faces but was disappointed to see that Coulbeck appeared to be on his own today. Celia was now sure that the man was Harry and was waving more vigorously and calling his name, not stopping until she saw the distant figure take note and begin to walk towards them. In moments, Harry had reached the slipway and having walked up it, he greeted them with a smile.

'Now then Coulbeck,' Ken said.

'Hello Harry,' Celia sang as he arrived, leaning forward and allowing him to peck her on the cheek. 'Out for a walk?'

'I guess so,' he answered, realising that the question was superfluous.

'You on yer own Harry?' Ken asked, still looking around.

'I am mate,' Harry answered, 'just stretching me legs whilst I've got the chance,' and then as an afterthought. 'Fancy a pint? My shout.'

'Why not?' Ken answered, 'if you're in the seat.' They strolled together across the promenade and were lucky to find some recently vacated seats on the crowded benches arranged outside a popular sea front drinking house. Harry disappeared into the dark interior of the pub, emerging minutes later, squinting, back into the sunshine, carrying a round metal tray containing two pints of bitter and a glass of lemonade. They toasted each other with a 'cheers' and quaffed their cold drinks in unison.

'Where's your mates today?' Ken asked.

'No idea Ken,' Harry answered.

'They've gone to Lincoln on the train,' Celia contributed. 'Shirley popped in yesterday evening to tell me she wasn't going to the dance and that they were planning a nice day out today.' She was smiling at the thought of the sweet young couple enjoying a day out together in the nearby city and she didn't notice Ken's glowering look of resentment at her words. But Harry did notice.

'What's that about Ken?' he asked suddenly, challengingly. He was in a strange mood and was not about to let slide the opportunity to vent his discontent.

'What's what about?'

'That look! Why did you roll your eyes like that, what's it to do with you if Shirley and Jens have a day out together?'

'Calm down Coulbeck,' Ken replied smoothly. 'I don't know what you're talking about.' But Harry was angry now. Angry, because he had seen the look that betrayed Ken Flett's unwarranted interest in Shirley. The suddenness of the altercation momentarily dumbfounded Celia; she did not understand what was happening and was clearly distressed.

'Stop it you two!' she appealed. 'You're ruining a nice day out and showing me up in front of these people.' Other drinkers had stopped their own conversations and were taking an interest in the sudden argument in their midst.

'It's not me Celia,' Ken appealed to her. 'It's him, he's a hothead. You know that.' He was trying to appear calm and in control, the sensible adult in the face of an irrational and unprovoked attack. Celia looked to Harry, her eyes silently imploring him to back down. He saw the look and despite his rising anger, managed to calm himself outwardly.

'I'm sorry Ceels,' he said at last. 'I shouldn't have gone off on one like that, it's just that I'm not sure that your husband's feelings towards Shirley are entirely appropriate.'

He said this calmly enough but the effect was explosive. Ken was on his feet in a flash, and Harry was instantly disadvantaged as the beer from Ken's pint glass slapped into his eyes, stinging them and blurring his vision. He felt a strong hand grasp his throat, closing his airways and he instinctively knew that a blow to his face was coming. Pinned by the throat, he also knew that he could not move to avoid it, so despite his blindness he launched a haymaking punch with his free arm. His clenched fist whirled into thin air and missed the target, but he felt the grip on his throat release as Ken was forced to step back to avoid the blow. He had bought enough time to cuff the beer from his eyes with the back of his hand, and with his sight restored he was up on his feet, moving fast and low to his left, preparing to spring his counter attack.

'No, no, stop it you two, stop it now!' Celia was on her feet too. She had thrown herself at Ken, placing her body between him and Harry, smothering herself around him, holding his arms down to his side. Harry saw that his opponent was helpless, pinned by his own wife, and he sighted a clear shot at Ken's exposed and defenceless face. 'Harry, no!' She shouted. She was looking over her shoulder at him, absolute shock etched on her beautiful features. He stopped.

'I'm sorry Celia,' Harry said at last, his chest still heaving. 'I'm sorry, I didn't mean to spoil your day out.' He turned and walked slowly away, still wiping beer from his face and hair.

'This isn't finished between you and me Coulbeck,' he heard shouted from behind. 'And you can keep your lecherous bloody eyes off my wife.'

Harry carried on walking.

CHAPTER FIFTEEN

The Hansen Freya cruised through a field of slush ice, her dark grey steel hull cutting smoothly through the white mass of floating hexagonal ice blocks that stretched as far as the eye could see in any direction. She was off the West coast of Greenland and after seven days at sea had almost arrived at the Labrador grounds. It was nearly midnight but daylight persisted, a soft eerie ghost of daylight but daylight nevertheless. Jens was standing on the foredeck, awestruck by the strangeness of the landscape. Neither day nor night, a faint milk white crescent of moon veiled behind chiffon clouds sat high in the pale blue marble sky. He looked around in wonderment at the panorama, marveling at the colour palette of ice whites and perfect blues shot with dusky pinks and oranges at the horizon to Freya's aft and vibrant indigo to the fore. Ghostly rainbows of light shimmered in rippling patterns in the sky to the starboard side, dancing, ethereal, the aurora borealis was welcoming them.

Most of the crew were amassed on the foredeck enjoying the remarkable spectacle. But they were not alone, even in this white ice-desert; about half a mile to her aft and just off the portside of her wake, another trawler accompanied Freya, also ploughing her way towards the Labrador banks. She was a Russian vessel, battleship grey and streaked with rust, they could just about make out the crew lining her decks, also appreciating the unearthly atmosphere and the northern lights. They watched her silently rising up and sliding down the undulating waves of Freya's rolling, surfless wake and apart from the clunking of the ice blocks that slid and bounced along her steel hull and the dull drone of the diesel engines, there were no other sounds to be heard. It struck Jens that the West Atlantic was an unnatural place.

Even the cold was otherworldly, it was more intense than any cold he had ever experienced before, a cold that you could almost reach out and touch. He felt the hairs inside his nose freeze solid; his breath billowed, a tiny fog curling slowly into the icy stillness. He had been seduced by the landscape into a state of deep reverie when a firm hand slapped down onto his shoulder startling him. He turned to see Percy Bennett's beaming but cold-pinched face. 'Best get yourself some kip Jens lad,' he said. 'We'll be at the grounds soon enough and you'll need all your energy then. I've just been up with the skipper and the weather forecast isn't looking too bright, we're heading into a pretty strong north westerly. It will make the last trip seem like a summer Sunday afternoon at Cleethorpes boating lake.'

Jens turned himself to face north west and felt the risings of a biting wind slice across his exposed face; he noticed the ship's rigging was laced with white ice from the sea spray and freezing rain, and he was happy to be sent below decks out of the Arctic conditions. Once settled in his bunk, he pulled his paper and pencil out of his kit bag and began to compose a letter to Shirley. He was hoping that Freya would cross paths with a homeward bound Grimsby trawler again and that his letter would be carried home to his sweetheart. He wrote lengthily about his feelings for her, about the precious days they had just spent together, the evening on the dunes and their lovely day out at Lincoln, and he wrote about his hopes and plans for their future. He wrote until he fell asleep, only to be woken by Percy Bennett with the news that they had arrived on the Labrador grounds and the trawl had already been shot. The ordeal of his labours would begin again soon.

*

Celia arrived at the bleached wooden topped table carrying two cups of tea and some buttered toast on a battered metal tray; she put the tray down on the table in front of Shirley and took a seat opposite her. They were sitting next to a window overlooking Cleethorpes promenade and had just popped into the cosy café on the spur of the moment for a sit down and a chat. Alice was in her pushchair next to the table, playing with her teething toy, an elasticated string of brightly coloured plastic clown figures. Celia had something on her mind though; she had not yet told Shirley of the fight between Harry and Ken and she felt that some sort of explanation from her was required, especially as she knew that sooner or later Shirley was bound to hear about this from somebody else. The only problem was; she didn't really know where to begin. She didn't fully understand what it was all about herself.

'Look Shirley,' she began uncertainly. 'There's something I've got to tell you.' Shirley looked up from cutting her toast with an enquiring look.

'I don't quite know how to say this, but I've got to tell you.' She paused to collect her thoughts. 'It's about your Harry and my Ken.' Shirley smiled inwardly at the reference to Harry being hers, but she continued to look puzzled. 'You see Shirley; they've had a bit of a fight.'

'No! Was anybody hurt?' Shirley asked, shocked.

'No love, nobody was hurt. In fact, it wasn't much of a fight really, because no blows were actually landed. It was more of a scuffle.'

'Why Celia, what started it?'

'I'm still not sure Shirley, that's the thing. Harry said something about my Ken's behaviour towards you and the next thing they were flying at each other. I had to get in the middle of them Shirley, I was scared to death.'

'I don't understand,' Shirley was aghast. 'There's nothing wrong with your Ken's behaviour to me, and it just doesn't make sense. I know Harry's protective of me but there's no need for that, it's bonkers.'

'I know,' Celia replied. 'I can't make head nor tail of it. I've had a long talk with Ken though and he's got a theory, but I'm not sure about it and I wanted to see what you think.'

'Go on,' Shirley said, intrigued.

'See, my Ken thinks it's got nothing to do with Harry protecting you at all and that he's made all that up just to give him an excuse to have a go at him.'

'But why would he do that?'

'Because Ken reckons that Harry is infatuated with me and that he's jealous of him.' She paused, letting it sink in. 'What do you think about that Shirley?'

Shirley did not answer immediately but thought for a while, gazing absently out of the window at the day-trippers and holidaymakers strolling along the prom.

'Well,' she answered at last, 'I know that Harry is very fond of you, he talks about you all the time and I've often seen him looking at you when he thinks nobody's watching him. I think he likes you a lot.'

'Really?' Celia was a little shocked but did not look displeased at this news.

'I don't know that Harry would want to attack Ken because of that though,' Shirley continued. 'It does seem very strange, but I wasn't there so I can't really say. It's a puzzle isn't it?' They both agreed that it was and they sipped their tea in silence until Shirley asked. 'And what about Harry? What do you think about him Celia?'

Celia was flustered but answered honestly. 'He's lovely Shirley. A smashing bloke! He's honest and hardworking and actually quite clever too, he's got some very interesting ideas.'

'And he's handsome too?' Shirley was partly teasing but was interested to know the extent of her friend's attraction to Harry Coulbeck.

'Yes, he is handsome,' she replied, blushing now, beginning to regret starting the conversation. 'But that's as far as it goes with Harry and me,' she continued, 'nothing could ever happen because I'm married. I know things aren't that brilliant between Ken and me at the moment but he's still my husband and Alice's father, and I would never be unfaithful to him.' They thought about this for a while.

'But you do fancy Harry, even just a bit?' Shirley asked.

'Yes, I suppose I do,' Celia confessed. 'But as I say Shirley, it could never be anything more than that, it's like a forbidden pleasure, something I can't help feeling even though I know it's wrong, but as long as I don't do anything about it, there's no damage done and I can secretly enjoy my little bit of wickedness. Do you know what I mean?'

Shirley thought about her own dances with Ken, about his masterful lead on the dance floor, the strength of his body held closely against hers, the fluidity of their movement together and she realised with a guilty shock that perhaps she did indeed know what Celia meant.

*

The Hansen Freya had passed smoothly enough through the silent ice fields but soon after had found herself in a battle to make any kind of headway at all against the fierce energy of a raging and heavy sea. Jim Cunningham was sitting in his captain's chair with his feet up on the console; he was wearing carpet slippers and was smoking a pipe. Apart from Freya's electrician and radio operator Pete Nutter, he was alone on the bridge. He was talking on the radio to an old friend, a man he had never actually met but had known over the crackling frequencies for many years, Captain Lars Korneliuson, skipper of the Norwegian trawler Lothbrok.

'Are you still fishing Lars?' Cunningham asked into the microphone.

'Yes we are, but I think this will be our last haul Jim,' the crackly response came in over the speaker with rounded Norwegian tones. 'The weather front is hitting us hard from the north west and I will take Lothbrok south to find easier waters as soon as we have the nets in.' Lothbrok had been fishing on the Labrador Banks for two weeks and was some hundred and fifty miles to the west of Freya. 'What are you going to do Jim?' Korneliuson asked.

'We've just arrived Lars,' he answered, 'and I'm not

about to call it a day yet, I want to see what Freya can do in a big sea, she's designed to fish in difficult conditions.'

'Yes Jim, you have the advantage over us, with your fancy new stern trawler, you can haul catches in much bigger seas than we can. So, I'll wish you good luck, but Jim,' he paused, 'don't push it! We've got very bad conditions here and you're just coming into it.'

'No worries, thanks Lars, give my best to the wife and kids.' Cunningham signed out. 'Looks like it's a bit blowy out there sparky,' he said to the electrician seated at the console opposite him. 'Now we'll get the chance to really see what this baby can do.' He hopped down from his high chair, walked to one of the bridge house's toughened glass windows and looked out from this vantage point at the wind lashed waves breaking in regular white explosions over the turtleback of Freya's foredeck.

'It will be interesting,' Pete agreed from his radio desk. 'It's hard to imagine fishing in conditions much worse than this. If we were on one of the old sidewinders we wouldn't even think about it.'

'We ain't jacking sparky,' Cunningham answered, still gazing out over the heaving sea. 'Believe me, we ain't jacking.'

*

Shirley was bothered by her conversation with Celia. She was so bothered that she found herself sleepless in the middle of the night. Sally was sleeping soundly in the other single bed in their small bedroom, she could hear her soft breathing, but Shirley's own eyes were wide open and staring at the bedroom ceiling. Her thoughts were in turmoil.

For as long as she could remember, there had always been two boys in her life, Jens Peter Thorsen and Harry Coulbeck. But it was not this that troubled her, it never had, it was just the way that things were between them and she knew that she loved them both, albeit in different ways. Jens was her other half, her soul mate and Harry was her protector and guardian. In her mind they separately embodied romance and respect. She had no doubt that her heart belonged to Jens Peter Thorsen, it always had done. From their early childhood she had known that they would be together for the rest of their lives, there could be no other husband for her. But now that Celia had confessed her own guilty secret, her illicit physical attraction to Harry, a spectre had been raised within Shirley, a spectre that she could not put to rest. Until very recently she could not have envisaged room or role for any other man in her life, but since she had started dancing with Ken Flett, she realised that she had started to feel something new, something totally different.

The dark ceiling offered no solace and no inspiration to a restless Shirley as she grappled with these new feelings. She knew it wasn't love; in fact the very concept of feeling romantic tenderness towards Ken filled her with revulsion. Nor was it respect, she knew too much about his surly and unpredictable temperament to see him worthy of her respect. This was something else, something she had not sought, but it was something that could not be vanquished through denial. She had to understand it and if she could do that, perhaps she could control it.

She considered the three men in turn. By asking herself how each of them made her feel, she sought to understand what they meant to her and how Ken fitted into her emotional equation. She needed to clear her head of this confusion, she had promised herself to Jens and she could not enter this new phase of her life with any confusion or doubt. She had to understand it.

She thought about Jens, sweet Jens. She smiled broadly in the dark, engulfed with love for her boy. She thought then about Harry, remembering their long talks and deep friendship, she felt safety and security in these thoughts, as if he were laying a protective arm around her shoulders. And then she thought about Kenneth Flett, imagining their dances together, recalling the feel of him against her. It was not love and it was not respect. It was something darker in her response, something animal.

And suddenly, in a heartbeat she understood and everything was clear again. It was not as she had initially feared with Ken, a sexual attraction. She did not desire him at all. She had those feelings for Jens alone. She only had to think of their night on the sand dunes just a few days ago to know that this was the truth.

She began to understand her feelings towards Ken, to see that she was responding to his authority, to his power over her on the dance floor. Shirley loved to dance and now she loved to dance with Kenneth Flett. He was masterful, he dictated her every move with his strong hold and polished technique. She was subjugated to him in the dance, a puppet in his arms and at last she began to understand. With Jens and Harry, she was natural, she could entirely be herself with them, unguarded and free, but Ken exercised the power of his will over her, he was the only one with whom she was not an equal partner. It was not the case that she was attracted to him; rather that he had imposed himself upon her.

The bedroom ceiling was already growing paler as the early light of dawn began to pierce the thin curtains and Shirley's tired eyes were at last closed in sleep as her mind released its grip on the monkey puzzle of her tangled relationships. She had found peace. She had no guilt.

*

An angry wind howled around the bridge of the Hansen Freya. Skipper Jim Cunningham, still wearing his carpet slippers and with his pipe held between clenched teeth was driving the brand new trawler hard into the mountainous waves ahead of her, taking them head on. He saw her hull rise with each successive wall of ocean and with a lurch in his gut, felt her pitch down into the voids beyond, crashing and shuddering with the impact. It was a potentially lethal rollercoaster ride. He glanced at the clock, the trawl had been down for nearly two hours, he would have to make a decision soon, the weather had got considerably worse in the last couple of hours but the boat was committed now and sooner or later he would have to get the catch in.

'Sparky,' he shouted above the noise of the engines and the screaming wind battering at the wheelhouse windows. 'Any chance of a break in the weather?'

'Sorry skipper,' he called back. 'There's not much good news I'm afraid. I've been picking up reports from other shipping in the area and from the weather station at St. Johns and it looks like there's another ridge of high pressure coming in from the west. It isn't going to get any better than this any time soon.'

Cunningham looked around his bridge at the array of equipment that would put most ocean liners to shame; he felt the reassuring growl of the two giant Ruston-Paxman diesel engines and had confidence in his vessel to weather the storm. But he knew that he had to get the trawl in and he had only a short window of opportunity to do it safely.

'Better get on with it then,' he said confidently to Pete Nutter, and picking up his tannoy microphone gave the crackly command to the deck crew. 'Haul time, haul time!'

Harry was in the mess room when the message crackled out of the speakers. He roused his team and they prepared for their duties, shrouding themselves in long waterproof capes and pulling on Sou'wester hats with their broad, tapered brims. They would need as much protection as they could get against the driving rain and the spray from the breakers they could hear crashing over Freya's hull. He led them out onto the working deck, feeling it heave and roll beneath his feet, but he knew that his team of experienced hands would set about their tasks without complaint. The steel deck was awash with seawater and slippery beneath their rubber boots, but after years of experience working in these conditions, they were all sure-footed and confident.

It was nearly midnight and although not jet-black night, the vessel was shrouded in a deep twilight made even darker by the blackness of the storm-ridden sky. Powerful electric arc lights illuminated the working deck; they glared off the wet metal decking and made a swirling light show of the sheet rain as it crossed their beams. The men only recently emerged from the bulk head were already glistening wet as they took their stations.

The winches were slowly drawing in the steel cables, taking the strain of the trawl, hauling its weight from the seabed below and fighting against the drag of the angry sea. The warps sang and thrummed under immense tension. Jim Cunningham, observing from the aft windows of his bridge smiled with satisfaction as Freya battled the waves. It would have been impossible to get a trawl on board a sidewinder under these conditions he thought, this is the future of distant water fishing, where machines did everything. Push button trawling.

'Here she comes,' Harry shouted. 'Now let's get her on the deck!' It was now the winch men's job to pull the heavy cod end of the trawl out of the sea and to get it safely onto the working deck. The trawl doors were stowed and the lighter bridle lines of the trawl gear had been hooked up to Freya's pulleys so that the winches could begin to drag the gear itself onto the ramp using the lines strung from two overhead steel gantries.

Cunningham was watching from the bridge and despite his confidence in his showpiece vessel, even he was nervous at this critical stage. Freya was pitching heavily into the great waves that crashed over her and especially whilst they were hauling in the heavy trawl she would be vulnerable. If it was a good catch, there would be thirty tons of dead weight hanging off her stern, pulling her around in the turbulent currents, acting like a giant rudder. If Freya slewed sideways in this heavy sea, she could be rolled and with men working on the exposed rear deck, that would be catastrophic. He bit down hard on his pipe stem and silently, desperately urged his team on.

On the deck, Harry had resorted to using his whistle to signal to his team, his voice inaudible above the roaring waves and howling wind. The bulging trawl was emerging from the water and he felt Freya surge forwards as Cunningham increased her speed against the prevailing waves. He glanced up at the wheelhouse and saw Cunningham's pale face through the glaring lights and sheets of rain. Harry guessed that the skipper wanted this over with as quickly as possible; more speed meant more power and less likelihood that they'd be turned by the net.

He smiled to himself, this is what it was all about he thought, we're the only buggers out here fishing in this, and we'll be filling our hold and getting back to Grimsby whilst everyone else is holed up waiting for the storm to pass. 'Tech-bloody-nology' he said out loud to himself as the fat trawl sprawled at last fully onto the deck, a torpedo shaped mass of gasping cod fish some three feet high, ten feet wide and twenty feet long. He could see their silver bellies and big bulging eyes compressed against the tight mesh of the bag.

At his whistled command, the mass of fish was winched into the air; it had lifted some ten feet when Freya lurched and the whole catch swung like a thirty-ton pendulum. The deck hands dived for cover to avoid being struck.

'Steady lads,' keep your wits about you, we're nearly there,' Harry shouted as loudly as he could, although he knew his breath was wasted in the gale. 'And you,' he shouted at the winch men, 'you've got the reactions of a pair of fucking bananas. Get that bastard tipped!'

Cunningham watched his catch, illuminated in the glare of the deck lights slowly rise above the deck below him. He pulled hard on the lever that opened the hatch and watched the section of deck begin to rise. Once it was fully opened, the bosun leaned forward and slipped the knot at the bottom of the bag. The fish began to discharge out of the open cod end into the holding pounds in the factory below. Cunningham smiled at Pete Nutter. 'We did it,' he said proudly. 'She's a beauty Pete, we did it, we've got the catch in and we've got the trawl emptied safely down below. Hansen's will be pretty pleased with us!' He watched the remnants of the catch dribble from the cod end into the plant and smiled at his achievement, pulling out his tobacco pouch to refurbish his extinguished pipe.

*

Jens had been below deck waiting for the catch. Although the plant crew were not exposed to the harsh weather conditions of the open working deck above them, they nevertheless knew that they were in the midst of a major storm. They were struggling to remain upright on their feet, it was as if a giant had picked up the vessel and was shaking her. Jens was dreading the gutting, knowing how treacherous it would be, standing knee deep in dead fish and working with the razor sharp knife whilst struggling to keep his balance.

They knew that the fish was on its way when the ceiling above them began to open. Rain poured in through the widening aperture as the sea tight hatch began to rise on its hydraulics, suddenly they were bathed in light from the arc lamps on the upper deck and the wind shrieked in and whipped around them. Moments later the first of the cod began to gush through the now fully opened hatch, thundering against the steel chute and into the pound. The fish came in pulsing surges as the trawl was raised higher and higher by the winch men. They swilled and swirled into the waiting pound, filling it and overflowing onto the deck. Percy Bennett looked across at Jens. 'It's a big one,' he said, amazed at the quantity of big fat cod fish that gushed through their ceiling into the factory.

'Even in weather like this?' Jens asked.

'Fish on the sea bed don't know what the weather's like up here,' Percy laughed back at the rookie. 'In fact, a bit of turbulence can stir up the water and get them up and feeding more, makes them easier to catch. Bad weather is good for fishermen if you've got a boat that can handle it,' he continued. 'And it looks like Freya is more than capable of handling just about anything. You'd better get used to this; she's going to catch a lot of fish Jens. Come hell or high water, you're going to be working through it all, and you know what that means don't you?'

'What's that mister Bennett?'

'Big fat cod and big fat pay packets,' he answered, making Jens smile and forget his earlier worries about the knife work. This was what he'd wanted, he reminded himself. The more I can earn, the sooner I can marry Shirley.

'Come on lads, up and at 'em,' Percy Bennett urged the gutting crew and they climbed over the waist high barrier and waded into the fish, knives ready in their hands. They began picking up fish, gutting them with practiced slices and hurling them away into the waiting fish washers. Jens was amongst them, working more steadily than he had anticipated. Once he'd found a sound footing the weight of the fish pressing against his legs as high as his thighs gave him stability he hadn't expected in the lurching and rocking vessel. Rain was still pouring in through the open hatch along with the occasional gush of seawater, thrown over the side of Freya's hull by the breaking waves above them. Jens worked as quickly as he could but as he paused to pick up a fish, he suddenly became aware that Percy Bennett was looking concerned, gazing up at the still open hatch.

He noticed Jens looking at him. 'That should be shut by now,' he said to him. 'There must be something wrong with the hydraulics, come with me lad,' he said. 'Let's go and see what's going on!'

On the bridge, Jim Cunningham had lit his pipe and waited for the net to be emptied, he'd watched until the once bursting trawl hung limp and empty from the pulleys and with a feeling of self-satisfaction, he'd flipped the lever to close the watertight hatch and seal the open deck, but the hatch did not move to close; it remained upright, leaving a gaping hole in his working deck. He flicked the lever again and again, but to no avail. The hydraulics had clearly failed. He picked up his tannoy microphone and with a whistle to grab the deck crew's attention he shouted his orders.

'Get that hatch down, the mechanics have failed, you'll have to do it manually.'

On the deck, Harry just about heard the command above the weather, but seeing that the hatch had not yet closed, he already suspected that there was a problem. He made his way over to it and gave it a hefty push; it was jammed rock solid and didn't move an inch, it was obviously a mechanical problem he figured. He knew that he should call for the ship's engineer to tend to it, but the deck was awash with water and the gunwales weren't clearing it fast enough before even more came crashing on board. Seawater was flooding through the open hatch into the lower deck. He called one of his team over with a message to go and get the engineer, whilst he continued working on the problem himself, he knew that every minute was precious. He had to do everything he could to prevent Freya taking on too much water down into her lower decks.

Harry dropped to his knees to examine the hinge mechanism more closely and leaning into the opening he saw that a metal bracket had worked loose during the opening and had trapped the hydraulic pipework that fed one of the pistons; it was blocked, with a kink preventing the release of pressure. He reached inside and grasping the trapped pipe gave it a tug. It did not move, but he had seen now that it didn't need to be pulled, it needed to be pushed backwards, away from the pinch point. If he could reach it, he could give it a push and hopefully release the kink. He slithered a little further inside the hatchway, and stretching as far as he could, he grasped the pipe again and pushed it with all his strength. He felt it move and then kick in his hand as the kink was released. The pipe vibrated with the surge of hydraulic fluid and he was suddenly aware that the steel platform was beginning to move above him, it was beginning to close on him.

Moving as fast as he could, Harry hauled himself backwards, turning as he did, fighting to get back onto the deck and out of the mouth of the closing hatch. On the bridge, Jim Cunningham could see what was happening but was powerless to do anything, the blockage had blown out a fuse and although he was wildly ramming the control lever it had absolutely no effect on the heavy metal door which continued to descend on his second mate on the deck below him.

Harry squirmed around, twisting his body painfully, grabbing at the rim of the closing door with one hand and looking for purchase with his other hand on the deck. He could see the deck lights, he was almost out and with one final, mighty effort he hauled his body clear of the closing trap door and onto the wet metal deck.

Searing pain coursed through his body, the trap door had closed onto his trailing left leg, crushing it like a massive guillotine. He heard, more than felt the bone break, and then he passed out.

With his damaged hand, Percy Bennett had struggled slowly up the metal ladder rungs onto the deck above. Jens was only one pace behind him when they emerged into a scene of consternation. The deck hands were swarming around the hatch, pulling it, heaving at it as they tried to open it. It took Jens some time to realise what was happening and then he saw Harry, prostrate on the deck, his leg trapped beneath the massive steel door. In seconds he was round Percy and by Harry's side. The crew were managing to lift the hatch now, six of them, straining with the massive effort. It inched slowly upwards and Jens pulled Harry clear of the opening, seeing his crushed leg slither behind him like the disconnected limb of a broken doll.

'Harry, Harry!' he was shouting. He pulled the prostrate figure to him and cradled his head against his chest. Percy Bennett had now arrived and out of his deep pockets produced a small bottle of sal-volatile. He waved the smelling salts beneath Harry's nose.

'He'll be alright lad, don't panic, I've seen worse than this,' he said. 'We'll have to get it splinted but he hasn't lost any blood. He's going to be okay.' Jens heard this and was further heartened to see Harry's eyes flicker open in response to the smelling salts. He looked up at Jens and managed a weak smile.

'And that,' he said, 'is how *not* to get a hatch closed. I hope you've been paying attention young Thorsen, it's a valuable lesson.'

The bosun arrived with the first aid box and moved to take Harry from Jens' arms. Jens stood up, but in his concern for Harry, he forgot his whereabouts on the deck and stepped backwards onto the top of the ramp. Percy Bennett saw Jens stumble backwards and instinctively reached out to steady him, but his fingerless hand flapped lamely against Jens' flailing arm, unable to get any purchase. Freya rose into a wave and Jens toppled further off balance. From the deck, Harry saw Jens falling backwards and despite his pain he managed to reach out and catch him by the ankle. Jens plummeted down the ramp towards the waves, dragging the injured Harry behind him. It was only by pure chance that Harry's free arm thrashed against the slender safety chain, grabbing it and halting their slide into the angry sea.

They hung, suspended together from the safety chain, it bit deeply into Harry's hand, he wanted to release it, to let it go and to end the pain, but he hung on. He felt the full weight of Jens, pulling them both downwards, down towards the sea, and he sensed with dread that he had only a tenuous grip on the very hem of Jens' oilskin trousers. His broken leg dangled uselessly and grotesquely by his side. He was in agony. He felt the oilskin, slimy with fish mucous slipping through his wet fingers. He was consumed with pain but he fought with every ounce of his strength against the darkening, against the ebbing of his consciousness. And at last he dreamed, and in his dream he heard a distant scream as Jens Thorsen slipped, inevitably, from his grasp and plunged downward into the roaring, icy, black water below.

PART THREE

CHAPTER SIXTEEN

October 1964

Shirley was woken by a gentle squeeze on her shoulder; she blinked her bleary morning eyes into focus and smiled when she saw Ken Flett's face looking down at her. He stroked her cheek and leaning forward, kissed her tenderly on the forehead, lingering momentarily, breathing in the fragrance of her bed warm hair.

'I've brought you a nice cup of tea,' he said. 'You just drink that up and by the time you come down, Celia will have some breakfast ready for you.' He patted her arm and walked to the door, glancing back at her with a smile as he left the room. Downstairs, she could hear Celia's voice talking to Alice and the vague clattering of kitchen sounds as the Flett household began the day.

After the shock of the news about Jens, Shirley had been inconsolable, taking immediately to her bed, refusing to speak, refusing food and weeping continually. When, after three days there were still no signs of her improving, her mother Gladys had despaired and called in the doctor for a house visit. There was not a lot that doctor Glendinning could do except to prescribe a mild sedative to help her sleep and to recommend they try to get her to eat some light foods such as soup and milk puddings. He also advised Gladys that she should encourage Shirley to accept visits from her friends. 'It will give her some other things to think about and help her see that she is not facing the loss alone,' he had said.

Gladys did not quite know where to turn to find the right visitors for Shirley, she could not ask Gwen Thorsen who was in deep mourning for her son. She knew that this would not be good for Shirley, and so she invited Dolly Coulbeck round to visit. But Shirley had not responded to her, turning her back and curling into a tight ball, refusing to speak. It was Dolly who suggested they should try Celia, remembering how Shirley had found comfort in her company after Jens had first gone away to sea, and how their friendship had flourished from then.

It had broken Celia's heart to see the ruin of her friend on that first visit; her once pretty features were distorted with grief, her eyes, sore and swollen with crying were almost unrecognisable. Having placed Alice safely onto the floor she had seated herself on the edge of Shirley's single bed and taken her silent friend's unresponsive hand in her own, desperate to impart even the smallest shred of comfort.

They'd sat together in silence watching little Alice shuffle speedily around the bedroom, picking up odd items wherever she could reach them and inspecting them with unbound infant curiosity. Finding one of Shirley's fur rimmed carpet slippers, she had stopped her locomotions and having seated herself once again in an upright position she'd tried to fit it onto her head. For the first time since hearing of Jens' death, Shirley had smiled.

Under Celia's gentle coaxing Shirley was eventually enticed to break her long silence. At first, her words were faltering, almost incoherent. Then they flooded out of her in a rage of grief, railing bitterly against her fate, speaking of the depths of her loss. Once this plug of pent up bitter emotion had been discharged, she had become calmer, more coherent and interactive, and taking both of Celia's hands in her own she had looked into her eyes and implored. 'Oh Celia, what am I going to do? How will I ever get over this?'

'You'll never get over it,' Celia had answered honestly. 'There will hardly be a day of your life when you will not think of Jens, but in time and with help from your family and friends, you will be able to cope.'

'I don't know about that,' her voice resigned, rather than despairing now.

'It's true Shirley,' Celia had pressed, 'and we're all here to help you.' She'd tried to think of other news that may gladden her friend and give her some comfort. 'Ken has made some enquiries at Hansen's about Harry. He's recovering in hospital in Canada. They say it will be a long job but they think they can save his leg, he's going to be okay.'

'I never want to see or hear from Harry Coulbeck ever again,' her voice venomous. 'He promised me that he would look after Jens. He lied to me. He should never have let this happen, it's his fault that Jens is dead.' Celia had been shocked at the starkness of Shirley's words and had tactfully changed the direction of their conversation, lifting Alice onto the bed and sitting her on Shirley's knee.

They'd played with Alice for a while, marvelling at her recent development, Celia noting again how her baby seemed to cheer Shirley. After a little gentle encouragement, Shirley was eventually tempted to take a light meal. It was just a bowl of soup, but it was the first proper food she had eaten for days, and sitting upright in bed with Alice at her side, Shirley had felt the first glimmering of hope that whilst she had been deeply wounded, somehow, in time, she would cope.

Over the next few days Celia's visits led to further improvements in Shirley's temperament until eventually she was able to face getting out of bed and getting dressed. A week after that and two weeks after the initial shock, she felt strong enough to return to work. During her absence, after meeting with the factory general manager, Ken had managed to arrange a different job for her, working in the office as an assistant to the planning department. She was to order in the boxes and other consumables used on the factory floor, making sure that they did not run out of the things that they needed each day to pack out the orders. This had been Celia's idea. She had felt that returning to a different environment with new colleagues, tasks and challenges would be beneficial for Shirley's recovery.

On returning to work, Shirley had immediately recommenced her afternoon visits to Celia's house after her shift; spending longer and longer with her each time, then staying for her evening meals and eventually overnight stays, sleeping in one of the Flett's spare bedrooms. Over time, she had virtually moved in, having brought over a good selection of her clothes and a few personal effects. She did not ever feel that she was intruding into their lives, Celia had been most welcoming and attentive and Ken too had not seemed to mind her being around.

Sometimes in the evenings, they would go for a spin in Ken's new car, an Austin Eleven Hundred purchased on a work credit scheme from one of the car dealerships in Grimsby owned by the Hansen Group. They all enjoyed these spins in the country; Shirley would usually sit in the front next to Ken whilst Celia sat in the back with Alice on her lap. They would bowl through the Lincolnshire lanes exploring the Wolds, finding villages and scenes that were new to them all, even to Shirley, a native of the county.

If the weather was fine and if they spotted somewhere that took their fancy, they would occasionally stop to enjoy a drink at a country tavern. Celia was delighted to see her damaged friend enjoying these small excursions, to watch her eyes twinkle again as she played with Alice and note that her conversation was gradually becoming less obsessive about her grief, and even chatting sometimes quite light-heartedly about Alice's comedic antics and about events at work. But through all of this, she steadfastly refused to talk at all about Harry Coulbeck.

*

The grey October morning shivered with premonitions of the winter to come and parchment leaves were swirling and tumbling in the chill breeze. Harry and Sid Coulbeck were sitting on a park bench, both wrapped in their heavy black overcoats. Harry's crutches were leaning against the back spell of the bench. He had just returned to Grimsby from St. Johns in Newfoundland where he had been taken after his accident. He didn't remember very much about the events immediately after the accident, he mainly remembered the intensity and depths of his despair at feeling Jens Thorsen's leggings slip through his wet fingers. The pain of his broken and crushed leg bleached into insignificance when compared to the agony of that loss.

There was so much to say that both men found words difficult.

'Will you go back to sea lad?' Sid asked his son.

'Course I will, as soon as I can Dad, it's all I know and all I can do. The accident hasn't put me off fishing, it was me own fault and I'll learn a lesson from it. I won't be so bloody stupid again.'

'How is the leg?' Sid asked after another lengthy pause, finding comfort in the mundane, the obvious.

'On the mend,' was Harry's oblique response. It was aching but he hardly cared. Three months had passed since the accident and the leg was clearly healing faster than his tortured conscience. He recalled blacking out in the very moment that Jens disappeared below him into the lethal sea, he recalled coming round later, how much later he did not know, but he remembered lying sweating in his bunk with a makeshift splint lashed to his leg. He remembered only brief moments of respite from the fevers and delirium throughout the interminable, sea-howling nights and days that skipper Jim Cunningham ploughed Freya through the storm waves at full speed to reach the shore. His memories of those two days were lost in dark fragments of pain and black anguish, half remembered, half dreamed.

Lucidity had not returned until the hospital bed in St. Johns. Only then did the full horror of the accident surface to his conscious mind. Only then did he realise the depth of his grief and feel the torment of his responsibility for Jens' death. He should have held on. Jens would still be alive if he hadn't let him go. It was his fault that Jens was dead. He hated himself for his weakness.

It was Saturday morning, but the park was nearly

empty. Nearby, a mother called out to a child playing dangerously close to the edge of the ornamental pond. 'Come here Christopher, you'll get yourself drowned,' she commanded in her Geordie accent. Harry heard her, noting her accent, an unusual one for Grimsby, but it was the urgency of her tone that struck him most of all. It stabbed at his conscience, reminding him once again of man's elemental and universal fear of drowning, the very horror that he had condemned his best friend to. He shifted uncomfortably on the bench. Sid was still finding words difficult to come by, but realising the depth of his son's distress he knew he must say something.

'Look lad,' he faltered, 'nobody blames you for what happened.'

'You're wrong there Dad,' Harry answered immediately.

'No lad, nobody blames you.' His voice was heavy with fatherly care. 'I know I asked you that question before you sailed and I believed your answer son. I know that you would have given your life to save Jens, and because I know that, I know that you couldn't have done more to save him Harry.'

'Well there's more than one person who blames me Dad,' Harry's voice was flat with the certain truth of his statement.

'Who's that then son?' Sid asked.

'Me, for one.'

'Well son, you're wrong. And I hope in time you'll come to see that. But I'm sure nobody else does.' He tenderly placed a hand onto Harry's shoulder and although he saw no outward sign, he was sure that he felt the spasm of a repressed sob tremor through his son's frame.

'Shirley does too,' Harry added bleakly. 'She won't

see me, she doesn't want to talk to me, she blames me.
She hates me.'

*

Ken was sitting in the small office used by the
factory supervisors. The room was sparsely furnished
with just two old wooden desks set side by side along one
wall, each with it's own chair. There was one spare chair
in the corner and two metal filing cabinets standing
against the back wall. There was also a calendar pinned to
the back of the door. It had a large photograph printed
on it depicting a naked girl driving a tractor.

He was completing his daily production paperwork
and looking forward to getting home. He was also
thinking about Shirley. It had been a slow job but with
each passing week he had seen her moods improving and
her old disposition returning. He knew that she was not
yet completely over the death of her fiancée but it had
been three months now and she was clearly well on the
mend. He was surer now than ever that she was
beginning to fall for him.

He was roused from his daydreaming with a start
when Percy Bennett entered carrying his own clipboard
and sat down at the other desk.

'Now then Percy,' Ken opened the conversation.
'Had a good day?'

'Not so bad,' he replied. 'Cut some good yield off
that Faeroe fish, it was nice and fat.'

'Heard anything about Coulbeck?' Ken knew that
Percy had been in touch with Jim Cunningham since his
trips on Freya and had been following Harry's progress
closely.

'He's just got back,' he answered. 'They put him on

the Freya in St. Johns, and she got into port yesterday. 'Haven't you seen him? I'd have thought he'd have been round to see that Shirley lass who's staying at yours.'

'He wouldn't do that,' Ken answered. 'She doesn't want to see him, he'll have been warned off by one of the wifeys.'

'That's odd,' Percy mused.

'She blames him for Jens' accident,' Ken explained. 'Thinks he should have stopped him falling overboard.'

'She shouldn't do that,' Percy answered. 'It wasn't Harry's fault at all. In fact he nearly got himself killed trying to save him. I've never seen anything like it.' Percy was reflective for a moment, and then he continued with difficulty. 'If anything Ken, I blame myself. The lad was in my team, it was me who took him up on the deck in a storm, and the worst thing of all is that if it wasn't for this bastard,' he held up his maimed hand, 'I could have caught him as easy as anything before he lost his balance.'

'It wasn't your fault mate,' Ken said, 'don't blame yourself, it was just one of those things. Some things are just meant to be.'

'You can't help it though,' Percy explained. 'You can't help going over and over it, again and again; I wasn't fit to be at sea, I had no right to be there, if it had been you on deck that night you would have caught him as easy as pie. I know that you're not a seafaring man Ken and I understand why you turned the job down, but I just can't help thinking that if it had been you instead of me that night on the Freya, then Jens Thorsen would still be alive today, and that lovely girl of his would still have her fiancée.'

CHAPTER SEVENTEEN

It was with considerable trepidation that Harry knocked on Gwen Thorsen's back door and eased himself into the kitchen, his body suspended and swinging between two wooden crutches. Gwen was sitting in her usual chair but Harry was shocked by how much she had aged since he had last seen her. Her hair previously threaded with grey had turned almost completely white now and her face was ashen and lined. She looked up at him with dark eyes and immediately stood to welcome him, placing her arms carefully around his neck so as not to overbalance him on the crutches. She held him for a long time in a tender embrace. He could hear the snuffle of her repressed tears.

'Sit down Harry,' she said eventually, stepping back and looking into his own watery eyes. 'I'll put the kettle on and we can have a nice cup of tea.' He manoeuvred himself into position and slumped backwards into the chair whilst she filled the kettle and tinkered about with cups and spoons.

'Look Gwen,' Harry began. 'I don't really know what to say but...'

'You don't have to say anything Harry,' he was cut short by Gwen, still with her back to him. 'That nice mister Bennett came round to see me as soon as he got back and he told me everything that had happened. In tears he was, cried like a baby in that very chair.'

'I tried Gwen, I tried my best.'

'I know you did Harry,' she turned, with tears in her own eyes now, she blinked and they trickled down her cheek. 'Mister Bennett said that you had no care for your own life when you tried to save Jens and that if it wasn't for the bosun grabbing your arm and dragging you back on board just as you passed out, you would have been lost too.'

'I wish I had been Gwen,' his voice was leaden.

'Don't be stupid Harry,' she replied outraged. 'You were lucky. You were spared and we should be glad of that, I can't blame you for it, I'm glad you made it. I never did want Jens to go to sea and everyone knew that. Jens knew it, but he had to go, and when you go to sea, you always take that risk. I think I always knew that this could happen. It's not your fault, it's nobody's fault, it's what happens at sea and we have to live with it like we always have done.' She sat down and poured two cups of tea.

'How's Frank taking it?' Harry asked.

'Better now,' Gwen replied, 'he was rocked at first but he's young and has got other things on his mind. He's left school now and has started at the bank, the one at the corner on Riby Square. It's not the career he dreamed of but he's enjoying it and he's getting on well. And at least he hasn't got any ambitions for the sea, I can take some comfort in that.'

'You can be sure of that Gwen,' Harry added. 'He's no fisherman is your Frank.'

'Oh, and another thing,' she added, this time with the

incongruous trace of a smile on her careworn face. 'I think he's got himself a girlfriend.'

'No, you're kidding me! Who's the lucky lady then?'

'Well, you'll never believe it, but it's Sally Lofts. He won't admit it of course, but she's been round here a lot recently and they seem pretty close to me. I don't know what it is about those Lofts girls, but they do seem to have a liking for my boys.' Harry smiled at this. 'Seriously though,' Gwen continued, 'she's been really good for him, helping him cope with the loss of his brother. It does remind me of how Shirley was with Jens after he lost his dad. Anyway, they're nice girls and I'm pleased for him, and it's nice to know that he can take an interest in anything other than a blooming book.'

They were both smiling at this when the back door opened and Shirley stepped into the kitchen. Obviously surprised to see Harry sharing a laugh and a convivial cup of tea with Gwen, she was stopped in her tracks, an astonished look on her face.

Harry began to struggle to his feet, grabbing his crutches and fumbling in his efforts.

'You needn't bother getting up, I'm not staying,' Shirley said abruptly, turning to leave.

'You're not going anywhere Shirley Lofts, you get yourself back here now!' Neither Harry nor Shirley had ever heard Gwen Thorsen sound so severe, but it did the trick and Shirley turned once again to face them as Harry, at last, managed to get to his feet. 'I'm not having it Shirley,' Gwen continued. 'I'm not having you blaming Harry for what happened. I'm not blaming him and I don't see why you should either.'

Harry and Shirley looked at each other in silence, listening as Gwen continued.

'Harry would have given his life for Jens Shirley, and

from what I've heard, he just about did. It's not Harry's fault that he got rescued and Jens didn't. He didn't save himself Shirley!'

Shirley was not looking at Gwen but at Harry when she answered. 'I know. But he promised to look after him, he promised.' Harry could not hold her gaze and looked to the floor.

'I'm so sorry Shirley,' he answered. 'You'll never know how much I blame myself for what happened. I tried my best but the sea was too strong, I couldn't hold him.' He sobbed at this and with an immense effort steeled himself against complete collapse. Shirley saw the depth of the grief in him, recognised it and felt the ice in her heart melt just a little bit. 'Oh Shirley, he continued, 'I don't blame you for hating me, it breaks my heart but I can see that you think I've let you down and I understand if you never want to see me again.'

She didn't answer but continued to look straight at him.

'I needed to see you just once though because I've got something for you.' She looked at him enquiringly on hearing this. 'You see, when they left me in Newfoundland, because they knew that I was a close family friend, they left Jens' kit bag with me so that I could bring back his personal effects.' Both Shirley and Gwen were now very attentive as he continued. 'I was just having a look through his stuff and I came across this,' he reached into his shirt pocket and pulled out a folded envelope. 'It's a letter for you Shirley,' he explained, offering her the letter. 'I had a quick look at it but I realised what it was and I haven't read it. Nobody has. He must have written it for you on the night that it happened.'

She reached out and with trembling fingers took the

letter from Harry's hand. It was only the second letter she had ever received from Jens and it would be the last. She couldn't take her eyes off it; it was precious to her beyond measure. They stood in silence for a long time until at last Shirley looked up with a smile of gratitude; it shimmered across her lips but could not be seen in her tear filled eyes. She turned and slowly walked towards the door.

'Thanks Harry,' she said quietly in a flat, abstracted tone, but she did not turn back, and then she was gone.

*

Shirley sought refuge in her old bedroom in her parent's house. She was lucky, everyone was out so she had the place to herself and she was deeply thankful for the privacy. She knew that she just had to be alone to read Jens' letter. Her hands were still trembling when she unfolded the wad of sheets out of the envelope; there were a lot of them, written in pencil. She smiled when she saw Jen's spidery handwriting filling them, both back and front. She began to read straight away, devouring the pages hungrily, but at the same time savouring every word.

My dearest darling Shirley,

I've just been up on the deck it was amazing. We've been steaming through a massive ice field, I wish you could have seen it Shirl it was like nothing you've ever seen before, I saw the northern lights flashing across the sky like an electric rainbow it was unreal. The whole sea was white with floating ice, the lads call it slush ice but its like billions of giant ice cubes, all sorts of shapes and sizes and as far as you can see, right to the horizon all round us. It was midnight but still light, like a summer evening at home and the ice killed all the sea sounds so everything was quiet, it was like I was in a dream. I was thinking about us and I could hardly believe how good things are turning out for us, we're so lucky. So I'm standing on the ship's deck in the middle of this ice field dreaming about you but I'm actually awake, it was brilliant and it made me realise how happy I am. When I think back to a couple of months ago when we had nothing and I was bored in the factory and earning rubbish money and we was just friends before we said I love you to each other and now look what's happened to us. I'm at sea where I always wanted to be or should I say where I know I should be and I'm with Harry who is the best friend anyone could ever have and you and me are engaged and have already got some money saved up for our future.

That last weekend was the best days of my life ever and I really mean that, when we went for our bike ride to Humberston and looked at the bungalows and dreamed about living in one, everything just felt so right and I knew deep down inside of me that one day Shirley, you would have one of those bungalows, it is like I could see you in the future. And that night when we made love on the dunes I have never felt feelings like that, I won't try to describe how you made me feel because I just can't write it down but believe me Shirl, nobody ever in the whole history of the world has ever felt happier than me on that night. And our day out at

Lincoln was really special too, it was like the first day that we'd ever done something as a proper couple, just the two of us. I felt a bit guilty about not asking Harry along but when we were together I knew that it was right to be just the two of us. I remember I couldn't let go of your hand, I couldn't stop looking at you and I wanted to kiss you all the time. Do you remember when we were inside the cathedral and we were looking up at the massive stone columns at that ceiling and the amazing coloured windows and do you remember how it made us feel? Well that's how I feel like all the time when I think about you. You are my cathedral.

No matter how long I live I don't think I could ever be happier than I was last weekend, it just isn't possible, my brain would explode! I really enjoyed walking up the hill at Lincoln and having that cup of tea and the scones in the old tea shop, I saw old folks looking at us and smiling like they knew how much in love we are and they were really happy for us. People are nice Shirley and one day we'll be the old folks smiling at young lovers because I just know that we will be together forever and nothing can ever come between us or split us up. Nothing can, nothing ever will because you will always be mine and I will always be yours. It will always be me and you and of course Harry too, I can't imagine ever not having Harry in our lives. I don't want to sound mushy or anything but Harry loves us both, he's like a big brother but much more than that and when we have children he'll have to be their Godfather I reckon so then we will actually all be a family, sort of.

So I was up on the deck at midnight in daylight in the middle of a silent white ice ocean and I was awake but I was dreaming about you and thinking about us and I know that whatever happens I am doing what I want to do, what makes me happy and makes me understand more about who I am. I'm sailing with the best mate a man could ever have and I've got the best most beautiful girl in the world waiting for me and I'm thinking that I must be the happiest man in the whole wide world.

Well, I'm getting a bit tired now Shirl and we'll be fishing soon so I'd better pack in and get some kip, so I'll just sign off by saying that I love you loads and can't wait for us to be together again. You are my eternal love.

Yours sincerely,

Jens Peter x

PS You are much prettier than Liz Taylor

*

Harry was propped up on his crutches in front of the jukebox in the public bar of the Lincoln Arms; he had been drinking for half an hour and had just finished his third pint. It was early evening and the pub was still almost empty, his only company was Belinda behind the bar and a handful of drunken Icelanders picking up where they had left off with their afternoon drinking session. He fed some coins into the slot and selected Goodnight Irene by Jerry Lee Lewis. The carousel inside the machine whirled and he watched the black vinyl disk get picked out of it's slot by the mechanical arm, rotate and lower in jerky movements onto the turntable. The needle fell and with a crackle the music burst from the speakers. He was still browsing the record listings, choosing his next disk when he heard a wolf whistle and an Icelandic voice calling out.

'Hello darling, what's a nice girl like you doing in a place like this, fancy a bit of sexy fun?' There was nothing out of the ordinary in this; it was after all, the Lincoln Arms and Harry took no real notice.

He turned clumsily on his crutches and started to make his way back to the bar and to pint number four. He was halfway back before he realised that the young woman who had just entered the bar room was Shirley Lofts. She was still standing just inside the doorway; her coat was flapping open, and her cheeks were flushed pink with the October evening chill. The Icelanders were openly leering at her and the one who had shouted out earlier was continuing with his entreaties.

'Darling, darling, come here and give me a kiss. I will show you a good time you pretty lady. Do you want to make it with a real Viking man?'

Shirley was not listening to him, but was staring straight at Harry, and Harry had stopped dead in his tracks.

'You have nice titties lady, come here and let me feel them,' the Icelander persisted, egged on by his laughing crewmates. But this was too much for Harry, coming to his senses now after the shock of seeing Shirley.

'Oi, scrob!' he barked out, stabbing an angry finger in the direction of the loud mouthed one. He still had his crutch tucked under his armpit and he waved it angrily in the air as he shouted. 'You just shut your fucking mouth or I'll shut it for you!' He knew that he represented no real threat to the Icelander who had four burly friends around him, but hearing Shirley spoken to like that had made his blood boil and he was ready to wade into a fight with one or all of them right there and then. Luckily for Harry, the Icelanders were out for drinking and not for fighting and the ringleader stopped harassing Shirley immediately, smiling good-naturedly at the angry English assailant with the red face, the broken leg, the two wooden crutches and the pretty girlfriend.

'Shirley,' Harry began, flustered by her unexpected appearance, 'what are you doing here?'

'I've come to see you,' she answered plainly.

'How did you find me, how did you know I was here?'

'It wasn't hard Harry,' she answered with a smile. 'I went to your mam's and she told me you had gone out for a drink. You weren't in the Corp so I came here and guess what - here you are!' He smiled at this and beckoned her over. Propping his crutches against the bar he heaved himself up onto a high stool. Shirley pulled another stool over and hauled herself up next to him. In the background the Jerry Lee record was playing and they sat and listened until the needle slid with a hiss off the disk and the only remaining sound to be heard in the bar was the guttural babbling of a five way drunken Scandinavian conversation in the distant corner. He ordered himself another pint of Hewitts and turning awkwardly on the high stool towards her he asked. 'What's it to be Shirl, Cherry B, gin and T?'

'It's a bit early for me yet,' she replied. 'I'll just have a glass of lemonade if that's okay.' The drinks were served and there was no excuse to avoid serious discussion any longer. 'Harry,' Shirley began tentatively, 'I've come to apologise.' She was not looking at him, but into her lemonade. 'I was wrong to blame you and I was wrong to take it out on you.' The words didn't come easily to her; she had been hardening her heart to him for three months since Jens' accident. All the time he had been recovering in hospital in Canada she had been shutting him out, refusing to answer his letters, refusing to hear his side of the story. She had been angry at the world and she had vented that elemental fury on Harry. But now she had come to realise that he did not deserve her vitriol, that he was injured, not just physically but mentally too, and that he had also lost somebody very dear to him.

'Why Shirley?' Harry asked. 'Why the change of heart? I thought you blamed me and hated me and I can't stand the thought of that, but I can understand it. I thought our friendship was over for good.'

'It will never be over,' she answered. 'Jens told me that in his letter. It was his letter that made me realise how important you were to him, and to me, and I know he wouldn't want me to blame you Harry 'cos you meant the world to him.'

'That's nice Shirl,' Harry took a deep glug of his ale to disguise his delicate emotional condition. 'He was like a brother to me, but more than a brother if you know what I mean.'

'I do,' she replied, delightedly. 'That's just what he said.' And then after a short pause she continued in a more serious tone. 'Reading that letter made me realise that Jens was truly happy at sea, probably for the first time in his sad, hard little life. He was really happy, and I think about that Harry and it gives me some comfort; thinking that he will never grow old, he will never become bitter and disappointed or broken and disillusioned, he died doing something that he loved, with somebody he loved, for somebody he loved, and you can't get better than that can you?

They raised their glasses between them and chinked their rims in a salute to Jens.

'You'll never know,' she continued, 'just how sorry I am about the way I've treated you and I don't know if you can ever forgive me, but I hope you can Harry.' She turned to look at him. 'I really hope that you can forgive me.' She did not know it, although she would soon learn that he already had. They sat and talked, just a little awkwardly at first, but their lifelong familiarity soon returned and they shared for the first time, their individual feelings of loss and regret. He listened to tales of her new job in the offices at the factory and she heard all about the several operations to mend his damaged leg and about his long recovery in St. Johns General Hospital.

Before he had finished his sixth pint, they had completely made up and by the time they said goodnight outside her parent's house, Shirley had confided almost all of her deepest feelings, cares and fears about the future to Harry.

CHAPTER EIGHTEEN

Shirley was sitting at her desk going through the order books and counting up the week's deliveries of cardboard boxes. She was good at the clerical work and enjoyed the achievement of balancing her stock figures. It was a simple but often challenging equation; she had to add her opening stock to the goods inwards deliveries and then compare this combined amount with the number of cases of product dispatched. If she has done this right, the balance of these two figures should be equal to the closing stock remaining in the warehouse. She had a good eye for detail and these routine exercises generally resulted in a happy outcome, but today she was struggling to balance the numbers. She had added it up three times already and was nearly a hundred and fifty boxes short. That was nearly half a pallet load, enough to reflect badly on her abilities and diligence she thought. She was clearly perplexed by this unaccounted anomaly and was still chewing the end of her pencil with a frown wrinkling her usually smooth forehead when there was a tap-tap on the glass door.

'If the wind changes, you'll stay like that!'

She looked up to see Alfie her old packing hall supervisor standing in the office doorway, a genial smile on his face. She smiled back; she liked Alfie and was genuinely pleased to see him.

'Hi Alfie,' she sang, 'how can I help you?'

'I've come to ask you to order in some more cardboard boxes to replace that half pallet that got wet in the factory last night and had to be dumped.' He did not understand quite why this piece of news brought such obvious pleasure to Shirley, but he did not complain when she hopped out of her seat and gave him a kiss on the cheek for his troubles.

'It's nearly tea break for my line,' he added smiling but a little disconcerted by her show of affection, 'why don't you pop down to the canteen, your little mate Dorrie will be there and you know she's been missing you ever so much Shirl.'

'Thanks Alfie,' she replied, 'I'll do just that. I'll just write out the stores requisition for your lovely boxes and then I'll get myself off to the canteen straight away.'

Five minutes later she was in the canteen with a cup of tea in her hand and another on the table waiting for Doreen to arrive. It was not typical for the office workers to use the canteen, generally they did not like the smell of fish that permeated into their clothes and lingered around them for the rest of the day, but Shirley had no such prejudice against the smell of fish and although she was wearing a smart grey blouse and her charcoal grey skirt she gave Doreen a big hug as she arrived in her fishy factory overalls.

'Hi Shirl,' she said cheerily, 'you okay?' Doreen had not seen much of Shirley since she had gone off work after the accident and consequently was a little cagey about what to say to her. She was pleased to note though that she seemed to be in a much brighter mood and she added. 'Has something cheered you up Shirl? You seem to be a bit more chipper today.'

'I've just balanced my cardboard boxes,' she explained. But seeing the mystified look cross her friend's face added. 'My stock, I mean. I've just balanced my stock of cardboard boxes.' The two girls smiled and Shirley added. 'Well, the truth is there's something else that has brightened me up a bit, it's Harry, he brought me a lovely letter back with him from Jens...' She trailed off at this.

'That's amazing,' Doreen said. 'Is it a nice letter?'

'Oh Dorrie, it's a wonderful letter. It was really upsetting to read, I cried like a baby, I cried so much I could hardly read the words but I read it over and over again and it's really helped me come to terms with what's happened Dorrie.' Doreen was listening intently to Shirley's outpouring. She continued. 'And the other good thing about the letter Dorrie, is that it's brought me and Harry back together again.'

'Oh Shirl, I'm so happy about that love. You two need each other more than ever now.'

'That's true,' Shirley agreed. 'There's just the two of us now, we used to be the Three Musketeers, now we're just the Dynamic Duo.'

'I know that you're still grieving Shirley and you're bound to have good days and bad days, but this is the first time I've seen you smile for months and that makes me so happy.' They instinctively clasped each other's hands and sat conjoined for moments before Doreen asked. 'You know what would be even better?'

'What's that Dorrie?'

'If you came down Pearson's on Friday night for a dance.' Doreen felt Shirley's hands, smaller and warmer than hers, stiffen at this and worried that she may have overstepped the mark, perhaps pushing Shirley too far, too quickly.

'I, er, I don't know Dorrie,' she answered at last. 'I'm not sure that I'm quite ready for that... yet. But it's a good idea, and something to aim for one day. You know, I might be okay if you and Harry and Celia was all there.'

'Well, just bear it in mind love,' Doreen concluded. 'Me and Col would love to see you out again.' She did not however, tell Shirley that since they had last spoken, she and Colin had become engaged to be married, choosing to stifle her own good news in deference to her friend's still tender feelings.

*

It was a cold, grey day, very different from the blazing July afternoon when she and Jens had last visited Humberston on their bicycles. After Jens' death, Shirley had retreated into a world of silence, and even when she had begun her recovery and subsequent return into society, she had still found it difficult to talk about Jens, and she had deliberately avoided doing so by fielding any direct questions about him with platitudes. But on Harry's return the floodgates had opened and at last she talked freely about her lost love, and about the dreams they had both shared before that fateful final trip. Harry was not a talker but he soon realised that Shirley did not need him to talk to her; she really just needed him to listen to the catharsis of her outpouring.

Harry's broken leg was well on the mend and a visit to the specialist at Grimsby hospital had confirmed that the surgery to reconstruct the damaged bone with steel pins and plates had been a total success. All he needed to do now was to rebuild the strength of his wasted muscles, and the only way to do this was through exercise. He was on his back in the living room, doing some of the stretching routines recommended by the hospital's physiotherapy team when Shirley had popped her head around the door, she laughed to see him prostrate and in such an unusual position. Deciding to take a few of her holiday days before the weather got too wintery for her to enjoy them, and knowing that Harry was bored at home, she had popped round to see if he wanted to have a day out with her.

Taking the 3C bus route out of town, they had enjoyed the journey through the tree-lined roads that stretched beyond the rows of terraced housing and eventually into the suburbs where newer properties stood further back from the road in their own green spaces. They had disembarked from the bus at a stop next to a cinder track where Harry had been obliged to hobble after Shirley as she headed off at pace, turning occasionally to shout at him to speed up. She was clearly impatient to show him something.

Soon, they arrived at a bungalow, it was the very same one she had visited with Jens just three months previously. It had grown since then, from the flat concrete base she had last seen; it now had walls and a sand grey pan tile roof, and even though there were still no windows or doors, the bungalow was beginning to take on the appearance of a family home. They picked their way carefully through the builder's debris and over the uneven clay clods that had been churned up by the heavy diggers and the lorries of the building site. They explored the shell of the bungalow, looking into each of the bare brick rooms in turn. Harry's face betrayed that he was somewhat mystified to find himself unexpectedly exploring a partly built suburban home on this cold

October afternoon.

'Shirley,' he said, 'why are we here, what's this all about love?'

'This is it Harry,' she answered spreading her arms and turning to indicate that she meant the bungalow they were now standing in. 'This is where I came with Jens on that last weekend, this is where we dreamed of living and bringing up a family together. This is why he went to sea; so that he could give us both a nice life.'

Harry swung himself to the empty window space and looked out across the road where some of the bungalows had been finished and were already occupied. Young children were playing in the front gardens, their mothers chatting over the low, creosoted wooden picket fencing. Everything was new; the bricks were clean and he marvelled at their brightness and the lightness of the mortar between them. It was something he had never really considered before, knowing only streets blackened by a century of soot and grime. The large picture windows with their freshly painted new wooden frames and the front doors glazed with dappled glass shimmered in the pale October sun, and even on a grey day like today he thought how they must illuminate the rooms and the lives of the people who lived in them. Clean, fresh, bright and new, he understood at last why Jens and Shirley would dream of a life here together; young people in a modern world.

'I get it Shirley,' he said. 'I can see what you dreamed of and I know why.' He turned to see her with tears in her eyes, she was not crying but the emotion was clearly difficult for her to contain.

'I just wanted you to see it Harry, it isn't just Jens that I've lost, it's our future too, everything we could have been together, all of our dreams have disappeared and nobody else can really understand that. I need you to know though Harry.'

He hopped towards her and reaching out one arm he pulled her to him. 'Thank you Shirley,' he said, consoling her with a squeeze. 'Thank you for sharing your dream with me, I do understand what you have lost.' His heart was heavy with the dull weight of the insight into Jens and Shirley's lost future. What made it worse, was that he could actually imagine Shirley living here in this clean, modern suburb, it just seemed right that she should be here, part of a new generation with new ideas and hopes, not just settling as he and generations before him had done, for a life in the footsteps of their parents.

'Well,' she answered, 'I'll just have to forget about it now though and get on with things.' She paused, then continued. 'Dorrie was asking if I was going to go dancing again, and I'm thinking about it Harry. Life goes on you know!'

'You should get out Shirley, but I'm not sure about dancing, I mean without Jens it will be strange for you won't it?'

'It will be a bit, but the truth is Harry, I was doing more dancing with Ken than with Jens anyway.' Harry stiffened at the mention of Ken and removed his arm from her shoulders so that he could better see her face.

'I don't like that Ken,' he admitted gruffly. 'I don't trust him and I don't like him being round you. I don't like the way he looks at you.' She frowned a little at this, her brow crinkled in puzzlement at Harry's sullen admission.

'Don't be daft Harry,' she said firmly. 'He's okay. I must admit that I wasn't sure at first, but Celia has been a brick for me, she's a really special person and apart from you, she's my best friend. When you weren't here it was

Celia who got me through the worst of it and Ken is her husband, so I've got no choice, I have to see him. Anyway, he's been ever so kind to me since I lost Jens, he's actually a really nice man once you get to know him a bit.' Harry didn't answer, thinking it wiser to say nothing rather than risk an argument or upsetting her, but he remained unconvinced by Shirley's plea on behalf of Kenneth Flett.

'If I did decide to go to the dance, would you come with me Harry? I know I would feel a lot more comfortable if you were there too.' It was not within Harry's power to deny Shirley anything she asked, so parking his resentment over Flett, he gave her a big smile.

'Course I will Shirl,' he answered, 'and who knows, if they play the Okey Cokey, I might even have a dance myself!' He swung himself between the crutches, putting his left leg in and out again, she danced around him, giggling and clapping as he sang the refrain.

CHAPTER NINETEEN

Friday night was the best night at Pearson's Palais de Dance and even on a cold October night like this one, the dance hall was packed with people, dressed up to the nines and ready for a good time. The night was very black; the cloudless sky was peppered with a rash of northern constellations but the Palais glowed brightest of all, dazzling against the backdrop of icy darkness. The tide roared invisibly somewhere in the distance, the rising and falling cadenzas of the breaking waves competing with the pounding beat and melodious tones of the music that escaped from the Palais into the night air. Harry had declined the offer of a lift from the Fletts in their new car, opting instead to arrive by taxi on his own. He stood on the opposite side of the road for a while, the collar of his coat turned up against the freezing wind that whipped into his face. He shivered as he took in the busy scene and wondered what this night would bring. In time he felt ready, and swinging his body between the two crutches, he made his way across the road between the cars and the buses and he paid his way into the venue.

It did not take Harry long to locate Shirley. She was

standing with Celia, Doreen, Ken and Colin at the bar, they were all chatting away and clearly enjoying a good laugh. He noted that the group had assembled around Shirley, and as their centrepiece she was the focus of everyone's attentions, Celia even had one of her arms linked with Shirley's. He hobbled up to the group and had his cheeks kissed by all three of the girls whilst Colin volunteered to get him a pint in. Shirley looked straight at him, with a broad, thankful smile. In his peripheral vision, Harry thought he saw Ken Flett sneering at him, but when he looked over Ken was smiling and had his hand outstretched towards him, offering a shake.

All eyes were on them so Harry took the offered hand and gave it a firm shake, feeling the considerable strength of Ken's returned grip as he did so. Colin arrived with Harry's beer and normal conversation was soon resumed as Doreen and Ken got back to teasing Shirley in a good natured way about whether or not her sister Sally and young Frank Thorsen could be trusted to babysit Alice without getting up to 'hanky-panky', as Doreen put it. Shirley was joining in with the ribbing and intimated that it was not Sally she was worried about but she feared for the safety of poor innocent Frank.

The Palais was filling up now and dancers were taking to the floor. Shirley's attention was taken by the colourful swirl of motion and it did not take long for Ken to realise that she was growing restless to join them. Moments later, they slipped elegantly onto the floor together and mingled seamlessly with the other dancers, joining them in the Viennese waltz.

Harry had managed to find a high stool and had installed himself at the corner of the bar, his crutches were propped up alongside him on one side and Celia was standing on the other. With Ken, Shirley, Doreen and

Colin all on the dance floor, Harry and Celia were soon enjoying catching up. She asked him about his injury and the progress of his convalescence, she asked about his reunion with Shirley but she did not mention the accident at sea and the loss of Jens. It was Harry who eventually raised the subject.

'Even though everyone tells me I'm wrong, I just can't help but blame myself Ceels,' he admitted. 'I was supposed to look after him and I let him down and I let Shirley down and Gwen too. I've let everyone down.'

'Hush now,' she put her small hand on top of his sea-hardened mauler. 'I won't listen to this Harry, none of this was your fault, you have to stop blaming yourself and you have to think about the future and not dwell in the past.' He smiled at her and shook his head.

'I wish it was as easy as that Ceels,' he swilled down the last inch of his pint and immediately caught the bar tender's eye with a nodding gesture at the tap. The beer was pulled and he ordered a gin and tonic for Celia whilst watching the ale gush in foaming squirts into the glass. Sensitive to the depth and strength of his guilt, Celia turned the conversation to lighter topics, telling tales of their evenings out in the new car and how Shirley had been getting on in her new job. Harry listened with interest, eagerly soaking up every morsel of news about Shirley's life since he had been away. He had just ordered another beer, although Celia had not even half finished her gin, when he felt a slap on his shoulder and turning to see who it was, he was delighted to see the grinning face of Bill Osborne looming over him.

'I heard that I might find you here,' he laughed, 'you being such a good dancer and all that!' Maureen was by his side and she pecked Celia on the cheek in greeting before turning to Harry and with her arms thrown around his neck, imparted a significant smacker on his lips. 'I'll get that.' Bill pointed at Harry's beer with a folded ten-shilling note, and catching the barman's eye he called out above the chatter. 'Another one of them and two gin and T's as well please mate.'

Celia protested but had the new drink thrust upon her nevertheless and the group assembled around the seated Harry in lively conversation. Celia noted with interest, that Bill did not mention the accident at sea nor did he ask Harry how he was faring in any way. In fact, Bill was behaving exactly as if nothing had happened and Celia observed that Harry had responded likewise. In contrast to his very recent bout of guilt-laden and morose introspection he now suddenly appeared to be jolly and hearty. She thought to herself that this was perhaps how these seafaring people had learned to cope with the constant presence of danger and tragedy in their lives, and although she thought it odd that something so significant could be looked over between two such close friends, she was at least happy to see Harry looking something like his old self again.

It was not until more beers had been ordered that Bill eventually asked about Harry's broken leg, and then only to find out when he would be returning to sea and whether he had a vessel sorted.

'I'm not going out on Freya again,' he told them. 'She's not a lucky boat for me, so I've been into the office to see Captain Taylor and he's put me down for Apollo again.'

'That's brilliant news!' Bill was over the moon to have his old friend back on the same crew again.

'I reckon I'll be a few more weeks getting over this,' he rubbed his damaged leg, the expression on his face betraying that even after twelve weeks of mending, the damaged thigh was still causing him considerable discomfort. 'But I reckon I'll be back at sea sometime after Christmas.' The two men raised their glasses and toasted Harry's return to the Hansen Apollo with a long swig of ale.

The house band were playing a rumba, the Latin American beat embellished with rippling arpeggios from the Spanish guitar and a syncopated back-beat of shaken maracas. On the floor, Ken was leading Shirley through the sensual moves of the exotic dance, holding just the very tips of her fingers of one hand, he backed away from her before drawing her in close, she responded with small, preening steps, allowing herself to be reeled in, twirled and pushed away again. Ken was a master of the rumba, his entire upper body poised and almost motionless whilst his hips moved fluidly in perfect harmony with the lilting, pulsing beat. Like a cat playing with a mouse, time and time again, he slowly eased her into him, his eyes never leaving hers, only to spin her away again each time. She was lost in the music, blind to any other couple on the dance floor; she was intoxicated by the rhythm and exquisitely teased by his smouldering technique. And then suddenly, surprisingly, gratifyingly, he took her into hold and they moved more closely together than they had ever danced before, hip to hip, they were swaying together, their faces inches apart. Eye to eye.

'Come outside with me, Shirley, there's something I have to tell you,' he whispered. They were so close together that she could hear him even above the amplified music. He turned and still holding her by the tips of her fingers, led her away from the dance floor, she followed him, obediently, step for step, still moving in time with the music.

From his vantage position at the corner of the bar, through the crowds of dancers and spectators Harry thought that he saw Ken leading Shirley away from the dance floor and towards the door. It was only the briefest of glimpses and he was not even sure of what he had seen, but he felt a shiver of presentiment that all was not well; there was something about the half seen girl's body language that disturbed him deeply. He looked around, raising himself on the spell of the stool on his good leg to gain a height advantage over the crowd and when after a few seconds he realised that Ken and Shirley were nowhere to be seen on the floor or in the bar, he knew that his suspicions were confirmed.

Collecting his crutches he slipped off the stool and without making any excuses to the others, picked his way carefully through the crowd towards the entrance and out into the cold night air. There were people milling around on the street, he looked around but saw no sign of either Ken or Shirley amongst them. Unsure of what to do next he made his way to the rear of the building and onto the promenade. There were fewer people here but still no sign of the missing pair. Beginning to doubt what he thought he had seen, he swung his way slowly towards the sea wall, and parking his crutches rested his weight on his elbows, peering out into the inky darkness of the Humber estuary.

In the distance he could hear the familiar sound of rolling waves, he closed his eyes in remembrance of the sea and wished himself back to full health and back on the trawlers far away from land and all of the problems on it. And then he heard something else, floating to him on the night breeze, maybe twenty yards away, on the beach side of the sea wall. It was the sound of voices in deep, intense conversation. He shuffled along until he was directly above them and recognising Ken's Scottish accent and Shirley's oh so familiar voice, he knew at last that he had found them. They were some ten feet below him, standing on the beach in the deep shadow of the sea defences. They were clearly arguing.

'I don't know what you're talking about Ken. You're crazy, there's nothing between us!' Shirley was impassioned and highly emotional.

'Don't deny it Shirley; there's no need to deny it anymore. Deep down you know it's true and now we both have to be brave and face up to it.'

'You're crazy!'

'Crazy for you, yes! And I know that you feel the same about me, I've seen it in your eyes, in your smiles, in the way that you look at me. You've been giving me the come-on for months Shirley, now let's stop playing games and admit what's going on between us!' His voice was growing louder and more urgent. Harry looked around and saw that the steps down onto the beach were some twenty yards away, back towards the Palais. They must have walked straight down onto the beach and wandered along for a while before they stopped to argue. Harry knew that he could not walk that distance on soft beach sand with his crutches, and he momentarily panicked with the feeling of helplessness that pervaded him. Down on the beach, the argument was rising in pitch as the two became more vehement.

'Stop it Ken, you're frightening me!'

'It's time to stop playing games now Shirley. It's been a lot of fun, but that's over with now. This is about you and me and nobody else. I know that you want me, so just give in to it. Everything will be alright, I'll look after you.'

'Stop it Ken, get off me!' She half screamed, half

begged.

'It's too late to stop, I just can't. We've gone too far!' His voice was pleading but steeled with intent.

'Get off me Ken, stop it!' There was a loud slap and a shocked scream from Shirley, her face had been slapped and by the sound of it, slapped hard. Harry was frantic now, unable to help Shirley just ten feet below him. Bellowing with rage he hauled himself bodily onto the top of the wall and launched into the black depths below.

He tried to land on his good leg but he was jarred by the suddenness of the impact and he buckled to his knees onto the beach. Rising awkwardly and trying to turn at the same time, he saw the white clenched fist looming out of the darkness towards him. It cracked hard and squarely into his undefended face. There was an explosion of pain. His nose was smashed and he was hurled backwards, sprawling into the sand. His eyes were seared with tears and blood from the blow and he squinted blindly, frantically pawing at them with the sandy cuff of his suit jacket, trying to restore his vision before the next attack came. But he was too late and he felt himself hoisted by his lapels. Two strong arms dragged him upright like a rag doll, he felt electric shocks of pain shooting deep inside his damaged thigh and fought against the dark pull of unconsciousness. Somewhere, far away in the distance he could hear Shirley screaming but he was half knocked out and her voice was faint and fading as though he were sliding under water. He thought about Jens slipping away from him, remembered the wet oilskins slithering through his fingers and he fought to summon back his strength. Through a squinted gap in his tears he saw Flett's head pull back in readiness to launch a head butt, saw his cold, mean eyes measuring the blow and he knew that it would finish him. In that brief moment of inertia, at the furthest point of the stretch backwards and before Flett's head began it's deadly forward motion Harry let fly with the handful of sand he had managed to pick up whilst Flett was man-handling him to his feet. His aim was spot on and the sand lashed straight into Ken's open eyes, blinding him and sending him reeling backwards. Harry was more stable now with his weight taken mainly on his good leg and his vision clearing, he had bought himself valuable seconds but Flett was recovering and the match was still grossly uneven. Harry knew he could not win a punching fight, so he opted to launch himself onto the still disorientated Flett. Leaping with his good leg and falling from above onto his prey, he managed to get one of his arms around Flett's neck and fortuitously caught a flailing arm and locked it up behind his back. The balance of power had shifted and although Ken was a strong man and bigger than him, Harry's years at sea hauling trawls on side winders had given him immense upper body strength and Ken was powerless to shake himself free as Harry's muscular right arm tightened around his neck, twisting it mercilessly. The two men were locked together in the sand, Harry now clamped to his victim like a vice. He was raging, outraged and furious at the insults and assault to his Shirley, his fury gave him even greater strength and he increased the pressure around Flett's neck, feeling the resistance as sinews, bone and tendon approached their breaking points. One last effort would do it he thought, he breathed a sharp breath through clenched teeth and tensed his muscles in readiness for the final twist. And then he became aware of Shirley's voice speaking calmly to him.

'Harry, no! Don't!' She was not screaming anymore, she was not frantic; she knew that she was safe; he had not let her down this time. He thought about her and her broken dreams and his heart overflowed with tenderness for her but he did not release his grip. He felt a hand on his shoulder and without looking up he somehow knew that it was Bill's. He must have wondered where he'd gone and like the best of friends had come looking for him. He opened his eyes and saw his friend's entreating look.

'Let him go Harry, he's beaten.'

So he let him go, and with Bill's help he struggled awkwardly to his feet, wiping sand from his face and clothes as he did so. Shirley came to him and put her arms around him more tenderly than she ever had before. He leaned his weight on her for stability and they embraced.

'Thank you Harry,' she whispered. 'Thank you so much! It was awful, he was touching me and he hit me, I thought he was going to rape me. You saved me.' She kissed his bloody face, holding it between her two shaking hands. Her lips sent shocks of pain searing through his damaged nose but he did not mind this in the slightest. Flett was still lying on the beach heaving for breath and coughing globules of blood and phlegm into the sand. And then, in that moment, they all became aware that Celia was standing on the promenade looking down at the scene below her on the beach. Her face aghast with the horror of what she had seen.

Ken looked up and saw her there.

'It's not what it looks like,' he managed to shout, his voice hoarse and strained. 'She came on to me and he's a bloody lunatic!' He pointed towards Harry with a wildly shaking finger. 'They're all fucking crazy here in this fucking town.' But Celia just looked on, speechless, pathetic and wretched with the shock of her betrayal. She was a ghost-white portrait of a disappointed and betrayed woman.

CHAPTER TWENTY

Two weeks had passed since the events on Cleethorpes beach when Harry and Shirley found themselves once again in the resort. It was a windswept and grey late October Saturday afternoon and Shirley was helping Harry with his exercise by accompanying him on a nice long walk along the promenade. They were both wrapped up warmly against the biting wind that lashed in off the turbulent Humber and Shirley's arm which was linked through Harry's, was there as much for mutual warmth as it was to give him support. He carried a single walking stick in his free hand. After half an hour of walking, Harry took pity on her and suggested that they take a warming cup of tea in one of the sea front caffs. The holiday season had long finished and only a few cafés remained open, but they found one up on the main road near the slipway from which the local fishermen launched their small boats into the sea. Although it was daytime, the café had the lights turned on and they tucked themselves into one of the snug booths, appreciating the steamy warmth and homely smells of toasting bread and frying bacon. Harry ordered two mugs of tea and some hot buttered toast for them to share.

'I wonder how Celia is,' he said. 'I hope she's okay.' Celia had not been seen since that terrible night when she had witnessed the fight between Harry and Ken on the beach.

'Well, I've got some news for you about Celia,' Shirley answered cryptically, her fingers fumbling at the headscarf knot beneath her chin and at last having worked it loose, flipping it away and preening her flattened hair back into life with her fingertips. 'I've been saving it till we got settled somewhere,' she added, happy now that her curls had sprung reasonably back into place. Harry was all eagerness to hear what this news may be and was surprised when Shirley produced a folded envelope from her handbag.

'I've had a letter,' she announced with something of a flourish.

'Can I read it?' he asked, reaching towards her.

'No you can't Harry Coulbeck,' she replied, snatching it away, out of the reach of his advancing fingers. 'You can't just go reading other people's letters, they're private and this letter is to me, not you!' He withdrew his hand, accepting the admonishment without question. 'Oh, there's no need to look all hurt about it,' she added teasingly, 'I'll read some bits of it out for you though, if you want.' He nodded and she removed several sheets of neatly written letter paper from the envelope and unfurling them she began to read.

'Dearest Shirley,' she began, her voice hushed for privacy but just loud enough for Harry to hear her across the small Formica topped table. 'You will never know how sorry I am for the way things worked out and for leaving without saying goodbye, but I hope that you understand and that you will forgive me. Once I realised what had happened on that awful night, I just had to get away as quickly as possible so I jumped straight into the first taxi I could find and went home. The taxi driver must have thought me a mad woman for I must have looked wild and poor Frank and Sally were surprised indeed to see me blundering in on my own and dismissing them very curtly. You must pass on my apologies to them both please, in truth I was out of my mind. Ken came home much later, he must have been very drunk because I could hear him falling into things and cursing dreadfully but I didn't see him as I had locked myself into the spare bedroom, the one that you used to use, and I stayed there with Alice by my side until it was light. I will not say that I slept for I didn't, I just watched the darkness turn to lightness through the fabric of the curtains and then I dressed us both and we left the house as quietly as we could, I could hear Ken snoring as we left. It took us a long time to get home, we caught the first train out of Grimsby Town to Doncaster and changed for Edinburgh, after that we caught another train to Aberdeen and arrived there in the darkness of late evening. I had telephoned my father from Waverley station in Edinburgh to tell him I was coming home and he and my mother were waiting for us when we got off the train in Aberdeen. I was tired and ever so sad but seeing them waiting there for us was such a relief, I could have just broken down and wept with happiness to see them both again after so long.'

Shirley had to wipe a tear from her cheek with the back of her hand at this point and she lowered the letter to see that Harry was listening with rapt attention to the story. She took a swig of tea to lubricate her voice for further reading and continued.

'I hate to admit it because I had been such a

stubborn know-it-all at the time and I had really made a big issue of it with my parents, but it seems that they were right about Ken all along. My father never did like him or trust him and he did his best to warn me and deter me from pursuing a relationship with him. It is unfortunate for us all that I did not listen to him at the time because so much upset could have been avoided, but Alice was on the way and in truth, I had fallen for Ken's considerable charms and believed all of his lies about how happy we would be together. I was a damned fool and you will never know how much I regret the things I did just to defy my parents and to prove to them that I knew better – I clearly didn't. But they have been brilliant to me Shirley, I have been welcomed back into their home and I am happy to be here, for a while anyway until I decide what I am to do next. I have made up with my father and of course Mummy just absolutely dotes on Alice, you wouldn't believe how good she is with her and how proudly she trundles her around in her little pushchair to show her off to all of her friends. I will have to be careful or baby Alice will grow up to be a very spoiled girl indeed, very much like I did I suspect.'

A further swig of tea was required and Shirley turned over the sheet and continued.

'I think I had known that there was something seriously wrong with my marriage for a long time but maybe I was just too proud to admit that I had made a mistake. Meeting you and your friends was the best thing that happened to me after Alice was born and I will always treasure our friendship. The kindness that Gwen and Dolly showed me gave me a lifeline at a time when I was very disillusioned and feeling very low. Then getting to know you and Jens and Harry actually gave me something to live for. I was so envious of your closeness, of the way that you so naturally and unselfconsciously cared for each other and looked after each other and I longed to be part of your lives. It is not an exaggeration to say that you restored my faith in human kindness at a time when my own life, cut off from my family and with a lone wolf of a husband was becoming increasingly solitary.'

Glancing down the rest of the sheet, Shirley made a 'blah-di-blah' noise, obviously skimming over the next few paragraphs before she picked up the story on the next page.

'I can't help but blame myself for what Ken did to you. I should have seen it coming, I should have realised what he was capable of. But I have to admit that I had absolutely no idea what he was thinking and I still find it almost beyond belief that he tried to press himself onto you. I heard you say to Harry on the beach that you believed he was going to rape you and although I don't for one minute think that he would have considered his attentions as rape, I have no doubt that no matter what you had said to him or did to him, he would not have stopped. I am so incredibly grateful that Harry had been watching over you (as he always does and always will) and that despite his injury he managed to save you from Ken that night. I am tempted to say that I wish he had gone further and had broken his neck as it looked like he was going to until Bill and you intervened, but that would be unchristian of me and although I hate Ken and even though he is Alice's father I hope to never see him again. But I should perhaps not go so far as to wish him dead, for we have seen too much of death this year.'

A fingertip quenched another budding tear and Shirley read on.

'When you lost Jens, you thought your world had

ended but you are still so young and have so much of life ahead of you and I was deeply happy to see you gradually recovering from the initial shock, and although you will always mourn Jens, I hope and believe that in years to come, the sadness will mellow into a sweet sorrow and that you will eventually find new happiness.'

She skipped over a few more sentences before resuming.

'So Shirley, I don't know if we will ever see each other again and although I sincerely hope that we do, right now I can't imagine how or when that will be. In the meantime though, I write these words as an explanation of my sudden disappearance, as an apology for allowing a situation to develop that threatened your safety and as a sincere thank you for the friendship and kindness you showed to me at a time when I needed it most. I will never forget you and Harry and Jens and I hold you all dear in my heart forever. Yours with love, Celia Gibson.'

She re-folded the sheets and returned them to their envelope; they sat in silence for a while, finishing their tea and nibbling the last of the now not-so-hot toast.

'That's a lovely letter,' Harry said at last. 'But why did you miss bits out?'

'They're the private bits,' she replied. 'Bits that she wrote for me and not for you.' Shirley was smiling so sweetly at this that Harry could not possibly take offence at his exclusion, but he equally could not help but be puzzled about the contents of the mystery parts of the letter. However, he did not press further and eventually they gathered themselves to continue their walk. They re-buttoned their loosened coats and Shirley produced the square fabric of her headscarf, folded it diagonally into a triangle and looped it once again around her head to keep the cold away from her ears. Once outside they headed off steadily along the promenade towards the pier. The wind had fallen whilst they had sojourned in the cosy café and although the tide was still roaring in against the sea wall, the walking was much more pleasant than before.

'Will it get completely better?' she asked, looking down at his damaged leg.

'Should do Shirl,' Harry answered. 'The doc' says that I might have a bit of a limp, but I should be almost as good as new again soon.' He looked out at the foaming tide and took in a deep breath of sea air. 'I can't wait to get back to sea though,' he added wistfully.

Their walk brought them eventually to the pier and seeing that the cast iron gates were pushed open, they took the detour, labouring up the incline and along the pier's boarded length to the very end, where they stood looking at the pale steel sky above them and the silt grey waters that were rushing in below them. He held onto the metal handrail for support, feeling the flaking paint peel beneath his grip, his fingertips probing the indentions worn into it from nearly a century of crashing waves and insidiously corrosive sea salt. He looked out across the estuary, past the forts, the defensive iron and steel structures that stood a mile or so out to sea, one on each side of the river mouth, guarding it against an invasion that had never come. He peered beyond them through half closed eyes towards the horizon. In more ways than one, he was half in his world and half in hers.

'You love the sea don't you Harry,' she said softly, observing the faraway look in his sea grey eyes.

'Shirley,' he replied after a long pause, a pause in which he was clearly absorbed in deep thought. 'I don't love the sea. Love is something I feel for the very few people who are precious to me, it isn't love that calls me back to the sea, it is something in my nature. It's like the tides, the drag of the ocean currents; they make their endless journeys around the planet, the same today, as they were yesterday, the same as they were a thousand, even a million years ago. Everything in life has a pattern Shirley, a cycle; like day always turns to night and like the changing of the seasons. The tide always returns to the shore, so a fisherman will always return to the sea. There is no sense to it, it is not a choice made out of love or ambition, it is just the natural order of things. Look at me! I'm just turned twenty-two years old and I'm already an old salt. I mean, look at these hands of mine, they're as coarse as emery board, they've been cut and nicked in a thousand places. I've worked the fishing banks from the Faroes to the North Capes of Iceland and Norway and I'm as familiar with the fishing grounds of Bear Island and the White Sea as I am with the pubs of Freeman Street. I know what it is to watch the Northern Lights play across a pale blue midnight sky and to watch silent bow waves rolling into the vastness of Greenland's ice fields. I didn't choose this Shirley. It chose me! It's in my blood and I am drawn back to it like the pull of the moon on the water down there beneath our feet.'

Shirley pondered this with a heavy heart, the inexorable inevitability of her lamentable fate made manifest in Harry's words. Eventually, after a long period of silence and with an immense effort, she wrenched an unborn truth from her lips.

'Harry,' there's something else I have to tell you,' he felt her body stiffen with the effort of what she was about to say, so he turned himself away from the sea to face her.

'Yes Shirley, go on, what is it?'

'I'm pregnant.'

The admission rushed out of her but her resolve melted immediately the words were spoken and she crumbled, moving into him, wrapping her arms around him and burying her face into the great chest of his overcoat. He did not answer her but still supporting himself with one gnarled hand on the battered rail, he placed the other tenderly around her neck, cradling her gently into him.

A flock of seagulls circled around them, calling out their harsh squawks as they floated on the chilled thermals that rose beneath their outstretched, white wings. They were scavenging, hunting for scraps of food in the out of season resort. They soon gave up on the two figures at the end of the pier and wheeled away en masse to hunt for discarded chips on the promenade.

'Well you know what's going to happen now don't you,' Harry whispered, his head bowed and his cheek resting against the smooth fabric of Shirley's headscarf.

'No, what's that?' she answered plaintively.

'We'll be getting married.'

'Oh Harry, don't,' she answered. 'I can't ask you to marry me just because I'm having a baby. It's not fair on you. You should marry someone who you really love.'

'But I do,' he answered firmly, 'I do love you Shirley, I think I always have.'

She pulled away from him to better see his face.

'Really?'

'Yes, really.'

'That's what Celia said in her letter, in the bits that I didn't read to you,' she confessed. 'She said that even though I would always love Jens, I shouldn't be blind to the fact that I had another man in my life and that man loved me just as much as Jens did.'

'She said that?"

'Yes she did, and a lot of other things too. She said that she thought you were a really attractive man, that you are kind and believe it or not, she even thought you were clever. If she hadn't been married, apparently, she could have fancied you for herself.' She looked at him with an incredulous look on her face. He laughed, delighted.

'Look Shirl,' he continued, 'it makes so much sense. You can't bring a baby up on your own and what kind of life would the bairn have without a dad bringing money into the house? The truth is, ever since you took me out to see that nice bungalow in Humberston I've been thinking how you deserve to have that kind of life. A life in a nice modern house, away from the dirty town, out where the air is clean and where you can see the sky without breaking your neck. I can give you those things Shirley. I'm going back to sea as mate on the Apollo. That means that I'll be getting paid a share of the catch on one of the best earning boats in the port.'

'But it's Jens' baby Harry, how would that make you feel?'

'I would be honoured,' he answered, his voice laden with the weight of sincerity. 'I loved Jens like a brother and I would bring up his child just as if it were my own. I can promise you that. It would be my way of paying my debt to him.' She looked deeply into his eyes and held his gaze for a long time; she knew that he was speaking the truth.

'So,' he said at last with the creases of a hopeful smile just hesitating at the outer edges of his lips and eyes. 'Have we got a deal?'

His arm still cradled her, sheltering her small face against the breeze that was now beginning to blow up from the cold estuary waters. He continued to hold her gaze and felt a tremor of anticipation as her eyes caught the faintest of twinkles from the pale October sunlight. She returned the smile more broadly and gave him the answer he was waiting for.

'Yes Harry we do, we have a deal.'

ABOUT THE AUTHOR

Mike Mitchell was born in 1958 in Cleethorpes, he has worked in the seafood industry since 1981. Mike is renowned both nationally and internationally in the field of seafood sustainability and has written on this subject in trade journals and in the academic press.

About this book: Whilst foraging in a store cupboard in the offices where he works on Grimsby docks, Mike discovered a number of old photographs and other materials, dating back as far as the 1940's. Amongst this find was an album of black and white photographs taken during the early 1960's, they were simple but compelling images of people going about their everyday work in the factories of the day. This set Mike's mind working; who were these people and what were their stories? Hope Street is the imagined story inspired by them, and although the people and events portrayed in this book are fictional, such stories of love and loss have been played out many thousands of times in the real lives of the people who lived and worked in Grimsby during the fishing years.

6950210R00172

Printed in Germany
by Amazon Distribution
GmbH, Leipzig